Thank you for your support!

BROKEN HALLELUJAH

JOANN MICHAEL YOUNG

Italics in scripture quotations have been added by the author for emphasis.

Printed in the United States of America

ISBN: 978-0-615-99036-1

THANK YOU, WITH DEEPEST GRATITUDE AND LOVE

First and foremost I would like to thank God for giving me the vision and courage to write this book. Without Him nothing in my life would be possible. I stand in His Grace and Mercy, always and forever.

To my beautiful two sons, C.J. and Terrance, Jr., to my mother and father, Mary and Joe, to my sisters and brother, Vickie, Lesia, Sharon, Ken and Rayvon, and to my nieces and nephews, Shaniece, Jasmine, India, Janel, Keith, Sankofa, Robert, Jr., Anthony, Jr., Dayvion and Rayvon, Jr., I love you with everything that I am. Your support and encouragement through all my trials and tribulations will always be heartfelt and forever treasured. Your unyielding love surpasses all things and because of you I have found the strength to be what God has purposed me to be. I love you all and I thank you for standing by me side by side, heart to heart, hand and hand. My love forever.

To the beautiful man in my life, John. Your belief in me, your support through all the times I needed that reassurance will be forever branded in my heart. I love you for who you are and who you inspire me to be. My love always!

JUNE 20, 2008

PRESENT DAY

Daddy was a preacher at the Missionary Baptist Church on the east side of Detroit. Every Sunday me and my brother would go to Sunday School and church service, most of the time staying after to help clean up around the sanctuary. Daddy always gave a good sermon, it was no wonder he was so highly respected in the community. Everyone looked up to him, always offering their help in one way or another. When Mama died folks had been coming over to the house cooking, bringing food, sending clothes, it's a wonder we had enough room to store it all. Daddy did a good job with showing his appreciation to everyone, "Thank You," had become a second language to him. He always said it doesn't matter how big a Bible you tote or how many scriptures you know, the true meaning of loving God is in the way a person lives, the good deeds they do, and he made sure his family led by example. We spent most of our Christmas and Thanksgiving days handing out boxes and baskets of food to those less fortunate. Other times we helped out the elders of the church by doing chores around their house or grocery shopping. One time, Mama, with barely enough strength herself, drove over to Ms. Jeannie's house to give her a sponge bath. A few months ago she had suffered a stroke and couldn't do much for herself after that, but Mama always made sure she was well taken care of.

Every Saturday night Daddy would gather the family around in the living room to read the Bible. His favorite Book was Genesis. He made me and my brother read one chapter each. I never did like it. All the big words I couldn't pronounce. It was a strange book with a language all its own. My brother use to say, "People don't talk like that," but Daddy would always explain it to us in a way that we could understand.

After Bible study we would get down on our knees and pray. Mama always led the prayer. She was a praying woman, always praying over something or somebody, especially her family. I remember her saying

Daddy was God's way of showing her that she must have done something right in her life. I never understood that. I always thought Mama was God's way of giving me and my brother the tender side of Daddy's heart. Lord knows she was the only way we were gonna get it. Never told her my feelings though, I loved her too much for that. The day she made her transition was just the way she wanted it, with me and my brother by her side and God's gift holding her hand and smiling upon her as she peacefully and graciously slipped away.

People always talked about how well Daddy was raising me and my brother without her, and how fine children we were growing up to be. Yep, my father was a dedicated preacher and pastor, but as far as me and my brother were concerned, he was a long stretch from being a Man of God.

MAY 20, 2008

DAY ONE - TRIAL

Mama use to say you could never prepare yourself for life. No matter how you plan and strategize your journey life has a way of derailing your course and throwing you into a pathway of unchartered waters. Waves so rough they capsize the very being of your existence. There are some that have the faith to rise above their adversities, but then there are others that sink below the surface, downward to the ocean's floor, drowning in their own dissent.

It wasn't long after Prosecution had rested its case that life's derailment beckoned its way through the first witness for Defense.

"I will have order in my court!" Judge Hallow demanded as he hammered his gavel over the unfavorable whispers of the courtroom. "I will clear everyone out if this disturbance does not cease immediately!" He turned his attention to Counsel. "Now, attorney Teller," he addressed in the most aggravated tone, "would you please approach the bench and explain to your client how this process works and in what manner she is expected to respond."

"Yes, Your Honor." Teller was a man of tall stature, rather eccentric. He possessed distractive behaviors that would aggravate the most composed person, tapping three times on the table with his fist before standing up, cocking his head to one side and putting his hand to his ear whenever a response was required, or staring off in the distance for ten seconds between thoughts before speaking. Well, at least that was my interpretation of it.

Teller stood and walked slowly to the podium, his torso slightly bent forward with his hands clasped tightly behind his back, "Did you understand the question?" he asked.

"Yes, Sir, I did."

"Well then I believe the court will be granted more than enough opportunities to hear what you have to say and the reasons you say them, but until then a simple, 'I do,' will suffice. Understood?" He cocked his head to the side and held his hand to his ear.

"Yes, Sir," I responded.

Teller gave a curt nod to the Judge and walked back to his seat.

Agitated, Judge Hallow cleared his throat. "Now let's try this again."

The bailiff approached the podium and stood directly in front of me. "Raise your right hand and place your left one on the Bible. Do you promise to tell the truth, the whole truth, and nothing but the truth so help you God?"

"I do," I said reluctantly.

The courtroom exhaled.

"Please state your name and age for the record."

I spoke low, nervous. "Faith…"

"Speak up please."

"Faith, 19-years-old."

"Last name?"

"Just, Faith."

Judge Hallowed peered over his glasses annoyed. "Miss Faith everyone has a last name."

"Daddy said last names were man-made rules, government labels signifying division amongst people. He said no one in the Bible had last names so who are we to defy God's way."

"Does Defense have witness's birth record on file?" Judge Hallow asked in a bothered tone.

"Yes, Sir, we do. I have a copy on hand." Teller retrieved the document from his briefcase and handed it to Judge Hallow who appeared more aggravated scanning the certificate than he did before receiving it.

"Let the record show that witness will be known by first name basis only." He handed the form back to Teller, a bit thrown by its contents.

"You may proceed."

Teller stared off in thought.

"*Today*, Mr. Teller."

He tapped the table three times before ascending from his seat, stood silent for a moment and then approached the podium. "Was God a significant part of your family's life, Miss Faith?"

"God *was* our life. Everything we did was based upon the word of God. Daddy made sure of that."

Teller turned to face the jury. "If God was such a pertinent part of your life then why respond '*no'* when being sworn in, Miss Faith?"

"Because the bailiff said, 'So help you God,' and God ain't never done nothin for me," I responded in a disdained manner.

"Are you angry with God, Faith?"

I dropped my head and chewed at the corner of my bottom lip. Not that I was ashamed or anything, I was just never able to hold my head up when speaking about God. "Nah. Not anymore. Use to be though. I use to get so mad I wouldn't speak to Him for days. That is until I realized that it didn't make a difference one way or another. If He wasn't listening to me when I wasn't mad at Him why would He listen to me when I was?"

"Ever wonder if God failed you, Faith?"

Prosecution stood in opposition. "Objection, Your Honor."

"On what grounds, Ms. Joy?" Judge Hallow asked.

"God is not on trial here."

Teller abruptly cut in. "Your Honor, I am merely trying to give the jury an open window to the complexity of these children's lives."

"I'll allow it, but with caution, Counselor."

Teller walked over to the table and picked up the black leather-covered Bible. He opened it to Psalms 34, and began to read verse 4. He stood with his back to me. "*I sought the Lord, and he heard me, and delivered me from all my fears…*" Are you familiar with this scripture at all, Miss Faith?

I could hear the pounding of my heartbeat over the stillness of the room. I dropped my head and closed my eyes for a moment, sketching in my mind the proverbial words that seemed to leave a bitter taste in my mouth. I waited. The queasiness in the pit of my stomach churned and I reluctantly willed myself to speak. I felt the bile burn my throat. "*They looked unto him, and were lightened, and their faces were not ashamed. This poor man cried, and the Lord heard him, and saved him from all his troubles. The angel of the Lord encamp around them that fear him, and deliver them. O taste and see that the Lord is good, blessed is the man that trust in Him…,*" I paused and swallowed hard. The lump cut through my windpipe, making it almost impossible to speak.

Teller turned slowly to face me. "Continue with verse 15, please, Miss Faith."

I would rather have bitten off my own tongue than to scar my mouth with tissues of propaganda and deceit, but knowing that the outcome would have been much worse if I hadn't I perjured on. "*The eyes of the Lord are upon the righteous, and his ears are open unto their cry.*"

Teller motioned for me to stop. I stared blindly ahead, afraid to blink. The atmosphere strained. I drew my attention away from Teller to the words engraved on the wall just above the entrance of the doorway. "In God We Trust." Aversion welled up inside of me and stuck to my insides like velcro. I could sense a haste of revulsion pumping through my veins. I quickly turned my focus back to Teller who urged me to go on.

"Verse 17, Miss Faith."

I bit through the grits of my teeth. "*The righteous cry, and the Lord hear, and deliver them out of all their troubles. The Lord is near unto them that are of a broken heart, and save such as be of a contrite spirit. Many are the afflictions of the righteous, but the Lord deliver him out of them all…*"

"Your Honor, what does this have to do with Defendant's line of questioning?" Joy interrupted.

I paused. Teller gently pressed his index finger against his lips.

"Allow us to get there, Ms. Joy," he responded without looking up, still engrossed in scripture.

"I'll allow it," Judge Hallow remarked.

Joy reclaimed her seat, but not without displeasure.

"Continue from verse 21," Teller spoke.

I didn't even have to think about it. I knew Psalm 34 like the back of my hand. It used to be an olive branch to my soul, the core of my protection. That is until God abandoned me and refused to comfort my spirit. I've felt a deep hatred ever since, a hatred that swelled inside of me and burned itself into the core of my being. I closed my eyes in an effort to block out the scrutiny of the spectators and recited the nauseating fill of scripture.

"*Evil shall slay the wicked, and they that hate the righteous shall be desolate. The Lord redeemed the soul of his servants, and none of them that trust in him shall be desolate.*" I opened my eyes. The room maintained its silence. Unsettled, I fidgeted with my hands, my troubled spirit evident.

"What does that scripture mean to you, Faith?"

"It speaks about redemption and deliverance, but God ain't never saved me from nothing."

"So, once again I ask, Miss Faith, ever wonder if God failed you?" Teller's back was still to me. Hand to ear.

"Yes, all the time. There were days when I would beg God to come and see about me, but He never did. No fault of anybody but my own though. On the surface I appeared righteous, pure of heart. But on the inside I was a hypocrite who was ashamed and confused. Hatred for Daddy consumed my soul. I despised him and everything that he represented. Daddy says, 'God knows your heart.' I guess I always felt God never answered me because He knew my heart was full of sin."

Teller turned to me. "*For there is nothing covered that shall not be revealed, neither hid, that shall not be known.*"

"*Your Honor…*" attorney Joy stood annoyed.

"Luke, chapter 12, verse 2, for those of you who are unfamiliar with biblical text."

"Sustain. Mr. Teller you have been forewarned."

Seemingly unaffected by the court's dissatisfaction of his conduct, Teller closed his Bible and approached the podium. "Faith, could you please point to the Defendant in this case and tell the court who he is?"

I gazed over to the attractive young man across the room who sat respectfully at the long oak wood table. He was a vision. Tall skinny kid, light brown complexion, dark hair and hazel eyes that glistened like the sun. He gave me a short smile as I gestured in his direction. "My brother, Rock," I said proudly. We looked so much alike, except I was a bit shorter, caramel-brown skin, dark shoulder length hair and hazel eyes, an attribute proudly given to us by Mama. I drifted in the moment, but Teller interjected my thoughts.

"Can you tell us about your relationship with your brother, Faith?"

I gave a warm smile. "He is my friend, my everything. He took care of me when I couldn't take care of myself," I hesitated, fighting hard to hold back the tears. "When I thought I couldn't go on he always made sure I did. He was the light in the darkest moments of my life, a ray of sunshine in the midst of clouds. He protected me when I should have been protecting him." I wiped my eyes with the back of my hand. The bailiff handed me a box of Kleenex. "My soul rejoices when I'm in his presence. He was the only one that could make me laugh when I had nothing to laugh about," I sniffed. "There were always reservations around other people, but with each other we could be ourselves with no inhibitions. Besides Mama, he's the only person who has ever made me feel like it was okay to be me."

"Have you two always had such a strong bond?"

"Yes, Sir, we had to. Nobody else was going to take care of us so we had to take care of each other." I suppressed my emotions.

Teller tapped the podium three times. The annoying sound echoed through the microphone. He pushed his hands inside the pockets of his pants and took in a deep sigh, staring off into the distance. “Miss Faith, take us back four years ago to August 15, 2004, after the passing of your mother. Can you tell us about that day?”

I reluctantly gazed over at Rock who appeared greatly disquieted by Teller’s request. His eyes held a stare of concern. Repulsed by the memories of that horrific day, I wandered back to one of the most humiliating moments of my life.

AUGUST 15, 2004

It's been months since Mama's death and Daddy is still angry with God for taking her away. He was fine for a while, but now he's become edgy, taking out his anger on me and Rock as if he wishes it was us that had died instead of Mama. Bible study has become more intense and his patience with us has grown shorter with each passing day. Rock spends most of his days outside playing, whenever Daddy allows it, and I've become obsessed with alienating myself from the world.

I've aged over the past year, my face show signs of exhaustion. Dark circles are starting to appear under my eyes from sleep deprivation and I look much older than a fifteen-year-old girl. Every day I awake is another day of confinement, incarcerated in my own world. Each day I pray for some ray of hope, some way to break loose from this cage I've been held in for so long. Mama use to say a person's journey is only as long as they make it. Mine seemed a lifetime.

The morning was gloomy and wet. It had rained all day into late evening. The fan Mama had for years was useless against the heat, which made the air more humid than ever. I stayed in bed most of the day depressed. Rock had gone to basketball practice at the recreation center a few blocks away. Daddy had just come in from a meeting at the church. He knocked on my bedroom door, but entered before I could respond. I was lying naked in my bed trying to get a little relief from the misery of the heat. Startled, I sat up, grabbed the sheet off the floor and covered my bare body.

"I just wanted to make sure you were okay, baby," he said staring at my exposed frame.

I pulled the sheet as tight as I could around me. I could feel the sickness creeping through my body. The nausea gradually increasing as Daddy approached me slowly and eased down on the bed."

"Daddy, please, Rock will be home soon." My voice trembled with the fear of an animal desperately trying to escape its predator.

"My God how you look like your mother.

"Daddy, please." I pulled away.

"Her skin was so soft, so flawless," he whispered as he ran his index finger up and down my cheek, combing my hair with his fingers.

"But I'm not Mama, Daddy. I'm your daughter." I could barely take a breath. Breathing seemed next to impossible.

He pulled me in close and stroked the nape of my neck with the bitterness of his mouth. The salty taste of my flesh mixed with his wet tongue aroused him to erection. My stomach churned with disgust as he groped my childlike breasts, squeezing and pulling the nipples until they hardened to a painful throb. "Please, Daddy," I begged. He slowly laid me down on the bed, removed his pants and climbed on top of me. The weight of his body pressed hard against my small frame. He pried my legs open with his knees and thrust his penis into my vagina. A dry heave strangled my throat and I released a choking sob, Daddy's perverted breathing heavy in my ear. Tears rolled down the sides of my face and I wept with the cry of a frightened child held against her will. Everything around me went dark and I lost all sense of self. With every foul stroke Daddy managed to take away all that was pure and chaste. He tightened his grip as he wrapped his arms around my waist and dug his fingernails deep into the flesh of my back, breaking the skin and releasing the flow of small amounts of blood, his penis growing more erect with each stroke. He penetrated harder, desperately thrusting faster and deeper inside of me. The stench of his perversion caught my throat and I fought to choke down the vomit. My body stiffened in the callous of his grip. The heaviness of his breath increased and he moaned like a dog in heat spreading my buttocks with such force I could feel the tip of my crack tear. I wanted to scream but the cry seized my chest and all I could feel was the stinging of the blood slowly running down the crease of my back. Daddy pushed in harder, his mouth wet with depravity. He released a loud moan as he withdrew his penis and ejaculated on my mouth. I gaged from the foul smell of his semen. Ashamed and empty I laid rigid.

He pressed his mouth against the wetness of my cheek. "*There is no one who always does what is right, not even one*." Daddy had a way of tainting the word of God with his twisted, adulterated way of thinking. "I will suffer the consequences of my sins, but those sins which I commit will only be judged by God." He climbed out of bed and grabbed his pants off the floor. Pulling the cover over my soiled body he kissed me gently on my forehead and walked out the room, closing the caged door behind him.

I finally felt myself breathe. The stench of Daddy's fluids on my body made me sick to my stomach. I grabbed the wastebasket by the bed and stuck my finger down my throat. I tried, with every ounce of strength I had left, to release the uncleanliness I felt permeating through my body. I vomited until nothing more would come up. My throat burned from the strain. I pulled myself off the floor and ran into the bathroom, turned the shower on full blast and jumped into the hot steaming water. The scratches on my impure body stung from the heat of the bath. I scrubbed and scrubbed, trying to wash away the dirt, the filth that didn't seem to wanna come off. My skin began to bleed. I had scrubbed my body raw. Consumed by my afflictions I stepped out of the stained water and dressed myself for bed. Afraid that Daddy would come back I layered myself with clothing, pulled my pink robe off the back of the chair and wrapped myself in the security of its warmth. I laid on the bed, bawled myself up into the fetal position and cried myself to sleep.

AUGUST 16, 2004

Severely depleted and suffering from sleep deprivation, I pulled myself out of bed and unwillingly met Rock and Daddy downstairs for breakfast. My eyes were red and swollen from crying, it was obvious I had been up all night. In a desperate attempt to avoid eye contact I dropped my head and quickly sat down at the table as far away from Daddy's view as I could, which proved difficult seeing that there was barely enough room for the three of us to sit in the first place. Rock's eyes held a mindful stare as he set the plate of scrambled eggs and sausage on the table in front of me. We had been down this road many times with Daddy, and once again my less than enthused attitude divulged the secret of his sexual degradation.

Rock grabbed a seat across the table from me and sat down to eat. An uncomfortable silence plagued the room. The only sound that was heard was the clacking of Daddy's fork against his plate as he stuffed down the last morsel of scrambled eggs.

"Why the somber spirit this morning daughter?" he asked glancing up from his newspaper with this condescending stare. Daddy was sixty-years-old and beginning to look his age. His skin had turned darker in some spots and began to sag around the eyes. His receding hairline was fully gray and he was in badly need of a shave.

"I'm not hungry this morning," I murmured through the remnants of last night's offense. I felt sick to my stomach. Being around Daddy was taxing to say the least. I placed my elbows on the table and hid my face in my hands. Rock eyed for my attention, but I was ashamed to look at him. I tried to tell myself that Daddy was a sick man, but the more I struggled to convince myself the more unapologetic he appeared.

Rock poured two glasses of orange juice and slid one across the table to me.

"So who's doing what today?" Daddy asked from underneath his newspaper. He took a sip of his coffee from the old coffee mug Mama had given him for his 50th birthday. It had the faded words "preacher" inscribed on the side of it and the handle was chipped from being banged one too many times. That was years ago, he was long overdue for a new one.

Daddy's greater than thou behavior never ceased to amaze me. I cringed as my mind raced with thoughts of last night. I rubbed my hands back and forth on my pajama pants trying to wipe the sweat from my aching palms. Emotions overcame me and I fought hard to hold back the tears. I struggled to make myself feel better, but as long as I was in Daddy's presence it seemed impossible. As I prepared to answer, Rock took notice and broke the silence, slowly running his finger around the rim of his glass.

"Well I thought I'd hang out here today and help with some yard work." He tapped the bottom of his glass on the table a few times before pushing it away.

"That's what I was hoping to hear," Daddy said in a matter-of-fact tone. "The backyard looks like a jungle and the shrubs could use a good trim. It's not suppose to be as hot today so it's a good day to get it done."

I appreciated Rock's intervention. I was relieved that the focus was taken off of me and put on him. It gave me a moment to clear my mind and get my thoughts together.

"Well, I guess I'll go upstairs and change," Rock said through a heavy breath. He pushed the chair away from the table and bolted up the stairs, leaving me uncomfortably alone with Daddy and my peace was short-lived.

For a moment I was paralyzed in my seat. Unable to move, that is until his eyes dug into me, causing a bone-chilling reaction to escape to a safe haven. I stood abruptly and started towards the stairs, but Daddy stopped me cold with his biblical antics.

"*Come now, and let us reason together, saith the Lord.*"

Frozen with fear I stood with my back to him. My legs were numb, they felt as if someone had buried them in cement. I closed my eyes in an effort to gain control of my nerves.

Daddy relaxed back in his chair. He leaned against the dull brown wall that was in badly need of a paint job, clasped his hands one into the other and rested them on top of his protruding belly. "*Though your sins be as scarlet, they shall be as white as snow; though they be red like crimson, they shall be as wool.*"

I said nothing as I turned to face my demon. To avoid giving eye contact I glanced around the small dim lit breakfast nook. Old pictures of family members hung on the cracked walls with large rusted nails. A gold-toned mirror, which had turned black around the edges, was hanging adjacent the family portraits. Besides the kitchen area, there was nothing more than a sofa, a curio cabinet and an antique chair in the family room that made the house a home. You could feel the summer heat coming through the thin pane windows, but the breeze from the rattling old air conditioner gave the house a nice cool feeling. I reminisced about Mama, how she use to sit at the table and let the stream of air blow her neatly combed bangs into her face. I missed her laughter, the scent of lavender that use to gently brush across your face whenever she walked by… my thoughts were interrupted by the sound of Daddy's voice. "Isaiah 1:18." I snapped back just in time for him to toss me a Bible coarsely across the kitchen table.

"Read Genesis chapter 4, verses 1 through 2."

Daddy hated procrastination so I immediately grabbed the Bible and opened it up to his request. My throat tightened as I read. "*And Adam knew Eve his wife, and she conceived, and bare Cain, and said, I have gotten a man from the Lord. And she again bare his brother Abel…*" Daddy rudely interrupted before I could finish the verse.

"Adam and Eve had two sons. Now read 4, verse 17."

"*And Cain knew his wife, and she conceived, and bare Enoch…*" he interrupted again.

"Stay there, make a mental note. *Cain…knew…his…wife,* what does that mean? It means his wife was kinship. He *knew* her. But, where did the wife come from if Adam and Eve had only two sons, Cain and Abel?" he cut me off before I could respond. "I'll show you. Now read chapter 5, verse 3."

"*And Adam lived a hundred and thirty years, and begat a son in his own likeness, and after his image, and called his name Seth.*"

Daddy rocked calmly back and forth in his chair. "Another son, Seth. Read 5, verse 4."

I was so nervous my mouth felt like cotton. "*And the days of Adam after he had begotten Seth were eight hundred years, and he begat sons and daughters.*"

"Speak up child I can't hear you," Daddy snapped at me as he thumped the chair upright to the floor. He sat erect as I finished the verse. "Read the latter, again."

"*and he begat sons and daughters*," I swallowed hard.

"Sons…and…daughters, which would suggest brothers and sisters. Now, if Adam and Eve were the first man and woman, and their children were the first generation then this scripture would obviously suggest that brothers would have had to have sex with their sisters to procreate." He slammed his hand on top of the table, startling me. "Simply stated, Cain married his sister and bore a son. Adam and Eve were commanded by God to go out and be fruitful, to multiply. Well how did God think they were gonna do it?"

White saliva formed in the corners of Daddy's mouth. It tended to do that whenever he talked too much.

"Incest!" he yelled. "Generations throughout the book of Genesis engaged in kindred relations in order to fulfill God's command. Isaac and Rebekah, Jacob and Rachel, Lot and his daughters," Daddy paused.

I clenched the Bible tight in my hands. Biting the right side of my bottom lip I found myself disgusted with Daddy's justification of incest. "What about Leviticus 18?" I asked in a defiant voice.

"The laws of Leviticus 18 were formulated to keep the Israelites under control. They were pagans, idolaters engaging in inappropriate sexual behaviors. Unlike Genesis, they were heathens, adulterers that were out of control and God needed order. The Bible is a historical book, girl, created for the signs of the times. You have to consider the going-ons when reading its word, haven't I told you that time and time again?"

Daddy was irrational and no matter how many scriptures I quoted from the Bible he would rebut with ones in his defense.

"That's not history, that's hypocrisy," I mumbled under my breath.

With no warning Daddy leaped up from the table and rushed towards me, in a fit of rage he slapped me across my face so hard I nearly lost my balance. My cheek stung from the force. Like a pit bull attacking a chihuahua he grabbed me by the hair like a ragdoll and dragged me upstairs into the bathroom. It felt as though every strand in my head was coming out by the root. Pinning me down with his knee in my chest, Daddy squeezed a large amount of toothpaste onto a toothbrush, clenched my throat, almost choking me, and brushed my teeth until my gums started to bleed. Alarmed and beside myself I fought to stand to my feet. Finally managing to rise to my knees I fell hysterical over the sink. Gagging for air I turned the cold water on full blast and spit out globs of blood and toothpaste into the rust-stained face bowl. Daddy's breathing was heavy. Being a large big-boned man around 230 pounds, he fell back against the wall wheezing, using every ounce of energy he had to catch his breath. I thought he was going to have a heart attack right there. Rock ran into the bathroom with his sneakers in hand. I was choking, my mouth was covered in toothpaste and I was still hanging on to the sink.

"What's going on?" he asked.

Daddy stepped over me and slowly pushed past Rock. "Ask your sister," he remarked walking down the stairs without looking back.

"Let me be, Rock," I wiped the tears from my face with the sleeve of my robe and picked myself up off the floor.

"Are you alright?" he asked concerned.

"Just another one of me and Daddy's heart-to-heart talks." I rinsed my mouth underneath the cold running water and grabbed a clean towel off the towel rack and dried my face. Rock watched silently as I walked down the hall to my bedroom. The sound of the door closing behind me was much like the bars of a jail cell being locked behind an inmate. Rock stood in the hallway alone, wondering what had just happened.

Later that evening Rock had convinced me to go to church. Daddy had a meeting with the deacon board and he couldn't think of a better place to be. It wasn't as though I had a choice in the matter. Daddy would have beaten me into submission anyway had I not gone, so I reluctantly dawdled along.

The drive over was quiet. Rock turned on the radio to break the silence. It was playing Bill Withers, "Grandma's Hands." That was one of Mama's favorite songs before she became so holy and righteous. I guess that's why Daddy didn't mind much when we listened to it. He would never say, but maybe he found some type of comfort in it too. Rock and I tooted up our lips and rocked back and forth singing along with the song. He turned up the volume. It was nice to smile again.

It was only a short drive. By the time the song ended Daddy was pulling up in the parking lot of the small store front church. We hurried out of the car leaving him a few paces behind. He yelled to us. "I'm going downstairs to my meeting. You two wait upstairs until I get out."

"Yes, sir," we synchronized. We swung open the doors. People were gathered in the vestibule waiting for the meeting to begin. We distributed empty hugs and kisses and continued into the brightly lit sanctuary. The atmosphere was serene. The stained glass windows that surrounded the walls were covered with images of God and His disciples bowing before Him. I took a seat at the end of the pew while Rock walked slowly down the middle of the isle and kneeled down before the altar in prayer. Didn't know what he was praying for, or why he was praying for that matter, but one thing's for sure, whatever it was would surely be in vain.

"When you pray, pray from the heart," Mama use to say. "Just tell God how you're feeling and what you need. No fancy talk or big words. Simply speak to Him, son, he already knows what you need before you ask Him anyway." Rock bowed his head and closed his eyes.

"When you come before God, show some respect," he remembered Daddy saying one Sunday morning. "Show some humility when you get in the presence of God. Give him a holy dwelling place."

"Preach Pastor, preach," he recalled one member screaming out.

Rock went over Daddy's past sermons in his head. It was a good thing he paid attention to God's Word during service because now, if only for a moment, he needed God to pay attention to him.

MAY 20, 2008

TRIAL DAY

"Faith, you and your brother seemed fairly close to the members of the church. Did you ever consider going to one of them about your father's molestation?" Teller paced back and forth only to pause for my answer.

"Objection, Your Honor, accusation, molestation has not been proven here."

"Sustain."

"I'll rephrase. Alleged molestation," Teller put his hand to his ear.

I swallowed hard. "No."

"Why not? They were Christians, people of God. One would assume that makes them trustworthy."

"Just because they went to church don't make them trustworthy. Christians are the most judgmental, unrighteous people on the planet. They wouldn't have believed us no way. Daddy had a reputation of being a good man, an honorable man. Everybody thought that we were going through psychological dilemmas anyway because of Mama's death. They would have just said it was the complicated grief that had us delusional."

"Complicated grief?" Teller asked.

"Yes, long lasting grief. At least that's what the psychologist told us. Daddy thought it would be in the family's best interest if we sought professional counseling to help us cope with Mama's death. An effort, he said, that would keep our family strong and help me and my brother to continue living a normal teenage life. For months we spent most of our days in and out of sessions talking to brain freaks, sitting for hours at a time while psychologists and psychiatrists tried to dissect our brain, asking one dumb ass question after another."

Judge Hallow sneered under his glasses, "Young lady."

"I'm sorry, Sir," I apologized.

Teller tapped his hand on his thigh. "And how did you feel about that?"

"I hated it, Rock hated it. Our life was an open book and everyone in the neighborhood and church knew of it, well at least what Daddy wanted them to know. Every move we made, every thought, every gesture was noted. How could Daddy expect us to live a normal life under those circumstances?"

"Did you ever mention your alleged circumstances to the psychologist?"

"No. I was afraid of Daddy and feared what he might do if anyone found out."

Teller paused for a moment before walking away and taking a seat. "No more questions, Your Honor."

"What?" I was confused.

Judge Hallow turned to Joy. "Does the Prosecution have any questions for this witness?"

"We most certainly do," Joy spoke in a confident voice. She was a very beautiful woman, well-polished. French manicured nails, thin arched eyebrows, short but very tasteful black tailored suit and her legs were so well-toned you could probably break glass on 'em. She wore her long black hair pulled back into a ponytail which showed off her thin light-skinned face. She walked up to me with her arms folded across her chest ready to strike.

"Faith, would you say your father secluded you and your brother from the church or other family members any time after your mother's death?"

"No ma'am."

"Did your lifestyle change in any kind of way that would seem suspicious or peculiar to other people?"

"No ma'am."

"What about behavior? Any change in you or your brother's behavior or in fact your father's behavior that would make someone question your home environment or the way your father treated you?"

"No."

Joy turned to the jury. "That's strange, an abused child would possess certain behaviors that would make one aware that rape, abuse or victimization is taking place in the home, or as you claim...alleged incest." She turned to me. "Withdrawal, acting out inappropriately in school or public, behavioral problems, unexplained bruises, fear of being around other people, isolation?"

"Objection, Your Honor. Attorney is not an expert in the field of child abuse," Teller remarked resting his chin in his hand.

"Sustain."

"You said your father was a Pastor of his own church. That can entail huge responsibilities for a person, wouldn't you say, Faith?"

"Yes. Daddy was a very hard worker. He held Bible class on Wednesdays, and Thursdays. He counseled members of the church when needed, and sometimes he would be called away to preach at other churches."

"Burning the candle at both ends per se?"

"Yes you could say that," I responded.

"He also taught Sunday School on occasions, am I right?"

"Yes."

"Your father sounds like a person with not much time on his hands. I assume a person would be tired after carrying such a full load. Rest would be all that's on their mind when coming home, wouldn't you say, Faith?"

"Objection."

"Sustain," Judge Hallow removed his glasses, frustrated. "Get to the point, Counselor."

"What time of day or night would you say these alleged sexual acts occurred?"

I glanced up at Joy. "Sometimes in the middle of the day, sometimes in the middle of the night, I never really looked at the clock."

"Did you ever scream or yell while these alleged acts were being committed?"

"Yes, several times."

"In the middle of the day?"

"Yes."

"And you are sitting here telling the jury that no one, at any time, heard you scream in the middle of the day, on a summer's eve where people are out in their yards, kids playing in the street, neighbors sitting on the porch. Yet, no one, not once heard you scream?"

I suppressed the tears. "I guess not…"

"You guess not? Did your father keep the windows open during the summer days?"

"Yes, all the time, but…" My nerves were beginning to get the better of me.

"Explain how your screams can go unheard if the windows were open." Joy paced back and forth in front of me. Every step became more intimidating than the next.

Rock clasped his hands in front of him and ran his thumbs across his lips. He tried desperately to maintain his composure during questioning. He knew I was hurting and wanted to protect me, that's what he did, he was my protector. Teller tapped his shoulder in an effort to calm him down. Biting his thumbnail, he remained silent.

"I don't know. Maybe no one was out on those particular days. I don't know."

"Highly unlikely," Joy said in a cynical tone. "What about visitors, did you have a lot of those?"

"Yes," I said throatily. People from the church came over often. Sometimes Daddy would hold meetings with the Deacon Board at home. Rock's friends would come over on occasion and hang out with him on the weekends."

"What about you, did you have friends?"

"Not really. I've never been much of a social person, more of an introvert, staying to myself."

"Before or after your mother's passing?"

"Before and after, that's just who I am, everyone knows it."

"And out of all the visitors that came over to your home, nothing seemed out of place to them, nothing abnormal?"

"If so they never mentioned it to me."

"Yes or no, Miss Faith."

"No." This lady was twisting my words, confusing my thoughts, making Daddy out to be the victim and me a liar. She didn't have to admit it, her arrogance implied it. Don't she know that my father didn't give a damn about me or my brother? How could she defend a man who instead of protecting his children inflicted nothing but pain upon them? A man that used the same penis to impregnate my mother to penetrate his own daughter, where in his diluted, twisted mind, had done nothing wrong. I searched around the room for an exit. I felt sick.

"Did your father ever take you to the doctor for any reason after your mother passed, annual physical, injuries of any kind?"

"Yes. My brother and I both had annual physicals."

"Ever had a pap smear or pelvic exam?"

"Yes, once…or twice."

"At such a young age?"

"No…I mean yes," I was speaking faster than I was thinking. I couldn't get my thoughts to catch up with my words. I needed a moment to gather myself. "Daddy insisted. He accused me of having sex…or something or other…with a boy."

"Did the doctor ever discuss with you any abnormalities that were found during these tests?"

"No…well not with me, but with Daddy."

"You stated that your father was aggressive with you during his alleged sexual acts, and you're saying that your doctor never discussed with you any concerns of physical abuse or sexual activity that would have shown up on your tests?"

"If he did, he told Daddy, not me."

"Were you sexually active with anybody at the time of these physicals, Miss Faith?"

I hesitated. "Yes I was."

"A boyfriend, a friend?"

My throat was tied in knots. I couldn't answer.

"Could you tell the court how many?" she paused. "One…two…three different boys?"

Rock's leg was shaking faster than a jack hammer underneath the table. He was losing his willpower to sit still.

"One," I said in a low voice.

"I'm sorry, Miss Faith, speak up so the court can hear you."

"One," my voice echoed through the courtroom.

"When did you end your virginity, Miss Faith."

I gazed down at the palms of my hands that were shaking and sweaty from the nervous tension endured by Joy's line of questioning. I cupped them one into the other in an effort to ease the strain. "14 years old," I said grudgingly.

"A year before your mother died?" Joy asked in a demeaning voice.

A knot tied my throat. Anxiety took over my body and I felt sick to my stomach.

Joy walked snappishly over to Prosecution's table, retrieved a document and returned to the podium holding it mid-air. "Let the record show that on the date of Miss Faith's physical, tests proved that she *was* in fact sexually active as her father had presumed."

The clanking of Joy's shoes against the courtroom floor as she walked self-assured back to her seat seemed louder than usual. I was beginning to feel overwhelmed.

"Counsel has no further questions."

Teller stood up. "I have one more question, Your Honor."

Judge Hallow nodded.

"Who did you end your virginity with, Faith?"

My face tightened. I had promised myself I would never share that sickening experience with anyone, let alone a room full of critics and reporters, but Joy had thrown me into a state of victimization and ridicule that left me no other choice. Humiliated and on the verge of tossing up everything I had just eaten, I blurted out the name, "Daddy!" It came out loud and wretched against the quietness of the room. My heart thumped. I could feel the razor blades cutting through the cavity of my soul. With a sense of vindication, Teller eased back into his seat.

Whispers of criticism charged the courtroom and Rock became irate as the cry of Psalms 35:1 tore from his lips. "*Plead my cause, O Lord, with them that strive with me. Fight against them that fight against me*!"

Judge Hallow banged his gavel trying to control the courtroom, but his efforts went unheard. I vomited right there at the podium, barely missing the feet of the bailiff.

Rock jumped up from his seat. Court officers rushed over to detain him. "*Let them be confounded and put to shame that seek after my soul, let them be turned back and brought to confusion that devise my hurt*!"

"Order, order in this court! Order I say! Counsel, control your client!"

Teller stood helpless.

"*For without cause have they hid for me their net in a pit, which without cause they have digged for my soul*!" Rock was belligerent.

"Bailiff, clear the courtroom now! I want everyone out!" Judge Hallow yelled over the noise as he continued banging his gavel. "This court is adjourned until eight a.m. tomorrow morning!"

The officers grabbed Rock, shoving his face into the table as they handcuffed him and took him into custody. His voice could still be heard from a distance, "*Let destruction come upon him at unawares, and let his net that he hath hid catch himself into that very destruction let him fall*!"

I paused, looked over at Joy who peered back at me. My response brought no further questions.

JUNE 28, 2008

PRESENT DAY

I've had insomnia these past few nights, lost all respect for humanity and prejudice has fluttered my heart like a cold winter storm that struck unexpectedly.

Summer's here again. It's beautiful this time of year, the flowers cover mother earth like a rainbow blanket. I pulled my long pink robe tightly around me, releasing myself into the warmth of its shelter. I gazed out the window into the half abandoned neighborhood. Several homes have been vacant for so long that squatters have begun living in them, the rest have been either burnt to the ground by arsonist or vandalized. Local thugs have turned the destitute house on the dead end of the street into a drug house. The wired fence that surrounded it stored two chained Rottweiler's in badly need of a bath. Dirt holes were dug throughout the poorly kept yard and the stench from the dog manure was almost unbearable. The windows on the side of the house were barred and the two in front were boarded up. The dogs ran around erratic, barking fiercely at the crack-heads that would come back and forth to the house at all times of the night.

The only beauty that was left of the neighborhood was an old field that set on the corner of the block that blossomed with beautiful sunflowers. Neighborhood folks use to say we had our own batch of sunshine right in the middle of the ghetto. I snickered to myself and glanced over at Ms. Eloise's house, the elderly woman who lived in the old yellow house next door to the neighborhood store. She was a sweet old lady, not very clean. She rocked in her old rocking chair every day at the same time. Her porch was full of old boxes of shoes and clothes that belonged to her late husband. She once told me that keeping his belongings around somehow made her feel like he was still with her. She talked about how they used to sit on the porch together rocking in their old rocking chairs talking the day away. She said that one day they even talked until the sun set and rose again. She described it as one of the most beautiful sights she had ever seen.

I always thought it strange that a woman would waste her days just sitting, not having much to do but wave at everybody that passed by, but Ms. Eloise thought differently. She said it was wonderful watching the neighborhood kids grow up. Some move out and start their own lives, and some stay where they are and eventually have their own families. She has seen things that have made her proud and things that have made her weep. Although she and her husband never had children, they treated the neighborhood kids as their own. Everyone on the block was saddened when Mister died. They came together to care for Ms. Eloise and do their best to keep her in good health. Mama called her the grandmother of the block. I don't think anyone deserved that title more than Ms. Eloise. I sometimes wonder if she and Mama ever talked about….I cut my thoughts short, walked back to the kitchen and poured myself a cup of coffee.

DECEMBER 24, 2005

I woke this morning feeling not quite like myself, although I haven't felt like myself for some time now, somehow I felt today was going to be a particularly unusual day. I had that eerie feeling you get when something is not quite right, that feeling you get in the pit of your stomach like something bad is about to happen.

Today was our annual Christmas Eve service at church and I was excited about it. Rock and I always look forward to this service because it's the time that he and I get to sing a duet together. Music was comfort to our soul. It was our way of escaping from who we were to who we wanted to be. For a brief time we could lose ourselves in the spirit and not battle with what was going on in the flesh.

I decided to wear my long white flowing dress tonight, but I couldn't find my black slip to go underneath. I searched high and low with no success. In the midst of my search I heard Daddy calling my name from downstairs. "Faith, girl you hear me calling you! Come down these stairs right now before I come up there after you! It's time to go!" he yelled with that impatient voice that I hate so much.

I looked up to find Rock standing in the doorway. He was handsome in his black suit and red tie. "Girl, come on. You know how Daddy gets if he's late for church."

"I know, Rock, but I can't find my slip. You can see clear through me with this white dress on."

"Well you better make it work because Daddy's patience won't last too long."

I didn't want to make Daddy angry before church service so I decided to take Rock's advice. I put my favorite red silk flower in my hair, threw on my long wool coat and ran downstairs to leave. I brushed passed Daddy who was standing at the end of the steps staring at me as if he could see every brain cell in my head.

"Ready, Daddy," I said as I rushed out the door to the car that had been warming up for nearly 15 minutes.

We pulled up in front of the church just in time for devotion. You could hear the Deacons praying and the congregation singing outside of the church. It was times like this that I appreciated the spirit of God. The music sounded so good that it marinated in my soul, and for a brief moment my brother and I felt safe and secure, and for the time being, that was good enough for us.

The church program was wonderful, well put together by the Christmas committee. Little Shanay and Tyrome played Joseph and Mary, and Sister Love's children played the three wise men. When Rock and I got up to sing we heard someone yell out "Sing children, sing." It was Mother Pearl from the front pew. She was what the church called a gate lifter. The person that you can count on every Sunday to praise the loudest and lead the congregation in worship. "Never be ashamed to praise your God," she would always scream. "Thanksgiving is in your praise. What you ask of God is in your praise." Mother Pearl had fought a lot of sickness in her life and was a witness to the miracles of God, her smile glistened as she raised her hands toward heaven. "Let your light so shine, children of God, let your light so shine."

Rock took the microphone first and decided to say a few words before our song. "I'd like to dedicate this to our mother," his voice cracked. "It was one of her favorite songs," he said throatily. "She suffered a lot in her last days, but I can't ever remember a moment when she complained about anything. So this song is for you, Mama," he said looking up toward heaven. "It's entitled, 'UP TO THE MOUNTAIN'." Daddy had a solemn look on his face and for the first time ever my heart wept for him. Regardless of the heartless way he treated us, we both knew that he sincerely loved our mother.

It was truly a beautiful song. I reminisced about Mama as we sang. Daddy dabbed a tissue in the corner of his eyes from time to time and emotions ran high throughout the congregation as the Holy Spirit filled the sanctuary. Rock's voice was strong and filled with emotion.

"I went up to the mountain because you ask me to,
Up over the clouds to where the sky was blue,
I could see all around me everywhere,
I could see all around me everywhere.

Sometimes I feel like I've never been nothing but tired,
and I'll be working until the day I expire.
Sometimes I just lay down, Lord no more can I do,
But then I go on again because you ask me to.

Some days I look down afraid I will fall,
and though the sun shines, I see nothing at all.
But I hear your sweet voice, Oooo comin and go, comin and go,
Lord telling me softly you love me so."

For a brief moment I felt a strong presence. It was Mama sitting in the back pew smiling at me. She looked so proud dressed in her white choir robe with a grin on her face that could light up the midnight sky. It was as though she came to tell me that everything was going to be alright. I stretched out my hand towards her. She smiled, blew me a gentle kiss and slowly faded away. Tears filled my eyes as Rock and I finished the song on a powerful note. We held each other tight, taking advantage of the stillness and tranquility of peace of mind. We never allowed ourselves to think about the nights end where we would once again be left alone to battle with the unspeakable sins of our father.

We arrived home around 10:00 p.m. and I was exhausted from the night's events. I took off my coat, hung it in the small closet of the hallway and rushed to my room. Daddy called out my name from the bottom of the stairs. I turned to catch a glimpse of his condemned face. There was this moment of silence, maybe five or six seconds, but to me it felt like a lifetime.

"What's wrong Daddy?" Rock asked standing in guard.

Daddy ignored his intervention and immediately started in on me.

"Girl, I can see straight through that dress. How dare you disrespect our Lord by coming to church looking like a harlot."

"Come on Daddy, no one saw, she had on her choir robe," Rock responded in my defense.

"Hush up boy, I'm talking to your sister." Daddy was furious.

Chill bumps invaded my body. That eerie feeling in the pit of my stomach was back. "I couldn't find my long black slip, and we were already late…I just made do with what I had."

"By exposing yourself like a prostitute?"

"No, Sir." My stomach churned with sourness.

Rock stood cold. Daddy paused for a moment and just looked at me with this blank look on his face. He stirred, no response, brushed passed Rock and went into his bedroom, closing the door behind him. Not knowing what to expect Rock and I remained quiet. A few seconds later we could hear Daddy playing the song "Hallelujah" by Jeff Buckley on his beat up old stereo. The familiar tune composed in my heart like the beauty of summer's end. Mama used to listen to this song every Christmas Eve, despite the cold brokenness of its meaning, its lyrics held the rhythm of both love and pain and that was something Mama mourned secretly everyday of her life. I brought my attention back to Rock who seized a fearful watch from the bottom of the stairs. Afraid to speak to one another we waited unknowingly in the darkness of silence.

Amid the serenity of the music, Daddy emerged from his room in a rage. He pushed passed Rock and charged me with a belt in hand. I turned to run, but he grabbed my ankle and pulled me down the stairs. Screaming, I clawed the steps trying to crawl back up. Rock jumped on Daddy's back in an effort to free me from his reviled grip. It was just enough force for my foot to slip out of his hand and paw my way back up the stairs and flee to my bedroom. He turned to Rock and charged him like an out of control bull. Seizing his hand around his throat he knocked him into the living room wall. Pictures fell to the floor leaving broken glass shattered everywhere.

"You think you man enough to stand up to me, boy!" Daddy was infuriated. He grabbed Rock by his suit jacket and dragged him down the hallway. Rock managed to come out of his jacket and run towards the front door, but Daddy caught him by the back of his shirt and threw him to the floor. He struck Rock with several blows from the belt. Trying to defend himself, he bawled up in the fetal position to shield the pain of Daddy's wrath. "I'll show you who's the man of this house." Daddy grabbed him by his pants, ripping them in the process and lugged him down the basement stairs kicking and crying. Rock tried to grab hold of the dry-rot banister but it didn't give much support. He stumbled down the corroded steps with a force that knocked the wind clean out of him, unbalanced he collapsed hard onto the concrete floor. Hardhearted, Daddy made his way back up the stairs in search of me, locking the door behind him.

Rock struggled to catch his breath. Exhausted, he stared up at the single bulb chandelier hanging from the brown water stained ceiling. Specks of mold appeared in the corners and the smell of mildew was making him sick to his stomach. The stucco walls around him were painted an ugly yellow color and the base had started to peel. Noises could be heard from upstairs and the sound of my screams echoed through the house. Helpless, he pulled himself up to his knees, raised his head and hands toward heaven and prayed that the love of God would protect me.

Daddy rushed up the stairs to my bedroom like an animal searching for its prey. I ran frantically into my closet and slammed the door behind me. "Open up this door, Faith! This is my house! You will respect me in my own house!"

I slid as far back in the closet as possible. I pressed my hands tightly over my ears trying desperately to drown out the sound of my father's enraged voice. "No, stop it!" I screamed. I heard a loud thump, my closet door flung open. Daddy grabbed me by my hair and pulled me to my feet. "No Daddy, please," I was hysterical, my heart felt like it was gonna burst through the cavity of my chest. "God, no, please," I begged with the mercy of life.

"You wanna prance around here like an animal with no sense then I'll treat you like one." He threw me to the floor. I fell on my hands and knees to break my fall. He kneeled behind me, took the belt and wrapped it around my neck, almost choking me, and buckled it as tight as it would go. He wrapped the strap around the palm of his hand, tightening it more and more with each grip. I managed to force my hand between the belt and my throat allowing myself just enough room to breathe.

"How dare you prostitute yourself before the church and defile holy ground with your loose ways." Daddy pulled my dress up, grabbed the crouch of my panties and ripped them off. I gasped for air. My heart raced as he called out scriptures from Ezekiel 43. "*Son of man, this is the place of my throne and the place for the soles of my feet. The house of Israel will never again defile my holy name by their prostitution.*" Exposing my genitals he pried his way between my legs, heaved my hips up and sodomized me with such force I almost choked on my own vomit.

"*They defiled my holy name by their detestable practices, so I destroyed them in my anger*." Daddy thrust his penis in me harder. The pain was so severe I couldn't scream. God knows I tried.

I saw Mama one more time that night. Her hazel eyes red from crying. Powerless and ashamed, she witnessed only a moment and then slowly faded away. Incapable of holding myself up any longer I lost my balance, my arms and knees gave way and I collapsed to the floor just as Daddy ejaculated. His incestuous howl was like a dog in heat.

I laid there on the cold hard floor wishing death upon myself. Praying that it would not come by the hands of someone else, but by my own father who had managed to destroy the last piece of innocence I had left in my young fragile body.

MAY 21, 2008

TRIAL

I was a mess this morning. I could hardly remember my name, too focused on yesterday's events to focus on today. A sudden wave of dizziness overcame me. I tried to calm myself but the hard pounding in my chest made it next to impossible to gain control of my nerves. I pray that nothing is disclosed today to make Rock lose it again in Court. Satan has a way of rearing his ugly head when things are at its worse. In the distance I could hear the clanking of hard-bottom shoes coming down the corridor of the court house. No one made a sound as the doors of the courtroom opened. There stood my brother, his hands and feet shackled, connected by a common chain around his waist. I cringed as our eyes caught glimpse of one another. Two well-fit officers escorted him to his seat at the defendant's table next to Teller. They treated him like he was a danger to society, a harbored fugitive that would escape at any moment. My hands began to tremble. I had a sick feeling in the pit of my stomach and I was suffering from a bad case of vertigo. "Please, Rock. Don't freak out on me today, not today," I whispered under my breath.

Judge Hallow entered the courtroom. He had an intolerant look on his face. "Mr. Teller, I assume you have spoken to your client and we won't have any more outbursts in my courtroom today?"

"Teller nodded in agreement.

"With that being said…you may call your next witness." Judge Hallow peered from underneath his glasses.

Teller tapped the table three times before standing up. He cleared his throat. "Your Honor, Defense would like to call, to testify by proxy, God's messenger to the stand."

The courtroom gasped. Joy immediately attacked Teller's calling of witness. "Inadmissible, Your Honor, this is absurd!" She jumped up with a force that nearly spilled her hot cup of coffee on her polished red suit. "Mr. Teller is making a mockery of this Court," her voice was high-pitched and bothered. "God cannot be on trial here. It is absolutely impossible."

The atmosphere shifted, yet remained perplexingly quiet.

Judge Hallow wrinkled his forehead, a baffled look on his face. "Counselors approach the bench." He was not pleased.

As usual, Teller walked slow, his torso slightly bent forward and his hands clasped tightly behind his back. My eyes remained fixed on Judge Hallow just long enough to notice his discontent.

Whispering, he placed his hand over the microphone. "Counselor what are you doing?"

Teller cocked his head to the side. "I intend to prove that a higher power caused my client to react in a way that was beyond his control."

"Your Honor, this is highly unethical." Joy was taken aback.

"I intend to prove otherwise, Your Honor. This individual will stand as God's witness as well as the cornerstone to my case."

"State did not receive this information during discovery," Joy's voice had taken a harsh tone.

"I assure you this was decided last minute," Teller responded.

"Counselor, do you live to wreak havoc in my courtroom?"

"No, Judge. I'm here to defend my client's innocence in every way possible allowed by law, and if that means I have to persuade the jurors to believe the most unbelievable story ever told in this courtroom, so be it."

There was a moment of incredulous silence. Judge Hallow peered at Teller with displeasure. "Do you understand the boundaries this line of questioning can cross?"

"I understand more the unpleasant circumstances my client will be subject to if sent to prison at seventeen years of age for a crime he did not commit." Teller stood firm.

Judge Hallow sighed. "I hope you know what you are doing,

Counselor." Despite his skepticism he allowed Teller to present his argument before the court.

Riled by the Judge's decision, Joy walked heavily back to her seat.

"Let the record show that I will permit Counselor's defense, but with limitations to my discretion," he added. "Mr. Teller you may present your case," Judge Hallow's voice was filled with reservation.

For a brief moment I thought Teller had lost his mind, but it only took me a few seconds to shake off this will never work feeling that surged through my veins. Tension fired through me as I sat erect and attentive in my seat along with everyone else in the courtroom, each as lost in their own thoughts as the next, waiting to see how Teller was going to proceed. I relaxed my nerves.

Challenged, yet confident, Teller stood. "Defense calls Dr. Skyler to the stand."

He was a short man maybe five feet or so with strong features and a large chin. His head was bald, his eyebrows and mustache was thick and gray, and he was wearing a drab black suit that although didn't do much for his physique, gave him a sense of power and high esteem. He was sworn in and Teller approached.

"Dr. Skyler, could you please express to the court your professorship and what qualifies you as a Biblical Scholar."

His voice was strong and emphatic. Who would have expected such a large voice would come out of such a small man.

"I hold numerous degrees from Princeton, Manchester, and Oxford. I have a B.A. in Religious Studies, a M.A. in Philosophy and Psychology, a Masters of Divinity in Christian Education, and a Ph.D in Theology. My specialties are Biblical Language, The History of Christianity, The Old and New Testament, and Hebrew Studies."

"Teller gave an impressive smile. "My goodness, you are God," he remarked sarcastically.

"Minus the divinity," Dr. Skyler beamed.

Onlookers sat amused.

Teller walked over to the table and picked up the Holy Bible. "Without getting into specifics, Dr. Skyler, could you please explain to the court, briefly, your view of what the Bible is or is not?" he put his hand to his ear.

"Well that depends on who you ask."

Teller turned in a sarcastic voice. "Well I thought I was asking you, Doctor."

Engaged snickers teased the courtroom. Judge Hallow struck his gavel. "Move on Counselor."

Dr. Skyler cleared his throat and adjusted himself in his seat. "First off, Christians must understand the Bible is a historical book with countless repetitions, imperfections and discrepancies, written not by God Himself, but by many authors over the course of hundreds of years. The Holy Bible consists of contradictory understandings, misleading idealizations, and different points of views. Many scriptures even entire Books have been omitted from the Bible, suggesting that Man has not only tampered with the word of God, but conformed it to Man's own satisfaction and biases, questioning its credibility and true form. Most of it, especially the book of Revelations should not be taken literally but more often figuratively. Jesus himself spoke in parables rather than literal terms, therefore leaving Man to his own interpretation."

"Are you telling us…Christians," Teller gestured around the room, "that the Bible is an imperfect book?"

"The modern Bible has numerous translations, King James, New King James, Amplified, New American Standard, New International, The Message Bible…versions that have transformed biblical language into contemporary language to be easily understood. Man is imperfect, so anything that is altered or tampered with by Man is flawed. The aforementioned translations were converted by mankind, therefore erroneous. Historically speaking, even the original translation of the Bible is questionable. Many biblical scholars inquire if today's Bible truly hold the original language of the early Hebrew Bible, was the language itself, in fact, properly or correctly translated into modern day scripture?'"

"Dr. Skyler, in your area of expertise, how many different languages would you say the Bible have been translated into?"

"If I am mathematically correct, sections of the Bible have been translated into 848 languages, the New Testament 1,168 languages and the Bible in its entirety has been translated into 438 languages. Combined, that's a total of 2,454 languages."

"You mentioned parts of the Bible. Can you be more specific?"

"Not all translations of the Bible include all books of the Bible. For example, the Tanakh, the Jewish Bible, consists of twenty-four books, the Catholic Bible has seventy-three books and the Protestant Bible has sixty-six books."

"Could this possibly be the reason division exist amongst the church?"

"Objection, Your Honor, Counsel is leading the witness?" Joy opposed.

"Sustain," Judge Hallow remarked.

"I'll rephrase the question. In your opinion, Dr. Skyler, can these various biblical translations cause division amongst people?"

"Absolutely…it's called religion."

"Religion…religion," Teller repeated to himself as he walked swiftly over to the table and picked up another Bible. "Religion!" he wailed as he held the books in the air, one in each hand. "I have here the King James Bible used by Protestants. The same Bible used by my client's father who was of the Baptist faith. The other book is the New American Standard version, which is translated in more modern terms for simple folks like us to understand." He handed the Bible to Dr. Skyler. "Stay with me for a moment, Doc." He flipped through the pages of the King James Bible. "I'm not here to debate religion, Dr. Skyler, but can you explain to us briefly how religion came about?" Engrossed in scripture, Teller never looked up. "And explain it to us in a way a four-year-old would understand."

"Simply put, different people had different beliefs, this triggered the foundation for division, and so religion was born," Dr. Skyler responded, once again shifting in his seat.

"Turn with me, Doctor, if you'd please, to one of my favorite Books of the Bible, First Samuel 31." Teller ran his finger down the words of the page until he found the scriptures he was looking for. "Read for me verses 4 through 6 from the New American Standard version so that the court may have clarity of what is being said." Holding the Bible in his right hand, Teller placed his left hand behind his back, bent his torso slightly forward and listened intently.

Dr. Skyler cleared his throat. "*Then Saul said to his armor bearer, Draw your sword and pierce me through with it, otherwise these uncircumcised will come and pierce me through and make sport of me. But his armor bearer would not, for he was greatly afraid. So Saul took his sword and fell on it. When his armor bearer saw that Saul was dead, he also fell on his sword and died with him. Thus Saul died with his three sons, his armor bearer, and all his men on that day together.*" Dr. Skyler enunciated each word, speaking in a deep and authoritative voice.

Teller leafed through the pages again. "Now, Dr. Skyler, could you go to Second Samuel 21, verse 12 and read that for me? Once again for clarity of the people would you please read from the New American Standard."

Dr. Skyler turned the pages generously and with care as if the Bible was respected as God Himself. "*then David went and took the bones of Saul and the bones of Jonathan his son from the men of Jabesh-gilead, which had stolen them from the open square of Beth-shan, where the Philistines had hanged them on the day the Philistines struck down Saul in Gilboa.*"

"Struck down?" Teller asked twitching. His OCD kicked into overdrive. "The King James version uses the word slain, when the Philistines had *slain* Saul in Gilboa."

"Yes, different terminology, but correct" Dr. Skyler answered.

Teller drew near to the podium with a rapt gaze. "Contradiction? Mistake?"

"Contradictions," Dr. Skyler confirmed.

Teller leaned in close, invading Dr. Sklyer's space. "In First Samuel 31, Saul took the sword and *fell* upon it, but in Second Samuel 21, the Philistines *slain* Saul." Teller paused in thought. Placing his foot upon the edge of the podium he slipped his left hand into the front pocket of his pants. "How can that be?" he asked in an inquisitive voice. "Both scriptures can't be true." Before Dr. Skyler could answer, Teller summoned him again. "Go with me once more to the Gospels. All four appear to be inconsistent of each other, but for the sake of time we'll just review two. First read Luke 23, verse 46. Once you get there feel free to start reading.

Dr. Skyler complied. "*And Jesus, crying out with a loud voice, said, 'Father, INTO YOUR HANDS I COMMIT MY SPIRIT,' having said this, He breathed His last.*"

"The King James' version says, 'And having said thus, He gave up the ghost.' Correct?" Teller asked.

"Correct," Dr. Skyler confirmed.

"Now, the Gospel of John, chapter 19, verse 30." Teller waited patiently. His eyes locked on Dr. Skyler as he read.

"*Therefore when Jesus had received the sour wine, He said, 'It is finished!' And He bowed His head and gave up His spirit.*"

Teller interjected. "Once again, King James says, "His ghost."

"Correct."

"That will suffice, thank you, Doctor." He walked over to the jury waving the Bible in the air. "Even the Gospels contradict each other on the details of Jesus Christ's last words. One scripture said Jesus cried out in a loud voice, 'Father, into Your hands I commit my spirit,' and then He gave up the ghost. Another scripture states, after He had received the sour wine He replied, 'It is finished!' and then He bowed His head and gave up the ghost. Contradictions, flaws, imperfections, the Bible is full of them." He sauntered back over to Dr. Skyler. "Amongst the various translations, contradictions and religions, can we truly peg the Bible to be an accurate book of truth or simply man's own interpretation of what they believe it to be?" He paused and stared at Dr. Skyler for a moment, waiting on a response.

"The Bible is many things to many people," Dr. Skyler remarked.

"Deceptive?" He turned his ear.

"Of course, the Bible can be very deceptive. If placed in the wrong hands it can become a very dangerous tool. The Bible is known to be at the core of religious crimes, holy wars, religious cults…"

Joy attacked. "Objection, Your Honor. Counsel is tainting the minds of this jury. We are not talking about a cult here, we are…."

"Aren't we, Ms. Joy?" Teller retaliated in a loud voice. We're talking about a man who used religion to physically, mentally and emotionally rape his children. A man who misconstrued the Bible for the sole purpose of controlling and manipulating innocent minds, creating this fallacy of superiority in an effort to mask the true inferior, inadequate, delusional person he essentially was." Teller tapped the top of the table three times.

My heart ceased to beat. Nobody could have described Daddy in a more truthful way. Teller was just being intellectually kind.

"Objection, Your Honor, this case has not been tried in its entirety." Joy was pissed off. "There has been no final verdict issued here. Counsel is being speculative and slanderous to the victim's character. I move to strike all latter remarks made by Mr. Teller," she demanded.

"It is so ordered." Judge Hallow leaned forward in a less than admirable way. "Mr. Teller, you will not try my patience or this courtroom again. One more incident like that and you will be held in contempt. Is that understood?"

"My apologies to the court, Your Honor. May I continue?" he asked in a more composed manner.

"You may," Judge Hallow responded still a bit agitated.

"Dr. Skyler, we often hear about children being abused for religious beliefs. What, in your opinion, do you think coerce parents to commit such brutal acts in the name of religion?"

"In religious concept, disobedience to your parents is considered soul damnation before God. Discipline is a way of avoiding eternal hell. Some parents believe they are helping their children by ridding them of evil doing and delivering them from the gates of hell. They inflict pain upon their child in the name of God. They believe scripture, '*spare the rod spoil the child*,' justifies physical punishment. Religion such as the Baptist faith, believe discipline is sanctioned by God. Proverbs 23 verses 13 and 14 seems to imply this by indicating, '*Do not withhold discipline from a child for if you strike him with the rod he will not die, but strike him with the rod and save his soul from death*.' These scriptures do not in any way entail abuse, but discipline, the teaching of a child to understand right from wrong, to respect and follow the law. These scriptures are rules for parents to guide their children in the right direction. To help them, not harm them."

"So you're saying that these, just as many scriptures, are taken out of context?" Teller asked.

"Absolutely, the Bible also says, '*provoke your children not to wrath, but bring them up in the nurture and admonition of the Lord*,' which means parents also have responsibilities to a child to not invoke abuse, ridicule, or undue cruelty upon their children, but to provide love, kindness and understanding."

"Through the spirit of God?" Teller asked.

"Yes," Dr. Skyler agreed.

"What about the Old Testament, incest, murder, drunkenness…also taken out of context?"

"The incestuous acts in the Old Testament are viewed by many Christians and religious groups as justifiable means to commit these same acts today. But these relations were only approved by God for reproduction of mankind, as Man could not procreate in any other way. This was God's order. But Man began to fall out of line with God's plan so He enforced strict laws against incest which can be found in the Mosaic Law, the Law of Moses."

"Can today's Christians be taking the Bible too serious?"

Dr. Skyler rubbed his hand across his forehead to the back of his neck. Taking a moment to massage the stiffness from sitting in one place too long. "That's a question for the ages, but I would definitely say in some instances, yes. As stated before, the Bible is historical doctrine. Parts of it, such as stories from the Old Testament, does not adhere to present standards and should not be compared to society today."

Teller turned his attention to Rock. "Tell us, Dr. Skyler, how can religious abuse affect the life or mental state of a child?"

Dr. Skyler sat upright. Resting his clasped hands in his lap, he took in a much needed breather. "Some children continue to turn to God for healing and strength, whereas others rebel. They become angry with God. They feel that God has turned His back on them or abandoned them in some way."

"Psychological behaviors?" Teller asked.

"If children continue to be abused in the name of God they are more likely to turn away from spirituality or Christianity as a whole. Religious abuse can have detrimental effects. Abused children may start harming or even killing themselves or others in the name of God. Withdrawal, seclusion, depression, aggressiveness towards others, even violence can develop."

"Violence towards the abuser?"

"Not always, but in some cases. Many times kids flee from their abuser, seeking refuge in a much safer place or environment. They sometimes fantasize about harming the person, even going to the extent of threatening them with harsh force, but they likely withdraw from these threats because of their fear of God or the abuser. The child has been taught to respect God and because God is seen as an authoritative figure, they also see their abuser in the same light, so it is highly unlikely that they will bring harm to that person, instead they may displace that anger or aggression towards other people. Resentment, hatred, all of these can cause demented behavior or sometimes the opposite. Children can turn from being extroverts to introverts. Abuse can be the origin of either meekness or hostility within a child."

Teller gave a confident smile. "Thank you Doctor, there will be no further questions." He trudged back over to Rock whose arms were crossed securely over his chest as if to safeguard his self-control. Teller bent low and whispered something in Rock's ear that made him smile. I would like to believe he was thanking him for today's restraint.

We sat in the courtroom for hours day after day, listening to Teller and Joy question and cross-exam witness after witness, only breaking once for a thirty minute lunch. Theologians, Psychologists and Psychiatrists took the stand one after the other. Teller fought hard to free Rock and me from the emotional and physical despair we suffered from our father, every now and again hashing it out with Prosecution. I sat adjacent to Rock who periodically looked over at me to make sure I was alright. At moments when testimony became too hard he would turn to me and whisper "Sweet Reverie." That was Mama's label for our "happy place." She would send us there whenever life became unbearable. It was a place where we could escape and go wherever we wanted to go, a place of peace and serenity. Mama used to go there a lot, especially when she was in pain. On the nights Daddy would argue and fuss to no end, Mama would take us into our bedroom, close the door and the three of us would gather hands in a circle and we would go to the most beautiful place, just the three of us. A place where heaven met earth and the waves of the ocean would carry us away to a terrain of tranquility and happiness. I always thought God never gave us much in life. Why He chose to take away the one true piece of happiness me and Rock ever had I'll never know. I'm still looking for the I.O.U. He owes us. I mean He didn't say it to me personally, but I wrote it down the day Mama died. I figured God had to owe us something big for taking away the one person who truly loved us. It's been five long years now God, so I think I'll cash in that I.O.U.

JUNE 30, 2008

PRESENT DAY

I decided to visit Ms. Eloise today. I hadn't seen her much since the trial and just wanted to make sure she wasn't in need of anything. Mama used to visit her every day, sometimes to help around the house, but mostly just to sit and talk.

The air was hot and humid. It was the middle of summer and a sizzling ninety-two degrees. I put my hands above my eyes to try and block out the beaming of the sun. Although Ms. Eloise only lived a few houses away, it was just enough distance to feel the sweat sticking to my skin like glue. You know that feeling you get when no matter how many showers you take that sticky feeling just won't go away.

I walked carefully up the cracked cement steps onto the old porch. The screen door was full of holes and half torn off the hinges. I knocked gently so not to do anymore damage to the door that had already been done. Ms. Eloise answered, her antique wooden cane supporting her frail body. Age spots covered her light wrinkled skin. Although she was of age, she was an attractive woman, a bit on the thin side. She was dressed in a homely floral red dress, and her long gray hair was pulled neatly back into a tight round bun.

"Why if it ain't the prettiest girl on the block," she said as she greeted me with a glass of cold lemonade.

"Expecting me?" I jokingly asked as I grabbed the ice-cold glass out of her hand.

"Just trying to cool the day's heat off of me is all. Would you like a glass?"

"No thank you."

"I think it best we sit out on the porch and talk. It's hotter than the devil's den in here. My house don't do much for air condition if you know what I mean." She smiled and slowly sat down on the porch swing that rested beside an old crate she used as a table. I handed her the glass of lemonade and plopped down beside her. We were silent for a few moments. The only sound that was heard was the squeaking of the swing as she swung slowly back and forth, sipping on her lemonade.

"My aren't you the prettiest little thing," she repeated gazing across the street at the field of sunflowers. "Yes you are. Growing up to be as beautiful as your mother, you are." She squinted from the beaming of the sun. Deathly afraid of storms though she was."

Ms. Eloise had a tendency to talk about several different things at one time. Old age I guess. I listened quietly.

"We both knew how terrified she was of storms, so when she would come down and visit me and Mister we would tell her that thunder was nothing more than God moving his furniture around in heaven." She smiled to herself. "I really don't know if she believed us or not, but it always seemed to make her feel better."

I touched Ms. Eloise's hand, my fingers caressing hers. "She loved you and Mister very much, Ms. Eloise, we all did."

"I remember the day she had you. I was her mid-wife you know?"

"Yes, ma'am, I know," I said respectfully.

"It was during Sunday morning church service, a terrible storm that day. The wind was so high trees were being pulled up by the root. Lightening lit up the sky like fireworks and the thunder sounded like World War II was happening right there at Missionary Baptist Church." She took a sip of her lemonade. "Yep, I think that's what sent your Mama into labor that day. Right when Pastor said, "Faith is…, there was a thunderous boom, and your mother let out a scream so loud we swore she must have received a personal visit from the Good Lord Himself." She snickered to herself. "Well, when your father found out that God had decided to bore you right there in His house, he nearly fainted. We all did, you were two weeks early you know."

I closed my eyes, recalling how often Mama used to tell me that story. She called it her "miracle story." I wonder if she felt as good telling it as I felt hearing it.

"Yep, you shot out like a bat out-of-hell."

I snapped back to reality.

"Didn't give me no time to prepare myself. I delivered you right there in church with the congregation looking on," Ms. Eloise smiled. "Oh yes, my child, you were definitely a gift from God." She tapped my leg lightly. "Your mother looked up at Pastor with those big angel eyes of hers and said, 'Faith…Faith is her name.'" Ms. Eloise nodded. "I couldn't think of anything more befitting, none of us could."

I found it hard to say what I really felt, but I spoke carefully so not to show her no disrespect. "My name and my life are two totally different things, Ms. Eloise. Me and faith ain't got nothing in common."

She turned towards me and clutched her wrinkled, but gentle hand underneath my chin. "Sometimes in life child our name is all we got, you hear me? It's all we got. If we don't hold it in reverence nobody else will."

I listened with no response. My condemned eyes stared back at her.

"Now, I've talked enough for the day." She carefully pulled herself up to her feet. "This old clock needs plenty of rest to keep on ticking." Slightly hunched over, she clutched her cane and walked slowly back into the house, the screen door creaking behind her.

I decided to sit for a while. I don't know if it was the heat of the day, or simply because I just didn't have any place else to go.

JUNE 4, 2008

TWO WEEKS INTO TRIAL

For days Teller and I went back and forth on whether or not to call Rock to the stand. I didn't think he was mentally strong enough to endure it, but Teller thought he would be our strongest defense against Prosecution. I fought him tooth and nail, but in the end Teller won the battle and called Rock as a witness to his own defense.

The courtroom was crowded today. People stood against the wall, waiting in expectation of what the day's events would hold. After that God thing, the trial had become a circus of spectators and reporters, even made headline news in all the papers. Church folks lined up outside, some in support of us, some not. Protestors rallied against Teller's defense and his unethical use of the name of God. Meanwhile, my anxiety kicked into overdrive. I was scared. Rock's not good under pressure and I didn't want our personal business out there for all the world to know. The physical abuse we suffered at the hands of our father was almost comparable to how cruel the media can be. They claim their job is to report the facts, yet they do everything but. Reporters are judgmental, arrogant and unremorseful, oblivious to the hearts of others simply to satisfy their own selfish needs, shoving the camera into a grieving mother's face that just lost her child to violence, interrogating a man who has just been wrongfully accused of a crime, around the clock surveillance of his home when he just wants to spend time alone with his family. They're obsessed with wrecking other people's lives, and Rock and I were no different. With no consideration of our feelings, they were making us out to be these twisted little kids who were caught up in the anguish of losing their mother. Perhaps in some way they were right. Maybe we *were* just two kids whose quiet cries and unheard screams were suppressed by the unconscious fact that the one person who protected us was now gone. Maybe we withdrew from everything and everybody and sought protection in the only two people we trusted, one another. Whatever the case, I couldn't help but to worry that our darkest hours and troubled days were far from over.

I was so fixed on the courtroom's atmosphere I didn't see Teller come in, but at first glance I noticed his unusual attire and judging from the looks of discontent, so did everyone else. He was dressed in a long black robe with a large red cross embroidered on the side of each sleeve. He looked like a preacher getting reading to deliver his sermon to a Sunday morning congregation. I sat nailed to my chair.

Rock was escorted into the courtroom unshackled, dressed in a dark blue suit with a white shirt and red tie, he looked stunning. Red was Mama's favorite color. She said it was symbolic of her love for us. Whenever we had to dress-up for a church function or social event, Rock would wear a red tie, I would wear a red ribbon in my hair, and Mama would wear a red scarf around her neck. It drove Daddy crazy, but it always put a smile on our face, and that's what mattered most to Mama.

Judge Hallow emerged into the courtroom, sat down at his bench and immediately probed Teller's apparel. After a moment of scrutiny he addressed the issue, a cold expression on his face. "Mr. Teller will you be so kind as to explain to the court your dress code today."

A tad bit arrogant Teller responded. "I think the robe speaks for itself, Your Honor."

"I'll tell you what I think, Mr. Teller. I think the only person who should be wearing a robe in my courtroom is me. Explain yourself, Counselor."

Joy stood offended. "Certainly you are not going to permit this, Your Honor?"

"Shouldn't I?" he replied in a patronizing tone. "He doesn't seem to be breaking any laws, Counselor, although I am curious as to the reason why you decided to dress in this manner today, Mr. Teller."

With a breath of uneasiness, Joy sat down.

"I feel it is pertinent to my defense today, Your Honor. It serves more as a metaphor rather than a statement."

"If I sense in any way that it becomes disrespectful or made a mockery of in these proceedings I will ask you to remove it. Understood?"

"Understood, Your Honor."

"Call your next witness."

"Defense calls Rock to the stand."

My nerves were getting the best of me and I began to tremor. I was a quiver away from having a nervous breakdown. Rock gave me eye contact. "Sweet Reverie," he whispered. I reciprocated. That calmed my nerves a bit, but only for a while.

Rock was sworn in and ready for questioning. Teller stood stock-still for a few moments. Careful not to stir up any emotional responses or outbursts, he was cautious in his approach. He started to speak, but paused, crossed his arms in front of him, and lifted his right hand to his chin. An awkward silence covered the room. Rock's neck was stiff. He looked nervous. But what else would you expect from a 17-year-old kid.

Teller cleared his throat and clasped his hands behind his back. "Mr. Rock, in the past few weeks we have heard testimony after testimony of a higher power and the existence, or non-existence of this higher power," he turned to Rock, "could you express to the court who or what God is to you?"

Rock's voice trembled from nerves, but became clearer as he continued to speak. "Well, Daddy use to say that God was this peculiar spirit that sometimes asked you to do peculiar things....things that you may not understand, but should never question."

"*Lean not to your own understanding*, per se?" Teller quoted.

"Yes, Sir."

"Can you clarify, or make clear these peculiar things that God would ask you to do?"

"Well He never asked us to do much of anything. It was more so God telling Daddy to do stuff and us not questioning it."

"Such as?"

"Well one day Daddy came home from church with a brown paper bag. He called me and Faith into the kitchen and asked Faith to open the bag and take out the bottle of red wine and box of crackers. Daddy opened the wine and poured all three of us a glass. He then opened the box of crackers and put them on a plate in the middle of the table. He said that since Faith didn't feel well that day and we missed communion at church, God told him to bring communion home to us. Faith hesitated and said that God wasn't the kind of God to get children drunk. But Daddy insisted, quoting the sacrificial scripture of Abraham and Isaac. He said that God would never tell him to do anything that would bring harm upon his children. So out of obedience we drank the wine."

"The entire glass?"

"The entire bottle."

"Go on."

"I felt dizzy like I was going to pass out or something, and I must have because when I woke up I was lying in my bed, Faith next to me. She told me I had gotten sick so she undressed me and put me to bed. Hung over from the wine and fearful of Daddy's unpredictable behavior, we stayed in our room the rest of the day."

"Did your father ever give you a reason as to why he made you drink an entire bottle of wine?"

"He said taking communion was sacred before God, and that the drunkenness was a form of punishment from the Lord for not taking part in one of the most holy experiences in a Christian's life."

"Did you believe him?"

"I believe that communion is sacred…yes."

Teller walked over to Rock. "But did you believe that getting you and your sister drunk was part of that sacredness?" He put his hand to his ear.

"Yes, Sir, the good book says, '*Whom the Lord loves he corrects, just as a father corrects the son he delights in.*' That's Proverbs 3:12."

The courtroom smiled in amusement.

Teller stood erect and clasped his hands behind his back. "You're very knowledgeable of the Bible for such a young age."

"Besides school books, it's the only book Daddy allowed us to read."

Teller turned and faced the jury. "Do you understand the word "reverence," Rock?"

Rock sat erect. "Yes, Sir, it was a word used often in our house."

"Can you tell the court what it means to you?"

"To love and respect all things that are holy," he answered looking Teller straight in the eye.

Teller walked over to the Judge's bench. "Do you see the robe that Judge Hallow is wearing?"

"Yes, Sir," Rock answered scanning the Judge's garment.

"And do you see the robe that I am wearing?"

"Yes, Sir."

"Would you say that you revere both?"

"Yes, Sir, but in different ways."

"How so?" Teller asked.

"Well, Judge Hallow's robe is a sign of worldly authority and your robe is a sign of spiritual authority.

"Rock, would you say that it's the garment you look up to or the person inside the garment?"

"The garment because it's a status symbol, it's what you wear that make people respect you. Daddy said it's the first thing people notice when they see you. It speaks of who you are before you can say a word."

Teller walked over to the jury. "And me? What does this robe say about me?"

"It doesn't speak of you as a lawyer if that's what you're asking."

"But I *am* a lawyer, Rock," Teller said putting his hand to his ear.

"No you're not, Sir. You're ordained by the holy garment, sacred before God. One to be respected and honored," Rock's voice deepened with respect.

Teller stretched his arms out wide. "It's a false symbol, Rock, a piece of material worn by man, used to manipulate."

"That is not for me to judge, Sir," Rock responded sharply. "False prophets will be dealt with by God."

Teller rushed over to the table and grabbed the Bible. He held it up high in the air. "*Take heed, lest any man deceive you. For many shall come in my name*," his voice echoed throughout the courtroom. What say you, Rock?

"My responsibility is not to man, it is to God. For every man must bear his own burden," Rock's voice was a little agitated.

Joy interceded. "Your Honor, Counsel is provoking the witness.

"I am not provoking the witness, Your Honor. I am trying to show the sick manipulation the victim implanted into this young child's mind."

"By quoting scriptures back and forth?" Judge Hallow asked in a constricted tone.

"No. By showing the jury that a mere piece of material can have such a profound effect on my client's mental state."

"Overruled," Judge Hallow remarked.

"Rock was there ever a time, during the alleged abuse of you and your sister, that your father would wear his pastoral robe?"

Teller's question had left Rock a bit troubled. He sat cold in his seat. He glanced around the room at the strangers who were sitting on the edge of their chairs waiting for him to speak. His eyes finally locked with mine. The thought of him answering that question sent a chill up my spine and brought Rock to the brink of uncontrolled emotions. He wiped the tears from his eyes with two quick strokes of his hand. It was as if he was waiting for me to say it was okay for him to answer…and I did. With tears in my eyes, I could only nod in approval.

Judge Hallow leaned forward, his glasses perched on his nose. "Did you understand the question, son?"

Rock sat for a tense moment, and then answered, "Yes, Sir, I did." His thoughts took him back to the cold memories of that unsettling day.

FEBRUARY 14, 2008

Four years have passed since Mama's death and Daddy's become more and more abusive from one day to the next. It's gotten to the point now that we've come to expect it. It's like we've become immune to it or something. Rock and I tried our best to live as normal lives as possible, but it got difficult at times, some days more so than others, but we coped the best we could and often found comfort in each other.

Today's Valentine's Day and as usual I'm sitting in front of the window watching all the couples walk by holding hands and such. Daddy never really allowed us to date, but I would often sneak out and see Rock's friend, Bishop, who is two years younger than me. Don't matter much though, because he's the most mature person I know. Not that I have anyone to compare him to, but he's sweet and kind, and he makes me feel pretty.

Unlike me, Rock would have friends over every now and again to play street ball or hang around and flirt with the girls walking up and down the street. But not Bishop, he was too busy flirting with me.

I had been sitting at the window for a while when I noticed Bishop and Rock coming up the street. My heart dropped. I jumped up, hoping they didn't see me, and rushed to put the kitchen chair back underneath the table. I took a deep breath, pretending to be preoccupied as they came through the front door.

"Rock is that you?" I asked as if I didn't know.

He walked into the kitchen, Bishop following with a single red rose in hand.

"This is for you," he said extending his hand out to me. He wore a black sweater, black overcoat, blue jeans and a black skull hat pulled so far down over his square forehead it covered his thick dark eyebrows. He had brown eyes, a pug nose and dimples so deep they looked like bottomless pits.

I smiled and took the rose. "Thank you."

He smiled and grabbed a seat at the kitchen table next to Rock.

"Nothing to eat?" Rock asked.

"I can make us a couple of sandwiches to tie us over until dinner."

Daddy would be at church for at least another hour and choir rehearsal didn't start until six. That gave us just enough time to eat and hang out in Rock's room for a while. We listened to Bishop's CD's he brought over and danced around the room laughing and giggling like kids. Although we were, Rock and I never got much chance to act our age, so it was nice. We danced until we were breathless.

It was getting late and Rock insisted Bishop leave before Daddy got home.

"Give me one minute," he said putting on a slow song. He took me by the hand and pulled me close, my breast resting on his chest. He leaned in close, his breath warm against my face as he gently kissed me on the lips. They were soft, like cotton candy. I closed my eyes and allowed myself to get lost in the moment, but the sudden stop of the music snapped me back to reality and I pulled away.

Rock stood stiff staring at the bedroom door. I turned to see Daddy standing in the hallway adorned in his pastoral robe and holding his Bible. There was a knot in the pit of my stomach. Bishop's arms were still around my waist.

"It's bout time for you kids to get ready for choir rehearsal," Daddy said in an eerie calm voice. "Your company should be making his way home."

"Yes, Sir," Bishop responded respectfully. "I'll see you later, Rock. Keep the CD. I'll pick it up another day." He gave me a warm smile and walked down the stairs. Silence fell over the room until the slam of the front door confirmed Bishop's departure.

"You whoring in my house, girl?" Daddy asked in a disturbed voice.

My body jolted.

"No, Daddy." Rock intervened as always. "Bishop came over to listen to some CD's is all. He was here for me, not Faith."

Fear overcame me and I couldn't speak. Daddy walked into the room and glanced over at the bed. The rose that Bishop had given me was lying on the pillow.

"You bringing that devil music up in my house, girl, defiling my holy home with that garbage?"

It was as though my heart jumped into my throat and was beating uncontrollably. Rock stepped in front of me.

"Bishop was here to see me, Daddy."

"Didn't appear that way to me, son, it wasn't your body he had his hands all over, wasn't your lips he was kissing on now was it, seemed to me he was more interested in Faith's flesh, than you." Daddy's voice was dry, his jealous eyes pierced through mine.

"That's not true Daddy. I brought him here. He came to visit me." Rock's voice was filled with supplication. "Faith had nothing to do with it. I swear." He felt his body stiffen.

"You pimping out my house, boy?"

"No Daddy. I swear."

With a forceful blow Daddy slapped Rock across the face with the back of his hand. He fell to the floor, his nose bleeding. "How dare you degrade your father's house! *He that worketh deceit shall not dwell within my house, he that telleth lies shall not tarry in my sight*!" He gave a hard stump with the bottom of his shoe into Rock's stomach. I dropped to his side as he doubled over in unbearable pain.

"Stop it Daddy!" I screeched. The resentment of seeing my brother wounded on the floor crippled me and I beseeched Daddy's mercy. "Please stop! I brought him to our room! I invited him in! Bishop was here for me, not Rock, for me! I clenched my chest to stifle my cries. "*Hold not thy peace, oh God of my praise, for the mouth of the wicked and the mouth of the deceitful are opened against me, they have spoken against me with a lying tongue.*"

Daddy stood with a wary eye. "You petition the Psalms of the Lord for leniency?"

"No, I plead the prayer of punishment for my sins."

"You employ the word of God for your wantonness!"

"I ask for just cause retribution!" My body shivered with bitterness. My face wet with tears.

"You little whore! You bring this heathen into my house, under my roof and appeal the Psalms of the Lord against me!" He grabbed a handful of my hair and drug me down the stairs declaiming Psalms 109 with the cunningness of his sour tongue.

"Please Daddy!" I screamed, trying desperately to escape the claws of my inevitable fate. I drove my knees into the wood of the floor but I could no longer hold my grip. I felt the stabbing of the splinters tear through my skin and the moist blood stream down my legs. Fatigued and breathless my body went limp. I know longer had the energy to fight. Irrational and winded himself, Daddy threw my depleted body onto the bedroom floor and drove his penis into the walls of my ravaged vagina.

Rock struggled down the stairs, but it was almost impossible for him to maintain his balance still disoriented from the hit. He leaned against the wall for support and finally managed to get to the bottom of the stairs. Weak and clutching his stomach, he banged on the locked door yelling for Daddy to stop. The stench of incest wrapped itself around the base of the walls and Rock could smell the vileness of Daddy's sordid act. With all the strength he could muster he drove his shoulder into the bedroom door tearing it from its hinges. He collapsed on the floor beside my stained body. I was lying on my back, my hair messy and my face wet from tears, my dress pulled up to my waist bearing my naked bottom.

Daddy zipped his pants and retrieved his Bible. "Clean yourself up for choir rehearsal." He stepped over me and Rock as if he was nothing and walked down the hallway into the bathroom.

I was more than a little tired when we arrived to church. My spirit was heavy and exhausted from fighting off Daddy. I had nothing left to give. Unrehearsed, I regained my composure long enough to sing the choir's request of Chester Baldwin's song, "I Still Hear Mama Praying." My heart swelled in my chest as I tried to make sense of everything that was going wrong in my life. The hatred Daddy had for me and the lack of compassion God had shown me. I struggled to find the words to the song just as much as I struggled to find the strength to sing it. All the hurt, all the pain that ached inside of me erupted and I found power through the serenity of the music.

I still hear Mama praying
I still hear Mama praying
and the prayer that she prayed has been keeping me day by day
oh I still hear Mama praying for me

When Mama bowed her head and knelt down in fervent prayer
she knew how to call on the name of Jesus
for she knew that he'd meet her there
oh she thanked him for health and for strength
but she never failed to pray for her children
saying Lord save them by your grace

I still hear Mama praying
I still hear Mama praying
and the prayer that she prayed has been keeping me day by day
oh I still hear Mama praying for me…

I felt trapped in my own body with no way of freeing myself. Feeling exhausted and on the verge of collapsing I couldn't hold back the tears. Mama's presence was so prevalent. I felt her spirit standing next to me singing every word, every phrase right along with me. It was as if she was praying at that very moment for God to save us for she knew in her broken-heart that there was no possible way that *she* could do it herself.

The choir sang with such strength and force:

Pray-ay-ay for me
Pray-ay-ay for me
oh I still hear Mama praying for me
oh I still hear Mama praying for me

By the end of the song Mama's spirit had soon departed and Rock and I were once again left alone to face our fears.

JUNE 4, 2008

TRIAL

I sat silent in the courtroom, biting at the corner of my lip. My body language said nothing for fear that someone would read my expression and put it on front page news. Rock looked flushed, his face pale. He wiped at his eyes with the sleeve of his shirt. Teller had removed his robe and was seated back at the defense table, his emotions unbalanced. There was an awkward stillness. Teller could feel the unsettling of the room. He rose to his feet, hesitant to go on. The last thing he wanted to do was feed off Rock's grief, but he had no alternative but to carry on. With a contained expression and heavy weight, he pushed forward.

"What happened after that night, Rock?"

He took in a deep breath and cleared his throat. "For weeks after that Faith suffered from broken hallelujah…"

Teller interrupted. "Broken hallelujah?"

"Mama said that's when life has beaten up on you so bad that you're too broken to praise. You've lost your strength, your will to trust God…" Rock's voice wavered and he pulled back for a minute. His eyes searched the courtroom until they caught mine. A look of betrayal seized his face. I granted an offhanded smile of approval and he regained his composure and continued on. "She was like a zombie. It was like Daddy had sucked the life out of her or something. She continued to sing in the choir and come to church and everything, but…but it was like she was there, but she wasn't there… If you know what I mean?"

"Go on."

"The abuse continued, sometimes physically, sometimes mentally, either way it affected us emotionally, especially Faith. The more Daddy abused her, the more withdrawn she became. It was like she was decaying from the inside out. I tried to give her strength, encourage her you know, tell her God would see us through this, but she wouldn't hear of it. She wouldn't trust Him, Daddy had taken it all." Rock brushed the tears from his cheek and dropped his head into a darkness deeper than the shadows of our past. He felt his heart skip a beat. He cleared his throat. His voice was hoarse and he was feeling dehydrated. Teller took notice.

"Would you like a glass of water, Rock?" Teller asked.

"Yes, Sir, thank you, Sir," he responded.

A nervous chill ran down the back of my spine and I couldn't shake off the uneasiness. Rock was breaking under stress and I could sense the tension inside of him growing. It disturbed him to reveal our most intimate secrets to a room full of strangers and I wasn't sure how much longer it would be before he lost his patience.

He took a few sips of water to tame the dryness of his mouth, but it did nothing to soothe the pressure.

"Are you okay to continue?" Teller asked.

Troubled, Rock looked around the courtroom at the onlookers. They sat in watchful silence. He had gone through critical testimony and they had taken mental note of every painful moment. He had invited them into our tragic world to feast on our suffering and they devoured it like hungry wolves. Stirring in their own selfish greed, they beckoned more and Rock's testimony fed their famished souls.

"Are you capable of continuing, Mr. Rock.?" Teller asked again.

Rock pushed aside the strain of judgmental faces and refocused his attention back to Teller. "Yes, Sir, I am." The words caught his throat and emerged as broken syllables. He took another sip of water to cool his parched tongue. "Could you repeat the question please?"

Teller paced the courtroom. "You were explaining to this court your sister's behavior the day after your Father had attacked the two of you for defying the rules of his house."

Rock found his train of thought. "Yes…at some point she became rebellious."

"What do you mean?"

"She became defiant. Sneaking out all kinds of night with Bishop, singing songs that Daddy totally disapproved of." Rock shook his head and snickered. "One day she sang "Son of a Preacher Man." That pissed Daddy off to the highest level. People at church just thought she was going through a phase. You know, over Mama's death and all. So they let her be. Funny thing about that whole situation was that Daddy left her alone during those moments. I couldn't quite figure it out, but I believe in his twisted little mind he thought of her as impure."

"Impure?"

"Yes."

"But he had already stolen her purity long before that." Teller replied in a disheveled voice.

"Objection, Your Honor. Slander," Joy disputed.

"Sustain," Judge Hallow agreed. "Counsel I am going to ask, and I rarely ask, that you avoid future attacks on the victim's character."

Teller nodded in agreement as he walked towards Rock. "Explain impure."

"Daddy was a biblical man, and Ephesians 5 says, there mustn't be a hint of sexual immorality or any kind of impurity or greed because these are improper for God's holy people, for the wrath of God comes upon rebellion and disobedience, so do not associate or be partakers with them."

"Teller cranked his head, disturbed. "You're telling me and the court that although your father allegedly molested your sister, he hypocritically looked upon her as impure because she was sneaking around having sexual encounters with another boy? Is this your claim?"

Rock uncomfortably straightened up his spine. "I can't apologize for my father's beliefs."

I wanted to sit there and support Rock, but the pain was too deep. His words caused me to feel an immeasurable amount of uncleanness, so I got up quickly and walked out of the courtroom door. Rock wanted to run after me and tell me that he was sorry, but he couldn't. His testimony was an act of love, and I understood that, but at that moment I felt like someone had knocked the wind out of me, I couldn‘t breathe. My anxiety was in overdrive and I needed some air. I stood there with my hand across my abdomen, feeling paralyzed. Maybe once I've gotten myself together I'd get the nerve to go back inside.

Teller was taken aback for a moment, but resumed. "Rock, explain to me in your own words your definition of sin."

Rock searched his thoughts and came up with a clear and precise answer, "disobedience to the will of God or God's law."

"And do you believe that the alleged acts of your father were sins?"

"We are all people of sin."

"But that's not what I asked you, Rock. My question was do you believe the alleged acts of your father to be of sin?"

Rock once again veiled the question. "Are you familiar with the Apostle Paul, Mr. Teller?"

Teller's face showed a tangled expression. "Yes I am."

"Well, in Romans 7, Paul speaks about sin in a rather interesting manner. It is defined as a pursuit of the flesh, an uncontrollable urge to do what is right, but justifies its own reasons for doing wrong. The influence of sin is a powerful thing."

"How so?" Teller urged.

Rock declaimed Romans 7 with the bearing of a minister standing before a Sunday morning congregation, his voice preached and direct. "*I do not understand what I do. For what I want to do, I do not do, but what I hate, I do*."

Aside from Joy's unmitigated disgust of Teller's entire approach to this case, she was fed up with his antics and disastrous line of questioning. She stood to interject.

Teller immediately interceded. "Counselor, please give us a moment before objection." He flipped the Bible to the book of Romans and respectfully placed it on the table in front of Joy who despite her opposition, reluctantly sat back down. Though he was aware the situation might get out of hand, he knew that this was something the jury needed to hear.

"*It is no longer I myself who do it, but it is sin living in me.*" Rock's voice was pungent and underscored. The room sat engrossed. Reporter's pens raced across their paper. Those who knew the Bible understood what he was saying. Those who didn't tried desperately to comprehend.

"*I have the desire to do what is good, but I cannot carry it out. For what I do is not the good I want to do, nor the evil I want to do, but this I keep on doing.*"

Teller stood in control, prepared to interpret every biblical word that came out of Rock's mouth. He bent his torso forward and put his hand to his ear.

"Are you suggesting that your father was a sinner who had no control over his sinful nature?"

Rock's eyes lifted to Teller. "Paul suggested that all believers of God battle with sin."

"So is that justification to break God's law?"

"My father struggled with sin, Mr. Teller. His comprehension of the word went much deeper than most people. He was obsessed with it. He believed the word of God was literal and he read it with conviction. 'We are a peculiar people who serve a peculiar God,' he would say. We believe in things we don't see and don't trust the things we do see. Everything Daddy did was based around the word of God. Whenever he did wrong he would find a scripture to support it. He was a prisoner to sin, but his beliefs were his beliefs, and Faith and I dared not question it."

"So he was a prisoner to the word of God?"

"*Oh wretched man I am*!" Rock continued on. "*Who will rescue me from this body of death? I myself, in my mind, am a slave to God's law, but in the sinful nature, a slave to the law of sin.*" Rock's forceful voice rose over the courtroom. He could be heard through the corridors. I pulled myself together and discreetly slipped back into my seat, hoping my presence wouldn't evoke a disturbance.

A gnaw of unease covered the courtroom. Teller paced back and forth. The sound of his spit-shined, hard bottom shoes traveled the room. He paused to give Rock a moment to contain himself and then continued questioning.

"Your father quoted that scripture much?"

Rock remained focused. He leaned back in his chair, rubbing the sweats of his palms across the thighs of his pants. "All the time, it was his way of justifying his wrongdoings to us."

"Were they justified?"

"Biblically?" Rock asked.

"Yes," Teller confirmed.

Rock thought for a moment before answering. "The Bible is a difficult book to understand. Many people died by the wrath of God's hand, so would you say that God was a murderer or justified by His actions? David committed many sins including killing the husband of his mistress, yet God still loved him. Were his acts justified by God's standards?" Rock paused again, gathering his thoughts. "You're asking me a question that I can't answer. In the natural world, no, his behavior is not acceptable, but I am a spiritual person, and in the spiritual realm people do a lot of things in the name of God, and in doing so they feel justified in their actions."

"Rock would you say that you have forgiven your Father?"

"God is a forgiving God. If he can forgive then who am I not to?"

Teller turned to Judge Hallow. I have no further questions for my client at this time, but would ask the court to allow me to redirect at a later time."

"Granted," Judge Hallow responded. Would Prosecution like to cross-examine?"

Joy stood up. "Yes, Your Honor, we would." She thumbed through a few pages of her notes before approaching the bench. "Mr. Rock, are you telling the court that you have no animosity against your father for the things he's done to you and your sister?"

"To say no would be lying. I do have some ill-will, but to carry around bitterness for the rest of my life would be too heavy a burden. For God's mercy I had to forgive Daddy."

"So forgiveness is expectant?"

"Yes, for believers of God's word. The Apostle Paul says '*Forgive one another, as Christ has forgiven you.*' If you are forgiving then God will forgive you, if not, don't expect forgiveness from God."

"So God is a just and merciful God, forgiving of all sins?"

"Yes."

She heaved a deep sigh and crossed her arms over her chest. "Mr. Rock, do you believe that God has exonerated your father of all his wrongdoings?"

My jaw clenched. I was becoming uneasy with this line of questioning. Edgy, I shifted in my seat.

Rock licked his lips. "Yes, ma'am, I do." His throat had become parched again which made it difficult to swallow. He ingested his own saliva in an effort to give himself some relief.

"Tell me," Joy voiced in a tone almost like a mother trying to coax her young son into telling the truth. "Was killing your father in some way a warped sense of your own forgiveness?"

Teller rose from his seat. "Objection, Your Honor. Witness has not been convicted here!"

"Sustain."

"If God is a forgiving and merciful God then not only has he forgiven your father for his sins, but he will also find mercy on you for your transgressions?"

"Objection, Your Honor!"

"Sustain. Counselor, you have been warned."

"*The Lord Our God is merciful and forgiving even though we have rebelled against Him*!" Joy recited.

Teller rose from his seat again. "Objection, Prosecution's accusations are indicative of a mercy killing. Murder has not been proven in this case."

"Which is what I am trying to establish, reasonable cause," Joy interrupted.

"Are you surmising that my client intentionally committed murder just to receive mercy from God?" Teller retorted. "That is absolutely absurd, Counselor."

"Are you suggesting your client has done nothing to be merciful for?"

"Are you suggesting that he has?"

"Isn't that the whole reason why we're here?"

Judge Hallow banged his gavel. "That will be quite enough, Counselors!"

Unable to restrain himself, Rock rose from his seat. Cutting through the tumult like a machete he divulged a stark charge that shook the courthouse to the foundation of its core. "I didn't kill Daddy!" he yelled, "God did!" His voice reverberated off the walls and the courtroom erupted into inconceivable madness.

I sat stunned, unable to move. The knot in my stomach tightened. The room was in utter disbelief. People's mouths were agape, reporters wrote erratically on their note pads, and eyes were glued to my reaction.

Judge Hallow continued to bang his gavel. "Sit down, Mr. Rock!" he shouted over the chaos.

Staggered by Rock's bombshell, Teller rubbed his hand across his head to the back of his neck, engulfed in desperation.

"I'm sorry, Faith," Rock pleaded. "I'm so sorry…I wanted to tell you…I did, but I knew you wouldn't believe me!"

I clutched the bench in front of me to hold my balance. Shock electrocuted through my soul as I felt the air leave my body.

"Sit down, Mr. Rock! I will have order in my courtroom!" Judge Hallow exclaimed.

Teller walked swiftly over to Rock, grabbed hold of his shoulders and forced him down to his seat. Rock had made a mess of things and he had to gain damage control. His defense was broken and he had to find a way to fix it.

Judge Hallow finally calmed the situation, but Rock's incredulous response stifled the courtroom and everyone remained in acute disbelief. Trepidation hung and we sat for a long moment waiting for the proceedings to recommence. Judge Hallow leaned forward and clasped his hands in front of him on the bench. He stared in displeasure and frustration. "Mr. Teller," he said in an irritated and not so pleased tone, "your client will contain himself throughout the rest of these proceedings or I will hold him *and* you in contempt…understood?"

"Yes, Your Honor," Teller responded shooting Rock a this-won't-be-tolerated anymore stare.

"Now, Counselor, do you wish to continue questioning the witness at this time?"

Joy stood up from her seat. "Considering the circumstances, Your Honor, Prosecution is not prepared to continue. We are requesting adjournment so that we may reassess our line of questioning in this case."

Judge Hallow rested his back against the chair. "Certainly understandable, Counselor, it is so granted. We will adjourn until…"

Teller interrupted. "Your Honor…I'm sorry, but if possible I would like to re-direct at this time."

Judge Hallow peered from underneath his glasses. "This is certainly unorthodox, Mr. Teller, but if Prosecution has no objections." He glanced over at Joy.

"No objections, Your Honor," Joy responded reluctantly.

"Granted, Mr. Teller, but you and your client have been warned."

"Yes, Your Honor."

Teller's case had run into a brief disturbance, but all wasn't lost. Somewhere in the ruins was clarification and he was intent on bringing it out. He unfastened his suit jacket, removed it, and hung it neatly on the back of his chair. Rock sat in grief, struggling to get beyond his troubled state, his hands tied in a knot of pain and worry. Teller pressed his hand deep in the front pocket of his pants and moved in to redeem the credibility of his client.

"Mr. Rock, on March 17, 2008, the police were summoned to your home because of a call from an unknown person who said to have heard gunshots coming from your address." Teller walked over to the table and picked up the deposition of the police officer who was first to arrive on the scene. "I would ask that the officer's sworn statement be put on record."

"It is so granted," Judge Hallow replied.

"Upon arriving to your home, the officer found your father lying on his back on the bedroom floor with one gunshot wound to the right shoulder and one fatal wound to the chest. Am I right?"

"Yes, sir," Rock said, tears welled his eyes.

"Also in his right hand was his Bible that also held a bullet hole that went straight through the book into the bedroom wall. Am I correct?"

Rock dabbed his tears with the back of his hand, "yes, Sir."

"I know this is hard, Rock, but it is very important that we go through each detail carefully in order to understand what happened that night. Do we understand each other?"

"Yes, Sir," Rock replied.

Teller leafed through the pages. "Your statement claimed your Dad had become increasingly hostile in the days leading up to his death."

"Yes, Sir."

"Can you elaborate?"

Rock dropped his head and assembled his thoughts from the clutch of his hands. "Daddy was unusually argumentative that night, carrying on about dishes not being washed and the house having the stench of old garbage. Later that day he fell into one of his rampages, but only this time rather than coming after Faith, he pursued me."

"In what way?" Teller asked.

Rock swallowed a gulp full of air. “Sexually,” the words rattled in his throat.

“Speak up son so the court can hear you.”

Rock raised his head into a sea of scrutiny. “Sexually” he retorted.

Teller waited for the jury to ingest Rock’s response. If he was going to regain control of this case it had to be now. He turned his attention back to the podium. “Son, I need you to explain to the court, in detail, what happened in the days prior to your father’s death. I will need you to take your time and inform me when it becomes too difficult for you to continue. If needed, I’ll give you a moment’s respite. Do we understand each other?” Teller studied the expression on Rock’s face.

Once again he glanced over in my direction, painfully locking his eyes with mine, searching for some sign…something…anything that would reassure him that everything was gonna be okay. But this time my face was empty, void of all comfort and understanding. Broken myself, I had nothing left to give. Feeling unaided and alone he stirred in disappointment. “Yes, Sir,” he responded, “it is.”

MARCH 15, 2008

We were hit with about three inches of unexpected snow last night, so Rock and the other neighborhood kids decided to get together and make a few extra bucks by shoveling the driveway and sidewalks of some of the neighbors' houses on the block. In the process they did Ms. Eloise's for free. Although it was the middle of March, Michigan's weather could be so unpredictable. A couple of years back we had a heavy snowstorm on the first day of Spring, instead of flowers blooming and the smell of fresh cut grass, there were snow blowers, shovels and kids pulling sleds up and down the street.

Detroit can get pretty cold during the winter, but I never wanted to move to a warmer climate. I loved the change of seasons, especially Fall. The leaves on the trees turned this beautiful fiery red color that kinda reminded me of the burning bush. Well, minus God's dramatic voice-over and all.

I turned away from the window to find Daddy staring at me. I didn't say anything…I didn't know what to say. I wanted to ask him what the hell he was looking at, but that was best remained a thought. His very presence made my stomach turn. I could feel my breathing getting heavy. My mind told me to walk away, but my body wouldn't allow it. My feet felt like they were nailed to the floor. I hadn't spoken much to God lately, but I managed to whisper a prayer somewhere in between fear and hate. I was out of practice with this whole prayer thing, so I decided to wait out His answer.

Daddy had a way of making you feel stupid. Not stupid dumb, but awkward stupid. You know that feeling you get when you are being chastised by your parents for doing wrong and then that big question comes, "Did you hear me?" and you nod your head yes and in that moment they just stand there and stare at you for a while until you start to feel stupid…yeah, that kind of stupid.

Just when I had given up on God's answer Rock came through the door. I started to give thanks, but hesitated, my prayer hadn't been answered yet because Daddy was still there.

Rock stumped the snow off his boots in the doorway and walked heavy footed into the house.

Daddy cut his eyes to his feet. "Were you raised in a barn boy?"

"No."

"Then take off those wet shoes in my house."

Rock removed his boots and lifted his head just enough to see Daddy piercing back at him, yeah…*that* kind of stupid.

After a few moments of eyeballing, Daddy gestured toward the kitchen. "Get in there and clean up that mess. You're so busy taking care of other people's homes you can't take care of your own, dishes still piled in the sink from breakfast." He turned to me as Rock brushed carefully passed him. "Don't stand there looking dumb girl, go help."

It took every ounce of mental strength to move my legs, but they wouldn't budge. I was too afraid to walk pass Daddy for fear of what he might do. His body blocked the doorway between the living room and the kitchen. I thought about making a run for it, but I had no place to go.

"Did you hear me girl?"

My body jarred from the tone of Daddy's voice. Adrenaline rushed through my veins and I lunged forward. I wanted to run out of the room, out the house and down the street, but instead I ran swiftly passed Daddy and into the kitchen.

"Get dinner started while you're in there," he yelled slamming the bedroom door behind him.

Sometimes I wonder if Daddy ever loved us at all. Even when Mama was alive he was passive with his affection. I can't remember one time when he said he loved us, or put his arm around us, or told us he was proud of us. My emotions rose. The only affection he'd ever shown was with his penis or his fist. Daddy was a constant presence that reminded me of everything impure. Flashbacks of abuse impaled my mind. I felt rotten from the inside out. Some days I would drink water until I got sick, trying to pee out Daddy's impurities filtering through my body. My stomach hurt, it always hurt. The thought of Daddy's fluids inside of me was like being infected with an incurable disease. I stood stock-still and closed my eyes, waiting for the moment to pass. Suddenly I felt a soft whisper in my ear and a gentle hand on my shoulder.

"Faith, are you okay?" Rock asked in a low voice.

I snapped back. "Yeah, I'm okay," I lied and continued my chores.

Rock clanked the dishes around in the sink while I prepared dinner, boxed macaroni and cheese, and meatloaf. Not my favorite, but all I could find in the almost bare kitchen. I set the table and Daddy came out to eat.

We must've sat quiet for an hour. Well at least it felt like one. It was never like this when Mama was living. Dinner time was family time. We would talk and laugh and joke about the people at church, it was fun. Not anymore. It's lonely now, the house doesn't have any life in it. We never laugh during dinner and Daddy hasn't said much about Mama since she died. It's like she took a piece of him with her. Personally, I wish she would have taken the whole thing.

Daddy picked up a morsel of mac-and-cheese along with a piece of meatloaf and stuffed it in his mouth. With a look of disgust on his face he spit out the food into a paper napkin and took a big gulp of water. "Did you check the expiration date on that meat?" he asked repulsed.

I jumped up, legs shaking from fear and ran towards the trash can. "I can check it now," I said anxiously grabbing the empty package out of the garbage. I tried desperately to read the date on the label, but it was too worn and faded to make out. Daddy snatched the slimy styrofoam tray out of my hand.

"It says October of last year... this is March!" he yelled as he thrust the tray into my face. I almost gagged from the stench of raw meat against my nose, the plastic stuck repulsively to my mouth. I tried to pull away, but he had a good grip on the back of my head, shoving it harder and harder into the nauseating package. Once again, Rock tried to fight him off, but Daddy slammed his head so hard against the wall he almost lost consciousness.

"Leave him alone!" I screamed as I charged towards him.

Daddy dragged me over to the table and shoved my face into the plate of macaroni and cheese. Grabbing a handful of meatloaf he stuffed it down my throat until I regurgitated. Pushing me to the floor, he took my own vomit and smeared it in my face. The puke blocked the tears flowing from my eyes.

"*Just as a dog returns to his own vomit, such does a fool return to his foolish ways*. Repeat it!" he yelled as he shoved my face deeper into the floor. "Proverbs 26:11. Repeat it!"

Hatred flared my heart and I wanted so desperately to tell him to go to hell along with his damned soul, to eat shit and die, but I shouldered the weight of imprisonment with no way of avoidance, so I shamefully repeated his degradation. "*Just as a dog returns to his own vomit, so fools repeat their folly*." I gagged on my own throw-up.

Satisfied with my humiliation he thrust my head into the floorboard and walked out.

I crawled over to Rock's side to make sure he was okay. Helpless, I nestled beside him in the fetal position and cried myself to sleep.

MARCH 16, 2008

Rock and I slept on the kitchen floor the entire night. The sound of Daddy's footsteps and the smell of old vomit on my face awakened me to the reminder of another vile day I was not ready to embrace. I desperately needed a moments peace so I laid unbending, pretending to be asleep, my eyes tracking the footpath of Daddy's every move. Goose pimples covered my body as I scanned the room of broken plates and globs of food scattered over the floor. I trembled from the thought of the night before, trying not to gag from the smell of my own throw-up that had dried to my face and began to peel. The brush of Daddy's leg against mine as he stepped over me and Rock like we were dogs lying in the middle of the road made me cringe. He had no soul, no sense of remorse for what he had done. He never did. He was what Mama used to call an onion, a person with no core. You can peel away all the layers and there's nothing there, just emptiness, a hole, no essence of being, nothing to define or validate you as a human.

The sound of dishes being thrown into the sink jolted Rock from his sleep. His head throbbed from the pain. It felt as though someone had put a bulldozer to it. He moaned as he tried to sit up. I felt pinned to the floor, my body ached. I wasn't sure if it was from sleeping on the hard floor all night or the roughness of Daddy's brutality. Either way it really didn't matter because before we could get up completely, he started in on us.

"The dead has risen," he said as he dried his hands on the dish towel thrown across his shoulder. "Rehearsal for the Elder's Dinner is at two, so get yourself and this mess cleaned up, you know how I am about the Lord's time," he said standing with his back to us.

Cringing from the pain in the back of his head, Rock stood to his feet. He extended his hand and graciously helped me up. We headed quietly out of the kitchen towards the bathroom when Daddy stopped us cold.

"I know you trifling kids are not getting ready to track pieces of food all through my house."

What do you mean through? I thought to myself. The bathroom is right next to the kitchen. If it was any closer we would be sitting on the toilet and eating at the same time.

Daddy reached into the cabinet, pulled out a large plastic bag and tossed it across the floor. "Take off your clothes right here and put them in this bag until you can wash them later."

Staggered by Daddy's request, Rock and I stood motionless. The scariest thing at that moment was the thought of getting undressed in front of Daddy with him standing there, scrutinizing our young bodies like a pedophile with a hard-on. I kept my back turned and pulled my dress up over my head. I could hear the sound of Rock's belt unbuckling beside me. Embarrassed, I avoided eye contact. I shivered from the cold air. I took off my bra and pulled my panties down to my ankles trying desperately not to bend over too much as not to entice Daddy. I reached my hand back behind me and took the bag out of Rock's hand. I balled up my clothes, put them in the bag and dropped it on the floor next to my feet. Rock and I stood shamefully nude. Although we were speechless, our humiliation spoke volumes.

"Rock, you go ahead and get in the shower, Faith can come in after you."

I swallowed the fear in my throat. Rock remained steadfast.

"Did you hear me boy?"

He stood unwavering, his fists clenched to his side.

"Don't stand there like a mule, boy. I said get to the shower?"

A look of repulse filled his eyes.

"Either you're stupid and you didn't understand what I just said or you've literally lost your mind," he said jabbing his finger into the side of Rock's head. "Now I said go take a shower and leave me and your sister be."

Rock struggled to conform, but the intrusive way Daddy had us standing there, naked and violated, shook him with resentment and he erupted into a volcano of rage. Words that seemed to hide themselves deep beneath the realm of his mind, waiting for the most opportune time to emerge, materialized against his will. "Noooooo!" he rebelled. His fists clenched so tight his palms started to sweat.

"Are you disobeying me, boy?"

Weary of Daddy's loathsome ways, Rock stood noncompliant.

"You defying my rules, boy, challenging my kingship?" He circled Rock like a shark. "Oh, I see son," he heaved, "you Absalom now, huh? Avenging your sister's rape, in the hunt for your father's death?" He raised his head and delivered an irrational soliloquy. "*Behold my son, which came forth of my bowels, seeketh my life!*" He eyeballed Rock who held a revolted stare.

Panic swelled inside of me. I felt Daddy's calloused hand touch the small of my back and move down to my buttocks. His depraved touch chilled my soul. My face blemished with tears.

"So what is it son, my life for your sister, or is it my kingship you seek?" His eyes bugged with iniquity as he fondled my body and provoked Rock to anger. "Absalom killed his own brother for raping his sister then fled for fear of his father's wrath, but after three years his arrogance caused him to return to seek his father's life and claim the throne as king." His tongue was sharp and crafty. "Are those your intentions, Rock, to claim my throne, or is it just hate that fuels your fire?!"

Rock's jaw tightened. "*Fear not, for this has been determined from the day that you raped my sister*," he said with hatred in his voice.

Daddy grabbed his face and squeezed it hard. "What did you say to me, boy?" He gave Rock an infuriating stare. "Does the Book of Samuel boil your wrath?"

He knew Daddy would relate to God's word, so he did just that, he used God's word against him. "*I anointed thee king of Israel, delivered thee out of the hands of death, gave thee thy master's house, yet thou has despised the commandment of the Lord to do evil in his sight*," Rock retaliated, snatching away from Daddy's firm grip.

"*Wash me thoroughly from mine iniquity and cleanse me from my sin for I acknowledge my transgressions, and my sin is ever before me*!" Daddy yelled as he gestured around the room in a crazed manner. It wasn't that he never admitted his sinful ways he just always found reasons to justify them.

Rock and Daddy combated scriptures like a tennis match.

"*Thou has despised me, says the Lord, behold, I will raise up evil against thee out of thine own house*!" drops of spit spewed from Rock's mouth as he uttered the wrath of God.

Daddy drew back his hand and slapped him across the face. He stumbled backward and fell to the floor. "*I will not be afraid of ten thousand people who have set themselves against me*!" Daddy yelled.

I felt something wet underneath my feet. I looked down to find myself standing in pee. Rock had urinated all over himself. I still couldn't find the strength to turn around. The thought of what would happen next put me on the verge of losing consciousness. In my moment of weakness I noticed a figure standing in the doorway. It appeared to be Mama. She had a look of despair on her face, hurt that seemed to sink down to the pit of her soul. I wanted to run into her arms, to feel safe again, but she seemed so far out of reach. Not saying a word, she fixed her eyes on my naked body and then focused her attention to Rock. Everything within him rose up and he exploded. Regaining his strength he charged Daddy with such force they went flying over the kitchen table onto the floor. Startled, I snapped my head around to find Rock on top of Daddy. He drew back his fist to hit him, but Daddy caught his arm mid-air.

"*Mine own familiar friend, in whom I trusted, which did eat of my bread, has lifted up his heel against me*!" Daddy yelled out as he thrust his knee into Rock's groin, forcing him to double over in pain. He rushed over to the kitchen drawer, pulled out the duct tape and ran back over to Rock. He pulled his arms behind his back and wrapped the tape around his wrists, bounding his hands together.

"No!" I screamed. "Daddy don't!"

"You see, son, Absalom was a patient man when it came to getting his revenge," Daddy remarked out of breath as he ripped the tape apart with his teeth and threw the roll across the room. "Unlike you, he kept his peace for two years before he killed his brother for the rape of his sister, but he had one fault when it came to conquering his father's throne," Daddy stood up and unbuttoned his pants, "he underestimated his father's ability and strength to fight back." Rock wrestled to stand to his feet with no avail. "It was that one mistake that led to Absalom's horrific death." He kneeled down behind Rock, reached his arm around and placed his hand tightly over his mouth. Rock struggled to break loose from Daddy's stronghold, but his strength was too overpowering. Daddy leaned in close and whispered in his ear. "So you see in the end my son, the final victory went to his father." He raised his torso, tilted his head back like a drug addict on the ultimate high and shoved his penis into Rock, sodomizing him like an animal in heat. Traumatized, Rock let out a grievous cry that penetrated my very being.

"Daddy…p-please," I whimpered, "don't do this…it's not right…," my voice faltered and cracked, I fell grief-stricken to the floor. "He's your son." Saliva spun my lips like a web as I choked on my own spit.

Muzzled by the fingers pressed against his restrained lips, Rock bit down hard on Daddy's hand, tearing the skin clean through to the bone, but he was unmoved. He held a tight grip on Rock's mouth while blood seeped from his hand onto the kitchen floor. Beads of sweat covered Rock's forehead and his afflicted body trembled like an epileptic going into convulsions.

"*O my son, Absalom, with God as my witness I would die for thee*!" Daddy cried as tears rolled down his face. "*My son, my son*!"

I sat there on the floor numb, unable to move. The disturbing realization that my father would commit such an abysmal misdeed terrified me. He was like a demon, possessed by the unclean spirits of his own mind. I tried to crawl to my brother's aid, but my own fears pinned me to the floor. By the time it was over they were both gasping for air. Weak and dazed, Daddy stumbled out the kitchen like a badly injured dog and retreated to the cowardly cave of his bedroom. Rock laid stricken on the floor. Lethargic from the emotional trauma, I crawled over to him and gently rested his head upon my lap. The yearning to take away his pain burned like an arrow through my heart. I wiped the blood from his mouth with my hand and stroked his cheek in comfort.

"I'm so sorry, brother," I whimpered. "I'm so sorry." I leaned over and gently kissed his cheek. Full of grief I cradled him quietly in my bosom, his face wet with my tears. The gaze in his eyes proved the hopelessness in his heart, a despair that weakened his spirit and left him empty and ashamed. A warm presence suddenly composed us, a security that could only be felt by a mother's touch. We couldn't see her, but we knew it was Mama protecting us the only way she knew how. She held us tight in her embrace, veiled us with a blanket of tranquility and slowly slipped us from Daddy's depraved claws into the comforting arms of sweet reverie.

JUNE 4, 2008

TRIAL DAY

The courtroom held a distressing still. Horrified looks covered the faces of onlookers. Judgmental voices mute, critical views perplexed, minds scarred by barbaric acts. Teller took a moment to recover. I sat fastened to my seat, my heart beating erratic. A feeling of nausea overcame me. I once again felt God's abandonment as I sat there gazing at my brother on the podium from across the room. His child-like eyes empty, broken from the painful past of a father who gave nothing, but took everything. The hatred in my soul harbored in my unrepentant spirit like a raped child in its mother's womb. I tried to pray, not for me, but for my brother, but the words buried themselves in the back of my mind and would not give life, instead they tumbled around aimlessly until they eventually plummeted into a dark hole of resentment and despair.

Judge Hallow cleared the sorrow in his throat. "Mr. Rock would you like to take a break?" he asked with deep concern.

Rock rubbed his hands across his face and dried his tears. Unable to look up, he gazed shamefully at the floor and shook his head. "No thank you," he responded in a low voice.

Judge Hallow turned to Teller who resumed questioning with much hesitation.

"Rock, was that the last you saw of your father that day?"

Moments passed before Rock spoke. Flashbacks of that night cut through his mind like a dagger. He could still hear Daddy's voice and Faith's repetitive screams ringing in his ears. Every repulsive stroke of Daddy's penis caused an affliction that overtook his body with weakness and fatigue. Although he said he had forgiven Daddy, doubt weighed heavily upon his merciful soul and he began to question his own forgiveness. Teller's voice broke his thoughts.

"Rock, was that the last that you saw of your father that day?" he repeated.

"Yes, Sir…um, yes, Sir," he stuttered. We all stayed in our room the entire day, even missing the Elder's Appreciation rehearsal, but we attended the actual event the next evening," Rock's voice was solemn.

"How was your father's demeanor that day?"

"Towards me?" Rock asked wiping away the tears with the tips of his fingers.

"In general," Teller responded.

"Erratic," he said regaining his composure. "All over the place, just like all the other days. He appeared agitated with the world."

"Did he address the incident that had happened the night before?"

Rock shook his head. "No, it was like it never happened. What difference would it have made? The damage was done and I had soon wanted to forget it anyway."

Teller paced the floor. "How did you feel about your father after that night?"

Rock hesitated.

"Did you hate him?" Teller stopped midway in his steps and put his hand to his ear.

Rock stewed in contemptuous silence.

Teller redirected. "Mr. Rock did you hate your father after that night?!"

An icy quietness froze the courtroom. Rock remained inaudible.

"Mr. Rock would you like me to repeat the…"

Rock broke in with a tearful rant. "Yes I hated him! I hated everything about him! I was his son, his only son, but he didn't care! He didn't care that he took away my childhood! He didn't care that he took everything from me and I can never get it back…it's never coming back!" Snot ran from his nose down to his mouth. He tried to wipe away the painful tears with the back of his hand, but they just kept flowing. He sniveled through the hurt. "He stole my innocence from me, my manhood and I wanted him dead, I wanted him dead so bad, but

I didn't…I didn't kill him!"

"What stopped you?" Teller struck back.

Rock continued to cry hysterically.

"What stopped you from killing your father, Rock?!" Teller's voice was aggressive, he approached the podium. "What happened that night? How did you get the gun? Where did it come from, Rock?"

"Bishop!" he yelled. "I got it from Bishop!"

"Why?" Teller cut in harder.

"He brought it over after I called and told him I was having trouble with some neighborhood kids."

"So you lied."

"I had to. I couldn't tell him the truth."

I was an emotional wreck and beginning to feel uncomfortable with the tension that was building between Rock and Teller.

"Then what happened?"

"Nothing."

"What happened after he brought you the gun, Rock?"

"Nothing!"

Teller walked swiftly over to the table and grabbed the police report. He rifled through the pages as the courtroom looked on. "Mr. Rock's fingerprints were found on the gun confiscated from the murder scene!" Teller waved the paper around in the air before slamming it down on the table. He hurried back over to Rock. "Your fingerprints were found on the gun, Rock. What happened next?"

Rock broke. "I hid the gun in my dresser drawer and I waited!"

"You waited, for how long?"

"I said I wouldn't do it…I said I wouldn't do it unless he hurt us again."

"Do what, Rock?"

"I prayed he wouldn't do it. I prayed with everything in me that he wouldn't do it again, that I was the last time, that after me he had done enough, but it wasn't enough…it would never be enough." He shut his eyes tight until fragments of that night flashed behind his eyelids. "After the Appreciation Dinner he came after her again. She tried to run, but he held her down. He pinned her to the bed."

"Pinned who to the bed? Who tried to run?"

"He beat my sister like she was nothing, like a dog lying in the street. He kept screaming that she was just like Mama. That she was going to leave him just like Mama did. Blood was on his hands and all over the sheets. I thought he was gonna kill her." Rock rubbed his hands intense across the thighs of his pants.

"So what did you do, Rock?"

"I ran to my bedroom. I could hear Faith screaming from downstairs. I grabbed the gun and rushed back down to Daddy's bedroom, but when I got there everything was silent. Faith was lying naked on the bed and Daddy was standing over her body dazed, like a zombie. Her face was bloody and she wasn't moving. I was scared…I was so scared." Rock wiped his face.

"What happened next?"

"Daddy grabbed his Bible off the nightstand next to the bed and held it up in the air. He turned and started babbling off scriptures to me."

"What did he say?"

Rock stared off in the distance as he tried to remember the sporadic details.

"What did he say, Rock?"

"He started quoting scriptures."

"What kind of scriptures?"

"Second Samuel 15:14."

"What did he say, Rock"

A cold chill ran down my spine.

"*Arise and let us flee, for we shall not escape Absalom*!" The words chiseled his lips

"His son sought to kill him? Is that what he meant, Rock, is that what he was trying to say?" Teller leaned in. "Why would he think you were out to kill him, Rock?"

"I had the gun pointed at him. I pulled the trigger, but I missed. I wasn't trying to kill him! I swear it! I was just trying to kill what he stood for. The word of God! He made it dirty, unclean! It wasn't what he thought! So I shot…I shot at the Bible and the bullet went clean through to the wall, but that's all I shot was one shot, I swear it! After that I dropped the gun!"

"Where did the other two shots come from, Rock?"

Rock seemed out of it, faraway, as if he was outside of his own body.

"There were two other shots, where did they come from?"

It was becoming impossible for me to stay in my seat. I wanted to jump up and run. My body shook from anxiety and I could barely draw a breath. I put my hand across my abdomen and tried desperately to ease the queasiness in my stomach. I thought I was going to faint right there.

"Rock, your father was shot twice, where did the other two shots come from?"

He rubbed the sides of his temples intensely as he tried to recollect the events that took place that night. "I remember dropping the gun after the first shot and Daddy staring at me with this blank look…but he…he wasn't staring at me, he was sort of looking through me. He was pale…he was so pale…it was like his soul had left his body or something. He crouched down on the floor to pick up his Bible that had been torn apart from the bullet hole. Pages were falling all over the place. He scooped them back into the Bible and stood up…" Rock wavered.

"And then?" Teller asked

"This cold presence overcame me…more like through me, like a gush of wind or something. The hairs on the back of my neck prickled, it was like it walked clean through me."

Teller cranked his neck. "*Walked*?" he asked.

"Yes, like passed through my body or something." Rock swallowed hard. "And then I saw her. As clear as I am looking at you, she was there. He saw her too. I swear to you he saw her. We both saw her…she was there!"

"Who was there, Rock?"

"My mother!" Bewilderment carried the courtroom. "As God as my witness my mother was there! She bent down and picked up the gun…right in front of me she picked up the gun and pointed it towards Daddy. She was crying and her hands were shaking. She never looked at me, she never said a word, but she was there."

"And where was your father, Rock? Was he still standing in the bedroom?"

"Yes, he was still there dazed."

"And, Faith, where was Faith, Rock?"

"She was still lying on the bed unconscious."

"What happened next?"

Joy intervened. "Objection, Your Honor, we're talking about a ghost here, this is highly unethical."

"Overruled," Judge Hallow remarked.

"What happened after your mother picked up the gun?"

"Daddy just stood there with this sinister grin on his face. I don't know if it was seeing Mama's spirit, or that he knew he had reached his own fate. He held the Bible out to his side and whispered Deuteronomy 32 under his breath. It was like he was giving his own eulogy."

"What was the passage, Rock?"

Daddy's voice echoed in his mind as he rambled on. If he closed his eyes hard enough he could almost feel Daddy reading along with him. "*To me belonged vengeance, and recompense, their foot shall slide in due time, for the day of their calamity is at hand and the things that shall come upon them make haste. See now that I am the one God, there is no god but me. I kill, and I make alive, I wound and I heal, neither is there any that can escape from me.*"

Teller charged in. "What did he mean, Rock? What was he saying?"

"God's judgment had come. Only God has the right to avenge."

"Rock, are you telling this court that *God* sent your mother to kill your father?" Teller asked in an almost disturbed tone.

"Objection, Your Honor!" Joy yelled out.

"Overruled, Ms. Joy." Judge Hallow retorted.

"Vengeance belongs to God. My father knew that. He was a man of the cloth, called by God to be a shepherd over many, yet he brought destruction to God's word. The man who has greater revelation will receive greater judgment, for unto whom much is given much is required."

"So God employed your mother to execute judgment?"

Joy chillingly intervened. "Objection, Your Honor!"

"On what grounds, Counselor?"

"Witness is not an expert in Theology. It's no way he can explain the actions of God, let alone prove that God allegedly killed his father."

Teller turned to Judge Hallow. "I am not asking him to explain why God allegedly did what He did. I am trying to get the court to understand what happened that night and why my client feels God allowed these things to happen. This whole case is built around the acts of God. Therefore, we must get into the mindset of my client and allow him to explain to the court God's actions on the night in question and to biblically support those actions. Now, in order to do that, Your Honor, he's going to have to explain his understanding of God's word, meaning his own interpretation of the Bible."

"I will allow it Counselor, but, once again, with limitations."

Teller nodded and turned his attention back to Rock. "Again, do you think God employed your mother to execute judgment upon your father?"

"Yes. It was God's retribution. Mama was our guardian angel, our protection from Daddy."

"If what you say is true Rock, why didn't she protect you and your sister on other occasions? Why did she wait until that night to stop him? If God is all-knowing, as you say, then why didn't He stop this a long time ago?"

"I don't know," Rock shook his head. "God doesn't work in our time. Our time is not His time. He acts at vital times, times that give Him glory. It's like asking why didn't Jesus come when he got message that Lazarus was dead, why did he wait four days even though he loved Lazarus? It was because he wanted to convince the people that God had sent him, that he was who he said he was. He wanted to give God the glory."

"Do you think the same holds true in this case?"

"Yes. Mama wanted to show us that God had not forsaken us, that it was time to show His glory." Rock sat unyielding.

Teller turned to the court, leaned his torso forward and clasped his hands behind his back. "Are you assuming that your father knew this? That God had sent your mother, the woman whom he loved, the one he married…to persecute him?"

"He stood naked before God, before Mama with her daughter's blood on his hands. His failure to protect us was evident. He knew it. The judgment of God is mighty; no man can stand against His wrath."

You could cut the tension in the courtroom with a chainsaw. Everyone was quiet, not a sound was heard, but a few shuffling of feet or coughs here and there from the dry mouths of spectators desperately needing to break for lunch. Teller walked back and forth, every now and again engaging his attention to the jury. He knew the difficulty of proving his case and the thin line between the boundaries he was crossing, but he needed to keep the jurors connected as much as possible to Rock, so he engaged his audience.

"Rock, you stated that your Dad knew his fate, how so?"

"It showed in his demeanor?"

"Did he run?"

"No, Sir."

"Did he in anyway try to defend himself?"

"No."

"So it was as though he was expectant?"

"Yes…sort of. Daddy was sick. It's like a person who continues to do wrong and wants to stop, but can't by his own power."

"Like a rapist or a serial killer who desires to get caught?"

"Yes, Sir, somewhere in his perverted mind he wanted to be rescued from his own corruption."

Teller quickly shifted gears. "What happened next, Rock? You run upstairs to grab the gun, you come back to your father's room, shoot one round into his Bible, he reaches down picks the Bible up off the floor and your Mom appears. What happened next?"

"She never looks at me, but I can see that her face is wet from crying. She crouches down, picks the gun up and points it at Daddy. I'm in disbelief. My heart ceased to beat. I can't believe what's happening. I'm thinking it's my mind playing tricks on me, you know, like temporary insanity or something." Rock's body chilled from the thought. "But it's not…she's real I kept telling myself. She's standing there, her hands shaking, she and Daddy just staring at each other. I was scared out of my mind, but all I could think about was getting my sister out of harms-way, so terrified as hell I walk slowly pass Mama into Daddy's room. He's stock-still, a statuette of sort. I picked Faith up off the bed and carried her back out into the hallway. As I kneel down to the floor I hear Mama whisper the scripture from Hebrews, '*It is a fearful thing to fall into the hands of the living God*,' and then two shots rang out. I haven't gotten Faith completely to the floor yet before the gunshots startle me. I quickly look up and I see Daddy lying on the floor. I couldn't see his face because of the position his body was in, but I knew he was dead because blood was everywhere." Rock battled to fight back the tears. "I…I look up at Mama and she's just staring at me with this sort of its going to be okay look on her face. My legs go numb and I can't feel my feet, so I'm just kneeling there with my sister in my arms." Rock swallowed hard as he dropped his head into his chest.

"What happened next?" Teller asked

Rock sat still.

"What happened next, Rock?" Teller asked again forcefully.

"I don't know…she just disappeared."

"What do you mean, she just disappeared? Did she walk away, fade into thin air? What?"

Rock fidgeted with his fingers. "She dropped the gun on the floor, smiled at me and turned and walked away. She just disappeared, I don't know, she just vanished."

Teller once again paced the floor. "*It is a fearful thing to fall into the hands of the living God.* What did she mean?"

Rock lifted his chin to eye level. "He willfully defied God's word and his disobedience cast God's judgment."

"Did you ever see your mother again after that day?"

"No, Sir, I didn't. Only thing I know is that the police is coming through the door, I'm handcuffed and Faith is taken off by the paramedics to the hospital."

Teller placed one hand on the podium and leaned in. "Mr. Rock, can you honestly say before God, under oath, and to this jury that everything you have told us here today is fact?" He surveyed Rock's face like an experienced lie detector sniffing out the truth.

"Yes, Sir, it's the honest to God truth."

Teller eyeballed Rock for a long minute before turning to Judge Hallow. "No further questions, Your Honor."

"Very well," Judge Hallow said with a deep breath, almost at a loss for words. "I'm sure we can all agree that it has been an exhausting day. I will dismiss Jury and court will adjourn and reconvene at 8:00 a.m. tomorrow morning."

JULY 1, 2008

PRESENT DAY

I have these reoccurring dreams that my home is possessed by demonic spirits holding me against my will. They have these disfigured faces, white eyes and sharp teeth, some with no faces at all. No matter how hard I try I can't escape. Two or more would hold me down while others pierce at my lungs, cutting off my oxygen until I'm unable to breathe or too out of breath to move. The fear jolts me from my sleep. Although I'm awake, they're still here. I mean, I can't see them, but I sense them. I can feel their presence hovering over me like a swarm of bees. It's like they've jumped out of my dreams into reality or something. I try to convince myself they're not real, but try telling that to my mind. I've been fighting demons all my life and now they're attacking my thoughts. Sleep was the only time I could truly find peace, but now, even that seems to be a battle.

I sat up, reached over and grabbed the ice cold water I kept in a thermos off the night stand next to my bed. I took a few sips to relieve the dryness in my throat. In between swigs I began to rationalize with myself. Maybe what I needed was my head examined by another shrink telling me my nightmares are just a result of the trauma from my childhood, or that the demons and feeling trapped inside my own home are all symbolic of Daddy and my desperate need to free myself from his incestuous misconduct. Yeah...well, here's to freedom, I thought to myself as I swallowed down the remainder of the ice cold water.

The trial has been going on for months now and I really don't know what to expect. The hate mail is piling up from people who accuse us of mocking the name of God, of being disrespectful to the Almighty Father. Well, where were these so-called-Christians when Daddy was defying the word of God, making a mockery of the church? I mean they run around the sanctuary screaming and hollering in the name of Jesus, but when it's truly time to answer the call no one steps up. Everyone acts like nothing is going on, as if they can't see what's happening right in front of their faces. Sure, they ask you how you're doing in their Sunday morning best, but really don't care one way or the other because they're belching out, "Praise the Lord," and walking away before you can give an honest response. Mama use to call folks like that deceitful Christians, people who pretend to be holier than thou, but secretly their sins are as dirty as the ground they walk upon. Guess that's why I never put faith in Man because Man would fail you every time...Daddy can certainly vouch for that.

Anyways, I diverted, Teller's coming over today to discuss the trial, but I don't feel much like talking, I'm exhausted. I haven't had an appetite for days and I've got this tightening sensation in my chest, I figure it's just anxiety. Teller is close to resting his case, and based upon his defense, the jury will either find my brother mentally insane or lock him up and throw away the key. Either way I'm left alone to live a life that wasn't much worth living in the first place.

I'm 19-years-old and already I feel used up, my body worn out. I've retreated so far within myself I don't know how to let anyone in. Not that many have tried, but those who have I've pushed away. My mind wanders back to Bishop, his warm smile and soft touch. Nothing ever came of that relationship, Daddy made sure of that. Anything I had to offer a man he took from me a long time ago. He left me broken and empty inside, a hollow shell yearning to be filled with something, anything conceivable that could make me feel whole again.

I don't know how to begin picking up the pieces in my life. It's hard enough to gain strength to climb out of bed. This morning all I want is to pull the covers up over my head and shut out the rest of the world, but I've got a long day ahead of me so I decided to shower and eat breakfast before Teller arrived.

Five minutes into my turkey sausage and wheat toast the doorbell rang. I took a few bites before wiping my hands on my pajama pants and greeting Teller at the door. He stood there for a moment with his head cocked to one side, waiting for me to invite him in. He was dressed in a long black oversized raincoat that covered his crisp white shirt and dark brown three piece suit, which I thought was sort of inappropriate for a Saturday morning home visit, but that‘s just me. The skies were overcast and we were expecting late morning showers, so at least he got the raincoat thing right.

I gestured for him to come in. He must have wiped his feet on the worn out doormat at least ten times before walking in...I've been meaning to replace that thing anyway.

"Something smells good," Teller said as he took a whiff of the air.

Yeah, it would have been nice to have a moment to enjoy it, I thought to myself. "Would you like a cup of coffee?" I asked.

"Thank you," he said taking off his raincoat and settling down into the old wingback chair. "Black, please," he added.

"Sure," I said walking back into the kitchen. I never drank the stuff myself, but Daddy always brewed a fresh pot every morning, so I managed to find an old can, with the expiration date worn off, pushed far back in the corners of the cabinet with enough to make at least a half-a-pot for Teller. I've noticed him drinking a cup every now and again during trial, so I prepared some just in case. I've often wondered how folks could drink two and three cups a day, I would jump right out of my skin, not to mention it gives me the runs.

I returned to the living room and cautiously handed Teller the hot cup of coffee.

"Thank you," he said before taking a sip. He placed the mug on the small wooden table and focused his attention to me. "So, here's where we're at, Faith." He leaned forward, rested his elbows on his knees and clasped his hands in front of him. "Prosecution wants to offer your brother a plea deal, a guilty plea in exchange for manslaughter which carries ten years with possibility of parole in five."

I shook my head confused, "Manslaughter?"

"Unpremeditated murder, Rock would be admitting to killing your father, but unintentionally."

"Do you think that's a good thing, I mean considering the circumstances?"

"No. Your brother is innocent. Taking a plea is an admission of guilt, and you and your brother are just as much the victims in this case as your father."

"So what do you suggest?"

"I suggest we let the jury decide. Granted, the evidence seems far-fetched, but so far-fetched that there's got to be some truth to it. I mean people just don't make up outlandish stories like this, especially when their life is on the line. The jury has got to see that, and it's my job to make sure that they do." He took another sip of coffee. "That's good stuff right there."

"So what do we do now?"

"*We*," he smiled, "will let the jury do their job. I did the best I could to build a solid case around Rock's testimony, the rest is left up to God."

"The best you could? Is that all you can say?" I ignored the God thing.

Teller took a couple more sips of coffee before he stood to put on his raincoat. "Considering the circumstances, Faith, that's all I got at the moment. This was a difficult case, and more difficult was gathering evidence or finding witnesses to testify to your brother's story."

"If what you say is true, Mr. Teller, then wouldn't it make more sense for Rock to take the plea?"

"No. I would rather fight this case to the end than throw in the towel. Rock will have a better chance at letting the jury decide."

So that's it? That's all we needed to talk about? You could of called on the phone for this, I thought to myself.

"You know, Faith, there's nothing wrong with sending up a prayer for your brother. Asking for a little help from the Man up above may be just what we need to help us get through this." He pulled the cuffs of his shirt out from underneath the sleeves of his coat and stretched out his hands towards me. "Do you know Matthew 18:20?"

I sat silent.

"F*or where two or three are gathered together in my name, I am there in the midst of them.*"

At that moment I heard the down pour of rain, a strike of lightning cracked the sky and thunder was heard, I figured it was a sign, but I couldn't bring myself to grab Teller's hands. I defied the gesture and indulged the Gospel of Mark, "*Therefore he could do no mighty works there because of their unbelief.*"

Teller humbly dropped his hands and walked towards the door. Before leaving he turned to me. "*When my father and my mother forsake me, then the Lord will take me up.*" He winked and closed the door behind him leaving me to my thoughts. I could no longer stomach my breakfast, so I sat on the sofa with my feet tucked comfortably underneath me and waited for the storm to pass.

JUNE 5, 2008

RECOMMENCEMENT OF TRIAL

Outside the courthouse looked like a three-ring circus. People were marching around with signs that said, "God is No Murderer," while others were selling t-shirts that said, "God Saves." The courtroom inside had become so overcrowded that the Sheriff wouldn't allow anyone else in. I tucked a strand of hair behind my ear as I discreetly glanced over at Prosecution's table. Joy was shuffling through papers and sipping on coffee. Judge Hallow's bench was empty and Teller hadn't arrived yet.

I took advantage of the composed opportunity and thought about Mama. You know how a certain smell or a particular time of year can make you think about certain events that happened in your life? Well, today was one of those days. I closed my eyes. The heat and humidity took me back to when me, Rock and Mama would sit on the porch and talk for hours. She would braid my hair while, "Have a Little Faith" played on the CD player from inside the house. We would grab hands and dance around the yard, free spirits laughing at life. Mama had a gift of making you feel good about yourself no matter how bad things got. Daddy, the cancer, and all the pain that came along with it never made her bitter, never took her joy. She was always smiling and whenever you were around her you couldn't help but to smile too. I was so absorbed in my thoughts I didn't see Teller and Rock enter the courtroom. The sound of Judge Hallow's gavel snapped me back to reality.

"Mr. Teller, it has been brought to the court's attention that you have an expert in Metaphysics and Paranormal Studies to witness on Defense's behalf. Is this correct?"

Teller stood up. "Yes, Sir, that is correct."

Judge Hallowed peered over his glasses. "Counselor you do understand that metaphysics overall is considered to be a very vague and implausible study…no disrespect to anyone's choice of profession, but because it's a matter of one's opinion and not scientifically proven, it would be deemed inadmissible in my courtroom."

"Yes, Sir, I understand that."

"Then why do you suggest I give you permission to address such a pointless issue?"

"Your Honor, if I may, metaphysics derives from the same concept as religion, yet you have allowed me countless times to address theology during this trial."

"Yes I have, Counselor, but theology is the study of God, metaphysics is not. Theology has specific doctrine, immeasurable amounts of historical documentation and sources to help support its existence. The Law itself is based on the very foundation of God. I cannot say the same about metaphysics."

"Your Honor, they both seek out to examine and understand the nature of existence and our purpose for being here in the first place. Problem is the world seems to think if it can't be proven by scientific facts or experiment then it must not be true. Whether we admit it or not we all have some type of metaphysical perspective or religious views about the nature of reality. I think we all can attest to the fact that there are things that exist separately from the natural world or beyond the range of normal human experience that at one time or another has happened to us that we cannot explain. Theology calls it divinity and metaphysics calls it the supernatural, either way they're the same, at least that is what I hope to prove here today."

Judge Hallow paused for a moment, taking caution to his response. "Very good argument, Mr. Counselor, but once again this is my courtroom and you are verging on the line of unethical. Let the record show that I will allow the testimony of your expert, but with limitations. As stated before, I will use my discretion as needed. If at any time your line of questioning causes derision to this case I will strike your expert from record and dismiss the testimony all together. Am I clear?"

"Yes, Sir."

"Very well, call your witness."

"Defense calls Dr. Wise to the stand." Teller lightly tapped the top of the table three times, unfastened the last button of his suit jacket and poured himself a glass of water before pleading his case.

Dr. Wise was a tall slender man, late forties, maybe six feet or more with long black hair pulled back into a ponytail. He must have been growing his goatee for years now because it hung down passed his chest. His blue jeans and black t-shirt gripped his frail frame so tight he looked anorexic. I figured he suffered from scoliosis or something because of the slight crook of his spine. Slumped over he made his way to the podium, ignoring the judged eyes filtering through the courtroom, and was sworn in.

Teller appeared tense. He drank the entire glass of water before approaching the witness. Rock held an unfitted look and I tried desperately to keep an open mind.

"Dr. Wise," Teller cleared his throat, "I would like to personally thank you for taking out the time in your busy schedule to be here today."

He smiled and gave a short nod. His teeth apparently stained by overindulgence of coffee and cigarettes.

"Would you please, for the court, tell us your area of expertise?"

"I hold a Master's in Metaphysics and a Doctorate in Paranormal Studies whereby I specialize in Angelology and Parapsychology."

He sounded like he was reading from an encyclopedia.

"Angelology?"

"Yes, the theological study of angels."

"Dr. Wise, is it possible to break down all of this terminology in simpler terms so that the court can understand exactly what it is you do?"

Thank goodness, I thought to myself.

"Sure. My profession is in the unexplained, in phenomena that's deemed physically impossible or have no scientific explanation such as angels, paranormal activity, strange or unusual sightings…things of that sort."

This was a long stretch for Defense, but Teller was determined to sway the jury into seeing Rock's testimony in a somewhat believable light, no matter how unbelievable it seemed.

"Dr. Wise, what is your belief in guardian angels? In your opinion, do they exist?"

He cleared his throat and grabbed the glass of ice water off the ledge of the podium. Although the cool air could be felt through the vents of the courtroom, the crowd of people seemed to be letting off body heat and absorbing what little air there was. Dr. Wise swallowed hard as he emptied the glass, his Adam's apple protruding through his neck like an inflamed tumor. He tightened his face and puckered his lips as if he were waiting for the brain-freeze to pass.

"In my line of work I have come across many people who have admitted to either seeing an angel or coming in contact with one when they were either in dire need of assistance or they were severely distressed. Many have described experiences of being pulled out of a burning car after a tragic accident, or seeing an angel when they have had profound grief or suicidal thoughts. Some angels have even guided loved-one's back from near death experiences. You see, Mr. Teller, the manifestation of an angel is never arbitrary but rather purpose-driven. They seem to appear at vital times, when they are needed most. Angels are not just simply help mates, they are summoned by God to provide comfort or help to loved-one's that require extreme assistance. This is why they are called guardian angels." Dr. Wise stroked his goatee. "To say to a person that angels do not exist is to say that God doesn't exist. They are one in the same."

"Can you clarify that statement for the court, please?" Teller leaned forward and put his hand to his ear.

"The Bible is understood to be the written word of God. The word "angel" is defined as a messenger of God, and throughout the Bible there are numerous accounts of angel visitations or interactions. In Genesis, chapter 18, three angels appeared to Abraham, one of the angels was clearly identified as God. In Genesis, chapter 19, two angels visited Lot, sent by God, to deliver him from the destruction of Sodom and Gomorrah. In Genesis, chapter 32, Jacob wrestled with an angel of who later blessed him with the name Israel. He himself proclaimed the angel to be God, stating, 'I have seen God face to face.'" He cleared his throat. "No one holds the supreme answer to the spiritual realm, but we would be wrong in suggesting it doesn't exist."

"These accounts are all from the Old Testament of the Bible. What about the New Testament? Are there any accounts between angels and humans in the New Testament?"

"Absolutely, I won't name them all because we will be here all day, but if I may, in the Gospel of Luke, Chapter One, an angel appears to Zechariah proclaiming the birth of his son, John the Baptist. Also in that same chapter, the archangel Gabriel comes to the Virgin Mary, proclaiming the birth of the Messiah, her son, Jesus Christ; and in Luke, Chapter 22, an angel appears from heaven to comfort Jesus during his moment of agony in the Garden, these are all pertinent accounts of biblical history. In each of these events an angel was sent by God to bring forth a message, or in the case of Jesus, an angel was sent to comfort. To deny angels is to deny God. Sometimes there are no scientific explanations for things, but it doesn't mean that it doesn't exist. Trying to explain the supernatural to science is like explaining God to an atheist, to them, if it's not seen, it's not there."

Teller crossed his arms over his chest. "Again, Dr. Wise, in respect to your area of expertise, how are angels regarded or described in appearance?"

"There are many variations. Many people have described angels as being human in appearance, maybe taking on the form of someone whom they have had an emotional attachment to in life, or a loved-one that has died, some even appearing as strangers. There were even cases where an irradiated figure gracing wings as high as six feet tall were reported. And as stated before, others have seen a light or a vision while dreaming, being in danger or having a near death experience. Many people have deemed angels as peaceful spirits who appear, provide help, and then strangely disappear just as quickly as they appeared."

Teller shoved his hands in the front pockets of his pants. He raised his head to the ceiling, examining it for a moment as if his next question was engraved in the cracks of the egg-shell colored paint. "Dr. Wise, in your opinion, would you say that angels have the power or capability to kill?"

Teller's question floored the courtroom. Agnostic chatters and disbelief swarmed from all sides. Some people protested blasphemy to God's name while others lied in wait for Dr. Wise's response. I sat asphyxiated in my seat. Judge Hallow banged his gavel and gestured his hand for silence. My eyes scanned Joy, waiting for her to object, but she never did.

Dr. Wise shifted in his seat…choosing his words carefully…trying not to offend the just any more than Teller's question already had. He poured himself another glass of water, sipped, stroked his goatee and met the gazed eyes of the judged room. "God created angels to solely carry out His perfect will and plan, whether that be to worship and serve Him in heaven, or bring forth His blessings or judgment on earth. In the Book of Daniel, specifically chapters 8 and 9, you will find profound evidence of God sending angels to warn and bestow judgment upon His people. The same holds true in the Book of Revelations. Throughout biblical times, angels, who move only according to God's will, have participated in the death and destruction of many individuals and nations who had chosen to deliberately disobey God's commands. Psalms 91, clearly states, '*He will give His angels charge over you to protect you in all your ways.*' This is evident of God's faithfulness to the protection of his people. His commands to His angels are not only to comfort and protect you, but to strike down those who come up against you." Dr. Wise scratched the side of his face with the tips of his fingers. The shaven stubbles sounded like two pieces of sand paper being rubbed together.

"If I am to speak directly from the written word of God, in my opinion, yes, angels have the ability to kill, but only if summoned by God."

His words were harsh, cutting through the courtroom like a dagger. Looks of contempt covered the faces of the jurors. To label God a murderer was blasphemy amongst the Christian community, and the trial was already getting enough negative publicity from the media. Dr. Wise sat calmly amid an outburst from one of the spectators, accusing him of being the anti-christ. He quietly stroked his goatee as the sheriff removed the viewer from the courtroom.

Joy lashed out. "Your Honor, this case has turned out to be nothing more than a constant degradation of God. I can no longer sit here and be a part of such disgrace. I move to strike Defense's entire case."

"On what grounds, Counselor?" Teller attacked.

"On the grounds of defamation and lack of evidence, this case is absurd. Defense has not presented one ounce of credible evidence to this court."

"By who's standards, Counselor, yours?" I am representing my client according to the information I have in this case and that information surrounds a superior being whether you choose to accept it or not. Furthermore, it would behoove you not to discredit my approach to this case. I've gathered the necessary evidence needed to build my defense and I've built it upon those facts. It is not for you to decide whether it is plausible or not, that is for the jury to decide." Teller retaliated.

"But your evidence is not supportive of a real person. You expect the jury to come to a verdict on the basis of a spiritual being?" her voice escalated.

"Well they have no other choice now do they, Counselor, because that's exactly who is alleged to have killed your client!" Teller stood firm with his neck cocked to one side and bug-eyed.

"I have had enough!" Judge Hallow seethed. He banged his gavel so hard I thought it would go clear through the bench. "I will see both

Counselors in my chambers now! Court will stand in ten minute recess!" He abruptly exited the courtroom with Teller and Joy in tow.

Judge Hallow's office was huge and dim, lit only by a small desk lamp that set next to a family portrait of his wife and two kids, one boy, one girl. On the wall was an 8x10 scroll with a gold border that read:

Deuteronomy 1:16 and 17: "*And I charged your judges at that time saying, hear the causes between your brethren, and judge righteously between every man and his brother, and the stranger that is with him. Ye shall not respect persons in judgment, but ye shall hear the small as well as the great, ye shall not be afraid of the face of man, for the judgment is God's, and the cause that is too hard for you, bring it unto me, and I will hear it.*"

Behind the desk was a large picture window with not much of a view. Dark colored drapes hung from each side, open just enough to allow the sunlight to pierce in. Against the wall was a tall bookcase that shelved stacks of law books that looked as though they had never been used.

Teller and Joy sat adjacent of one another. Judge Hallow stared across the desk with a displeased look on his face.

"I have never, in all my years on the bench, experienced such disrespect between two Counselors. Not only have you taken it upon yourselves to break the rules of my courtroom, but there are two kids out there whose fate lies in your hands and you are acting more juvenile than they are."

Joy dropped her head like a disobedient child being scolded by her father. Teller sat reserved. Although he didn't say much it was evident the complexity of the trial was beginning to take its toll.

"I have had the privilege, in the past, of presiding over many of your cases and I have always had the utmost respect and regard for both of your work, but I will no longer tolerate your indignant behavior in my courtroom," he criticized. "Now, Mr. Teller, I understand that this is a difficult case to try, which is why I have allowed the evidence I have so far, but my main concern at this juncture is the absence of any eyewitnesses who can attest to your client's claim. Although his sister was present at the time of the murder, not even she can substantiate to what happened that night."

"Which is why Prosecution move to dismiss," Joy remarked, this time with considerable empathy.

"Your Honor, I know I don't have very much to go on, but I am fighting for a young man who has been imprisoned all his life. No decent human being should have to suffer the way those kids have suffered and I will not be a part of a system that has failed them thus far."

Judge Hallow leaned back in his chair and clasped his hands behind his neck. "Mr. Teller, emotions can be a very strong suit in which one could wear in a very detrimental way. It has the ability to distort the truth and influence our judgment. Could it be that your concern for the welfare of these children are making you bias in this case?"

"Granted, I'm grasping at straws here, Your Honor, but I would never have taken this case pro bono if I thought for one second that my client was not telling me the truth. He's innocent and I intend to fight with every fiber of my being to prove that to the jury, even if that means fighting a ghost."

Judge Hallow paused for a moment, engrossed in thought. "Very well, Mr. Teller," he leaned forward and clasped his hands on top of the desk. "I am denying Prosecution's request for dismissal." Joy looked displeased. "I have presided over a lot of trials in my lifetime, but none as unconventional as this one. In order to judge fairly I must remain indifferent to all involved and that means accepting things that I wouldn't accept under normal circumstances, to the extent of the law. If we can all respect these terms and conduct ourselves in a civilized manner I'm sure this case will go as smoothly as possible from this point forward," he gaped over his glasses.

"Yes, Sir," they responded.

He turned his attention to Joy. "Does Prosecution plan to cross-examine Dr. Wise?"

"No, Your Honor, but we are prepared to recall Mr. Rock to the stand."

"Very well, court shall reconvene."

Recess felt like an eternity. When Teller returned to the courtroom he had a solemn look on his face. Judge Hallow took his seat at the bench and Joy returned to the Prosecutor's table. She leaned over and whispered to her assistant who listened intently like a kindergartener being told the secret of his life. I felt nauseous. Teller's disposition made the air even more threatening as he took his seat next to Rock without saying a word.

Judge Hallow cleared his throat. "I would like to thank everyone for their patience and apologize for the disruption. At this time court is back in session." He glanced over at Teller. "Does Defense have any more questions for this witness?"

Dr. Wise, who had been sitting for a while, looked as though he was in desperate need of a cigarette and a cup of coffee.

Teller stood. "No, Your Honor, Defense has no further questions."

"Very well," Judge Hallow turned to Joy. "Does Prosecution wish to cross-examine?"

"No, Your Honor, but if it pleases the court Prosecution is ready to recall Mr. Rock to the stand."

Judge Hallow gestured to Dr. Wise. "Thank you for your patience Doctor you may step down." He searched the room. "Could someone please escort Dr. Wise safely out?" Dr. Wise's fragile and thin structure resembled a bent stick figure as he exited the courtroom unscathed.

Rock approached the bench like a condemned prisoner walking to his execution. The distance between the defense table and the witness stand felt like a mile. Looking haggard and worn and barely holding on to what little dignity he had left, Rock once again presented himself before the court to be judged.

"Let me remind you Sir that you're still under oath."

"Yes, Your Honor," Rock said in a nervous, shaken voice, his heart beating a heavy rhythm as he awaited Prosecution's attack.

Joy flipped through the bound pages of court documents, which looked more like a book rather than a transcript. She stopped midway, tapped her index finger at a particular point and smoothed the pages out with the palm of her hand. She stood in position. "Mr. Rock, you stated in your earlier testimony to Defense that you called your friend, Bishop, to request a gun. Could you tell the court how many days prior to your father's death did you have that conversation with your friend?"

"That morning."

"What morning?"

"The morning of the shooting."

"The day after your father attacked you?"

"Yes, ma'am."

"How many hours would you say there were between your father's alleged attack and your calling Bishop?"

"I don't recall."

"Nine…ten hours, maybe?"

"I don't remember," Rock repeated a little agitated.

Joy walked around to the front of the table, leaned carefully back on its edge and crossed her legs at the ankles. "Were you still angry with your father at the time you requested the gun from Bishop?

"Yes, ma'am, I was."

"And what was your intent for the gun?"

"Protection."

"Protection for you or protection from your father?"

Rock looked perplexed. "Isn't that one in the same?"

"No. Protection for you is premeditated. Protection from your father is self-defense."

"Objection, Your Honor."

"Sustain."

"Mr. Rock, rather than you and your sister calling the police at any time regarding the alleged attack, you chose to seek out a gun and take the law into your own hands."

"Objection, Your Honor, speculation, furthermore, there's no evidence proving witness's sister had any knowledge of him obtaining a gun."

"Sustain."

"I'll rephrase. Mr. Rock, you had ample opportunity at any time before and after your father's attack to call the authorities, tell a neighbor or notify anyone of your father's alleged abuse. Yet, you chose to acquire a gun, under your own volition, and take the law into your own hands.

Rock shook his head. "No, that's not true. I only got the gun for protection, not for the intent to kill anyone."

Joy looked down at the documents held tightly in her hand. "Your exact words to the court were, 'I got the gun from Bishop; I wanted to kill him; I hid the gun in my dresser drawer and I waited.' It's right here in black and white, Mr. Rock. That was your testimony, those were your words."

"No, you're twisting my words I never said I wanted to kill him."

"So what are you saying to this court? In the midst of anger and hatred, not even 24-hours after your father's attack, you sought to gain possession of a gun not for the intent to kill, but for what purpose?"

"I told you to protect me and my sister." Rock felt his temper rising.

"And what did you think that protection would involve with a gun?"

"I don't know."

Joy approached the podium. "Do you know the sole purpose of a gun, Mr. Rock?"

"Yes, Ma'am I do."

"And did you know that purpose when you obtained the gun?"

"Yes, Ma'am I did."

"Yet, you expect this court to believe that you acquired that gun with no inclination of vengeance?"

"Objection, Your Honor Counselor is badgering the witness?"

"Overruled."

"What were you thinking when you asked for the gun, Mr. Rock?" Joy stood cold, her words digging, waiting for that moment of weakness when Rock would implicate himself with his own words. "Your dad had just sodomized you, his only son, an innocent child, you were angry, consumed with hate. You did what any human being would have done under those circumstances."

Rock shook his head. "No. That's not true."

She kept digging. "You watched as he raped your sister. She was lying lifeless on his bed, covered in blood. You couldn't think. You thought she was dead. You retrieved the gun, came back, pointed it at your father…"

Teller quickly intervened. "Objection Your Honor, badgering!"

Anger grabbed at Rock and he lost all self-control. "I had to protect me and my sister!" he cried. "He took my manhood! He raped her almost every night! He did nothing but inflict pain upon us day in and day out! What was I supposed to do, wait on him to kill us?!"

Teller watched as Joy set the bait.

"All he ever did was hurt us and beat us! He never loved us! He wasn't a father, he was a monster! He destroyed our childhood! We were kids! We just wanted to be kids…" Rock's voice broke as tears welled in his boyish eyes.

Joy pounced on the opportunity like a cat devouring a mouse for lunch. "Was that your reason for getting the gun, Rock?"

"Yes!" Rock's voice leveled to a low breathless tone. "I got the gun to kill him. Is that what you wanna hear? I wanted him dead. He didn't deserve to live. He abused us in shameful ways. He didn't deserve to be called Daddy. He didn't deserve God's mercy" Rock's lips quivered. "But, I didn't kill him. I wanted to...but I didn't...I didn't kill him." Rock's chest heaved up and down as he struggled to catch his breath. He erupted into a strained helpless cry.

At that moment all wind left my body. I lost sense of where I was. The only thought in my head was to run to my brother's aid, to redeem myself for not being able to protect him from that horrible night. I rushed to the front of the courtroom to console him. The bailiff started towards me, but Judge Hallow gestured for him to stop. I ran straight into his arms. We stood there, motionless, holding each other tight, protecting each other from the rest of the world.

Overcome by emotion, Joy spoke in a nearly apologetic tone, "Prosecution has no further questions for this witness, Your Honor."

Judge Hallow turned to Teller, "Does Defense wish to call any other witnesses?"

Teller clasped his hands behind his back and leaned his torso slightly forward. "No, Your Honor, Defense rests its case."

"Very well, court will adjourn for the day. Counselors will be prepared to present closing arguments at 8:00 a.m. Monday morning.

As the courtroom slowly emptied out, Rock and I stood there for a while huddled together, comforting one another with our faces buried in each other's arms. To the world we were two kids fighting against all the odds, but to us, we were simply brother and sister fighting to be free.

JUNE 7, 2008

Teller spent the rest of the week working on his closing argument. Pieces of torn and balled up paper covered the home office floor. He sat staring at the computer, an empty blank screen glaring back at him. He hit delete so many times his index finger had begun to cramp up. What could he say that hadn't already been said? If there was ever a time he needed God, he needed Him today. He slid open the desk drawer and pulled out two bottles of prescription pills. Pressing firmly down with the palm of his hand, he opened the caps, popped one of each pill in his mouth and chased them down with water. The pain in his joints was becoming unbearable and the weakness of his muscles grew more aggressive by the day. His eyes hurt and he felt fatigue, so he decided to take a break. Maybe a warm bath will help soothe the pain. In the courtroom he had skin as thick as a rhinoceros, but away from all the legal jargon and expectations the tough skin shed like a snake. Behind the walls of his home, in his own private space, he suffered from multiple sclerosis, a disease that caused him chronic pain. He hadn't had a relapse in months, but the stress from the trial exacerbated the symptoms. His body had become weak, exhausted from trying to prove something that wasn't there, chasing a ghost, that at times, appeared to have no intentions on getting caught.

Teller stepped cautiously into the warm bath, even the slight move of his neck radiated pain down his spine. He eased himself down into the tub, careful to grab hold of the handle attached to the wall to help support himself getting in and out of the tub. He leaned his head back and closed his eyes. Drifting into deep thought, he wandered back to his childhood. To the cruel days when his father was an alcoholic, the nonstop beatings he had to endure as a result of too many drunken nights. The screams of his mother's voice as she tried desperately to pull him from the grips of his father's belted hand that lashed down so hard it left welts that bruised the skin and swelled for days. The nights filled with lying awake to the cries of his mother being repeatedly raped; the liquor bottle thrown into the fireplace after a long night of binge drinking; the igniting of a fire that stirred a frantic rescue of a mother carrying her son to safety, only to seal her own demise in search of a love that would never be. A child left hopeless, standing on the curb, waiting for a mother that would never return, but later be found lying next to a husband that not only beat the life out of her, but took her life, trying to save his.

The sound of broken glass from drunken bottles penetrated his mind. The heat from the hot water jolted him out of his thoughts. The tub had overflowed onto the floor. Teller tried desperately to reach for the faucet, but the pain was so severe he could hardly move. He pulled himself out of the tub and stumbled back into his office. Grabbing the cell phone off the desk he dialed 9-1-1. Overcome with excruciating pain, and unable to hold his balance, he collapsed to the floor before the paramedics arrived.

JUNE 8, 2008

"Mr. Teller, I know you are a very busy man and you have been through a lot in the last twenty-four hours, but if you don't hold your arm still so I can check your blood pressure you will find yourself in here longer than expected." The pretty nurse in the blue scrubs smiled as she attempted to take his vitals.

Teller had been admitted into the hospital and only had two days left to prepare for his argument. His pain had subsided and he was feeling better. He ignored the nurse as he went about writing and scribbling on his note pad.

"Well, Sir, looks like I got here just in time. I think you'll be needing this." Judge Hallow walked around to the other side of the bed, grabbed a chair and handed Teller his laptop.

"Everything looks good, Mr. Teller. I'll come back later to check on you," she gave a warm smile and walked away.

Judge Hallow crossed his arms and cleared his throat. "Looks like you're pushing yourself a little hard, Counselor."

Teller hiked his eyes just enough to give a short grunt. "Mmh," he said as he focused his attention back on the computer.

"Yeah, well, you won't do yourself or those kids any good if you don't start taking better care of yourself."

"On the contrary, Judge, I won't be much good to anybody if I don't finish this closing argument before Monday morning, besides it was just a little heat exhaustion, that's all. I feel much better now. As a matter of fact they said I could go home today. Just waiting on a couple of test results and my release papers," Teller said engrossed in his work, never once looking up.

"I can push the closing arguments back a few days if need be, Counselor. Maybe take a day or so to regain your strength." Judge Hallow tucked his chin into his chest and peered over his glasses.

Teller eyes quickly shifted. "Sir, I don't need any extra days. I have two, and I assure you that is more than enough time to gain my strength and prepare my argument to be heard before the jurors on Monday morning. As I stated before, it was the heat, but I'm fine now. There's nothing to be concerned about. No reason to go rescheduling any dates on my behalf."

"Well, heat exhaustion or not my friend, our body has a way of telling us when we're over extending ourselves whether we want it to or not. And yours is speaking loud and clear." Judge Hallow stood up from the chair. "Neglecting yourself for the sake of others, Counselor, is simply not worth it. We should never be too busy to take care of our temple," he said slipping his hand deep into the front pocket of his trousers. "I've never heard a man on his death bed ever say he wish he would have taken more time to work harder." He patted Teller on the shoulder and walked away.

"Eight a.m. Monday morning, Judge," Teller yelled from behind.

Judge Hallow gave a wave of his hand. "Can't tend to others if you don't tend to self, Counselor," he replied and strolled out of the room never looking back.

JUNE 10, 2008

The day before court Teller decided to pay Ms. Eloise a visit. He needed more relevant information for his case and she was the only person he knew of that could halfway give him what he needed. Her telephone number wasn't listed so he drove to the other side of town by chance. He didn't have an address, but he remembered the house from visiting Faith on numerous occasions during the trial. He had hoped she wouldn't be home. He didn't want her to think he was sneaking around behind she and Rock's back, but he needed as much information as possible to plead his case. The drive over wasn't too bad, mostly freeway and main streets. He pulled up to Ms. Eloise's and turned off the car. Faith's house sat on a remote part of the street and looked isolated and lonely as always. He opened the car door and quickly walked up to Ms. Eloise's front porch, knocked on the half-hinged screen door and waited for her to answer. He glimpsed around the destitute home. Torn shoe boxes were piled head high and old clothes hung on a rollaway cart. It looked more like a rummage area than a porch. He was about to knock again before the door slowly creaked open. Ms. Eloise peeked through the hole in the torn screen.

"Ms. Eloise?"

"Yes."

"Ms. Eloise, my name is Mr. Teller. I am the Defense Attorney representing Mr. Rock in his criminal case. I just need a minute of your time if you don't mind, ma'am."

"Defense attorney?" she asked

"Yes, ma'am."

"Well isn't that nice," she said impressed.

"I just need a moment ma'am."

She slowly pushed the door open and invited Teller in. The inside of the house wasn't much better than the outside. An old rusted fan rattled loudly as the blades forced themselves to blow out as much air as possible. It set inside a half opened window that was propped up in the corner by a stick. Clothes, that appeared to belong to a man, were thrown across the yellow floral sofa. An aged-old corn pipe rested on top of a wood table next to a torn leather chair, whose seams were held together by duct tape.

"That was Mister's chair," she said as she gestured for Teller to sit down. "I've never allowed anyone else to sit in that chair until now," Ms. Eloise gave a proud smile.

"Thank you ma'am," Teller said humbly."

"Mister passed away years ago, but I keep some of his stuff lying around so I won't feel so lonely," she said easing down into her wooden rocking chair. "It gets so quiet around here at times."

"I imagine so," Teller said respectfully.

"Are you married, Mr. Teller?"

"No ma'am, I'm not," he smiled.

"Well, don't worry yourself too much," she said in a gentle voice. "I'm sure there's a young lady out there who can't wait to be snatched up by such a fine gentlemen as yourself."

Teller smiled politely. "I surely hope so, ma'am."

Ms. Eloise leaned back in her chair and crossed her sagging legs at the ankles. Her withered hands relaxed in her lap. "Now Mr. Teller," she said. "What's resting on your heart?"

For a moment Teller sat quiet. He drew in a deep breath and released it. Ms. Eloise waited patiently, her drooped gentle eyes attentive to his every move. He tapped his knee three times with his fist and leaned his head slightly to one side. Besides his reluctance, she noticed his obsessive-compulsiveness just as much as he did her hoarding, but instead of criticism, they chose respect, and made no mention of one another's odd behaviors at all. Teller took off his suit jacket, removed a white handkerchief from the inside pocket and dabbed the sweat from his forehead. Wet stains formed underneath the pits of his shirt and the sleeves were beginning to stick to his arms.

"It's always so hot in here, would you like to sit out on the porch Mr. Teller?" she asked dabbing the piece of kleenex she had in her hand across her face.

"No thank you ma'am. I'll be fine," Teller lied with deliberate intent to avoid Faith. He laid his jacket on the arm of the chair and looked up at Ms. Eloise. He had procrastinated long enough and decided it was time to explain the reason for his visit. "Ma'am I'm sure you're fully aware of the serious case brought against Mr. Rock."

"Yes, Sir, I am. So is everyone else in this neighborhood."

"Yes, ma'am, but I'm sure you know much more than just whispers going around the neighborhood. Faith tells me she talks to you quite often about the case, that you're sort of like a grandmother to she and her brother."

"Is that the purpose of your visit today Mr. Teller? To find out what I know about the case?"

"No. I was hoping we could talk about Rock and Faith. The case is set to go to the jury for deliberation tomorrow and I need more personal information for my closing argument."

"Personal?" Ms. Eloise asked with uncertainty.

"I know of the unfortunate circumstances surrounding their father, details I won't discuss because of client-attorney confidentiality, but what I don't know is much about their life outside the home, friends, school, their relationship with the kids in the neighborhood, I was hoping you could enlighten me."

"Mm," she mumbled taking a quick moment to think. "Those children never really had much of a life, especially Faith. Rock would come out quite often to play that street ball with the rest of the kids in the neighborhood, but Faith...," she shook her head, "Faith, that poor child. I never saw much of her after her mother died. She would sit on the porch by her lonesome, or come visit me every once and a while, but other than that I can't tell you much."

Teller leaned forward. "What about their mother? How was their demeanor when she was alive?"

"Like children, happy, running around here without a care in the world. They attended church a lot though, too much if you ask me. Too much of anything is not healthy. Even the good Lord himself rested. But you couldn't tell that to that Daddy of theirs, and their Mama, she loved that man, so. She would do just about anything to keep him happy."

"So they had a pretty decent relationship?"

"If you call decent arguing all the time, shucks, she came down here many of nights with those children in their pajamas. Mister and I use to let them sleep here just to get a little peace. Sometimes that's all a person want is a little peace and quiet you know. Not fussing all the time. That's no way to live, that's no way for anybody to live."

"Were there any signs of abuse?"

"To who?"

"The mother."

A wary look crossed Ms. Eloise's face. Teller took notice.

"Yes, but not as often as with the children though. Sometimes she would have a bruise or a scratch here and there, but nothing to make a big fuss over." She felt a pang shoot through the pit of her stomach.

"What do you mean by not often?"

"He would never hit her intentionally. At least that's what she told me and Mister. She would get caught in the middle of the struggle is all, trying to protect her children. She loved those kids and she'd do anything to keep 'em from harm." Ms. Eloise began rocking slowly back and forth in her chair. "Nobody around here really knew about the abuse but me and Mister, if so, they never mentioned anything about it. Folks round here pretty much mind their own business, you know, keep to themselves."

Teller cocked a questioning eyebrow. He waited out his words to say the right thing, but nothing fair or impartial would fit his response.

"I sense judgment, Mr. Teller."

"Depends on one's perspective, ma'am."

"Shrewdness may not have been my strong suit Mr. Teller, but I only did what was asked of me," her aged voice slightly raised. "That poor girl was afraid child services would take those kids, and I wouldn't be a part of that. I wouldn't be a part of that guilt. Yes, now maybe it was my choice to say nothing, but it was her choice to stay. She could have taken those kids at any time and left, but she didn't. That was her choice, not mine, so if anybody's going to be condemned here, Mr. Teller, it won't be me. I did nothing wrong," Ms. Eloise rambled on in guilt.

Teller sat disturbed.

"I did all I could short of begging her to leave, but she wouldn't. I didn't know much of what went on in that house down there Counselor, but I knew enough. Me and Mister both knew enough to remove her from that situation, but she wouldn't hear of coming home. I guess she felt living with us was much worse than living with him so she took the lesser of two evils..." Her expression abruptly changed, a heavy look scarred her face and she appeared stricken. She quickly altered her focus and silently indulged herself into her rocking.

Stumped, Teller shifted to an upright position. He could feel the adrenaline speeding up in his body as his heart pounded in sync with the squeaking of Ms. Eloise's chair.

"Forgive me, ma'am…" he said almost breathless.

Ms. Eloise's eyes darkened much more than what they already were. The twinge in her chest felt like she was having a heart attack, but she was sure it was just the years of lying and deceit that was finally catching up with her. She waited for the pain to past, but it never did. The words hurled from her mouth so fast Teller needed a moment to collect his bearings.

"She was my daughter, Mr. Teller."

The magnitude of Ms. Eloise's confession hit like an earthquake and shook Teller to his core. Flabbergasted his heart stopped, only to beat erratic again. He didn't know whether to stand or sit, so he stood. "*Who's* your daughter?" he asked off-balance.

Ms. Eloise never lifted her head. She fidgeted with the torn piece of tissue clutched in her hand. "Their mother," she sniffed, "their mother was my daughter." She fixed her eyes on Teller who looked on with disbelief. The squeaking sound of the rocking chair and the rattling of the fan echoed the room. Teller cleared his throat and broke the awkward silence.

"Does Faith and Rock know about this accusation?"

A tear crept down her cheek. Her emotions had been suppressed for so long they demanded the right to emerge. She hesitated, knowing the answer to that question wouldn't be as simple as asked. She took in a deep breath and exhaled through the dryness of her mouth. "No, Sir. Their mother thought it best they didn't. It was plenty of times me and Mister wanted to tell the truth, but their mother had her reasons and those reasons had to be respected."

Teller's face took on a dissatisfied look. "What reasons could a mother have for not telling her children who their grandparents are, especially these children, they had no one."

"They had us, Mr. Teller," she snapped. "No, not in a way that you may approve of, but they had us, and yes, the children have been through a lot in their young years, that's exactly why we decided not to tell 'em. It would have just made a mess of things. It was just all too complicated."

"Forgive me, but which part was messy and complicated, the part where you didn't do anything to protect the well-being of those children, or the part where you all collaborated to deny them the comfort and security that could have come from knowing their grandparents?" Teller's words fell hard upon Ms. Eloise. She grabbed the armrest with her left hand and her cane with the right. Shaking and trembling, she slowly pulled herself to her feet.

"We've got no business talkin bout this. Giving Mister reasons to roll over in his grave."

"I'm sure your husband has had enough reasons to roll over in his grave without the assistance of me," his unacceptable response proved to be a contentious dilemma.

"I won't discuss this business any further!" Ms. Eloise yelled, vexed by Teller's derogatory remark. "You have no idea the weight I've carried on my shoulders all these years or the burdens I've had to bear keeping this secret. No need for you to provoke me any further. I would ask that you leave my home now."

"Well what do you suppose I do with this news, Ms. Eloise, huh? Rock is my client and I have viable information that could change the entire outcome of this case. Furthermore, I am his attorney and I am obligated to disclose any evidence I have regarding this case with him at all times, it would be unethical if I didn't. So please, help me to understand. Give me a legitimate reason on why I should withhold this information from my client."

His petition forced her words. "Mister is Faith's father!" Her detrimental response caused all strength to leave her body. Her knees weakened and she felt faint. Teller rushed to her side and gently lowered her back down into the rocking chair.

Numb and weak himself, he stumbled back against the wall directly behind Ms. Eloise. Short of heat exhaustion he removed the handkerchief from his front pocket and wiped the sweat from his face. He rested against the dull painted wall and stared silently across the room at the worn clothes thrown carelessly across the sofa, the duct taped chair with the corn pipe on the table, and the hamper full of old shoes with dust so thick you could write your name in it. Like a rush of wind and almost a sense of paralyzing revelation the troubled secrets of the home gave life, each one giving way to the other, terrorizing screams of a child's cry, a mother's plea for forgiveness of a father's sin, and one helpless child giving birth to another. Teller's body felt heavy. The pain of his joints wouldn't allow him to stand any longer. He walked slowly over to

Mister's chair, drawn by a presence that seemed to impound him, he sat quietly down. Unable to speak, his lips parted slightly, but remained wordless.

In a broken voice, Ms. Eloise elaborated over the thickness of the silence. "She was 13 years-old when it started. It was months on in before I realized anything was happening, such a free spirit, full of life, and then withdrawn, quiet, not much to say about anything. One day she come runnin out her bedroom into the kitchen cryin and carryin on, so I ask her, I say, 'what's wrong child?' she standing there looking as scared as a deer in headlights. 'Papa broke me,' she said. Her white night gown was stained and blood was running down her leg. She had started her cycle, but to her, Mister had done an unjust." For a moment Ms. Eloise looked a little older. The bags beneath her eyes had darkened and drooped slightly lower. Teller stared voiceless. The only thing to be heard was the continuous clatter of the fan. She pressed the tissue tightly against her eyes to dry her tears. With a troubled heart she continued.

"After that I resented Mister, so. I couldn't bring myself to look him in the eyes, yet alone have relations with him. I couldn't stomach it. We had tried for years to have a child, finally at the age of 40 I conceived. It was a miracle. She was God's gift to us, and this was his recompense? Violating his own daughter, having sex with the seed God planted?" Ms. Eloise paused. The disgust in her voice tweaked into a softer tone. "I wasn't sure if it was because I came to know, or that God had His hands on him, but he had a sense of remorse, a sense of guilt that consumed him. He hadn't touched her in months and as often as he could he begged for our forgiveness." She paused for another moment. The house was hot and humid. She reached over and grabbed the hand fan she brought home from church service off the crate next to her chair. The handle resembled a large popsicle stick with a square piece of cardboard stapled to the top. It advertised Dickerson's Funeral Home, a beautiful sanctuary with cherry wood pews and large pillars that held the most beautiful floral arrangements. It was hard for Ms. Eloise to fathom her own funeral, but maybe she'd consider Dickerson. She waved the fan back and forth in a swaying motion to relieve herself of the heat. She sat unspoken for a long moment. Her eyes watered and her bottom lip trembled as a tightness caught her throat. She forced a swallow and continued.

"Mister was a good man in many ways, Mr. Teller. I know that's hard for you to understand right now, but he done a lot of good, a lot of good for his family which is why I stayed." She shook her head. "I never fully forgave him though. I couldn't. I had a mother's heart and my mother's heart wouldn't let me forgive him completely." She grabbed two or three fresh tissues out the box. "How could I forgive such a selfish and vulgar act?" She choked back the tears. "But overtime I learned to trust. I did, Mr. Teller. I trusted Mister enough to leave her alone with him...only until I ran to the market. I hadn't done it in six months, but he'd proven himself trustworthy so I figured it was okay," she rambled on, sometimes jumbling her words in confusion. "I don't know, Mr. Teller, call it a mother's intuition, but every impulse in my body turned on. I couldn't feel my heart beat. My nerves had gotten the better of me and I couldn't move. I'd gotten all the way to the store's parking lot, turned the car off, but couldn't get out." She clutched her hands to her chest. Agony shattered her voice with every syllable she spoke. "I turned the car around and with everything in me I rushed home. The front door was closed. I...I couldn't remember if it was open...if I left it open when I went to the store, but it was closed. I couldn't feel myself breathe. I pushed the door open and there was Mister on top of my baby. Her panties down...I...I swear all life left me. I swear I died." She cried painfully.

Teller could no longer sit and endure Ms. Eloise's anguish. Even more so than her grief, her health was very much a concern. He wanted to continue their conversation but quickly restrained himself. The urge to go on was suppressed by her dropped head and tear-stained face. Feeling somewhat responsible for her poignant mood, he managed to limp like a wounded dog over to her side, the agonizing pain that burned in his joints deepened with every step. He rested his hand gently on her frail shoulder, praying for God to ease her troubled soul, to give her some sense of comfort amid her distress. Emotionally exhausted, she took in a slight breather. The much needed respite was followed by a flow of tears that seemed to consume her for so many years.

It was a long while before Ms. Eloise and Teller spoke a word. She inhaled and exhaled slowly until her breathing slowly leveled off. She took a moment to get her emotions under control. With a light and weak voice she forced herself to release the bondage.

"Our family kept to ourselves after that. I helped her raise the baby for a couple of years, but she left home, married young and moved here. I couldn't bear to be separated from her so Mister and I bought this house…," her voice broke. "I just wanted to be close. No one knew us, not even her husband, she wanted it that way. She was ashamed of Mister, of me for staying with him. Eventually she started coming around. Her visits were sporadic, but got more frequent after the abuse. We never mentioned the past. She chose to continue running from it in hopes that it would just all go away. Funny thing though, in all the running she did she landed herself right back into the arms of her father, only this time it was her husband."

Teller's pain was excruciating. His muscles tightened like a vise. He walked leisurely over to Mister's chair, picked up his jacket and grabbed the prescription bottle from the side pocket. He opened it and choked down two pills without water. The air felt empty and still. He turned to Ms. Eloise who looked exhausted, as if she had nothing left. Pain carved the wrinkles of her face like the sketching of a portrait, outlining the pain that only a mother could feel. Memories of his own mother sprang forth and he thought of all the mothers who had ever endured, who had ever suffered for the sake of their children. The realization that no other human form outside of a mother could ever know her strength, the power of her love could never be surpassed. Nothing in life could ever equate to her love. It pierces through the heart like a flamed arrow burning in the deepest pit of her soul and shapes her very being. A love that starts in the womb, dwells for nine months, and somehow manifests itself into a human being that forms an unbreakable bond that would be impossible for any man to ever experience, feel or understand. An immeasurable love that would make her give of her mind, her body, her soul, to the extent of extreme actions if ever that bond was threatened.

Teller stared into Ms. Eloise's sorrowful eyes, the origin of broken hallelujah had carried itself through two generations and somehow made its way into his own past, and for the first time he caught a clear understanding of the incalculable means a mother would go through to protect her children, even if it was sacrificial to her own well-being. With a deep sense of compassion he walked quietly over to Ms. Eloise and gently kissed where her wrinkled forehead and gray hairline met. Overwhelmed and still in a state of disbelief he sauntered over to the door, his joints taut in a hinge of debilitating pain, pulled the fragile screen door open and quietly left Ms. Eloise with a heavy foreboding of what's to come from the dark secrets of her broken soul.

JUNE 11, 2008

CLOSING ARGUMENTS

Teller arrived to court twenty minutes early, about the same time as Prosecution. Joy greeted him with a firm hand shake. She appeared more relaxed this morning, even managing to slip in a slight smile that somehow exposed her relief to finally have the trial reach its end. Teller had been up all night, but felt revived and ready to tackle the day's agenda. He laid his briefcase on top of the table, removed its contents, clasped his hands in front of him, closed his eyes and said a silent prayer. He asked for guidance, for covering, for strength to present his case suitable to God, to represent Him in reverence and honor, after all, He was the one actually on trial here, not Rock. Teller raised his head in enough time to be greeted by Judge Hallow with a content nod as he took his position at the bench. Rock was escorted in a few moments before the jury and everyone took their appropriate seats.

Judge Hallow wasted no time. "Is Prosecution ready to present closing arguments?"

Joy stood. "Yes, Your Honor, we are."

"You may proceed."

Joy approached the jury box, crossed her arms in front of her and addressed the court. "Ladies and gentlemen of the jury I would like to say on behalf of the People of the State of Michigan, thank you for your patience, dedication and time you have given diligently to this case. I know this has been a long and sometimes bumpy road, but I am confident that the evidence presented to you during this case has proven, beyond a reasonable doubt, that the Defendant, Mr. Rock, committed the heartless murder of his father on March 17, 2008. The facts have shown, and Mr. Rock has admitted in his own testimony that he willingly went out, acquired a hand gun from a friend with the sole purpose of protecting himself from his father. You have heard indisputable testimony from police officers who stated they had arrived at

Defendant's home to find the victim nude, unarmed and helpless, lying in a pool of his own blood. The gun confiscated at the scene was proven to be the same gun obtained by Mr. Rock earlier that day and used in the murder of the victim. Defendant's fingerprints not only encased the murder weapon, but in his own words admitted to firing a shot at the victim while he stood defenseless in his own home. Now, let's take a moment and recollect the events leading up to that fatal night. The Defendant alleged that he and his sister had been beaten by the victim during a dispute over dinner the night before. The following morning they endured the humiliation of standing before their father and each other naked, their young bodies violated and exposed. Thereafter, his father, the one man in this world who was supposed to love and protect him, did the unthinkable, the most horrific act a father could do to a son, he sodomized him, his own son, each painful stroke stripping away his innocence, his dignity, the only purity that defined him as a child. Think of the contempt he must have felt. The anger, the hatred that drove him to pick up a gun, hide it in his dresser drawer, wait on his father, and then when the opportunity presented itself, shoot and kill him in cold blood." Joy paced the floor.

"Now let's remember, Mr. Rock and his father were not the only two individuals there that night. As testified by Defendant, his sister, Faith, was lying unconscious on the bed in their father's room. It was also alleged by Defendant that there was a fourth party involved, the resurrected spirit of his mother whom had died years prior. Counsel wants you to believe that not only was this figurative person present, but she was in fact the one that pulled the trigger killing the victim in his bedroom. The problem with that accusation is there has been no solid evidence, nor viable scientific fact to prove this theory, and the only other person who could testify to this sighting was passed out on her father's bed unresponsive." Joy clasped her hands in front of her and lowered her head in thought. "Let's deal with that for a moment ladies and gentlemen. According to paramedics' testimony, Miss Faith was coherent when they arrived to the house that night. The medical records showed that she had gone into shock, but was conscious upon arrival to the hospital. She was traumatized and shaken by the acts perpetrated upon her young body, but the medical records prove that the trauma did not render her unconscious, it merely made her body weak and caused her to collapse. Prosecution has demonstrated and presented proof to you through expert witnesses that a person who is unresponsive, or in Miss Faith's case, in a state of temporary shock, can be jarred back to consciousness by a loud noise such as the loud piercing sound of a gun going off." She turned her focus to the jurors. "Ladies and gentlemen, Defendant's own testimony states there was not one shot, but three shots fired that night, one while his sister lay inert in their father's bed, and two, as Defendant claimed, inflicted by his dead mother as he knelt down with his sister in his arms adjacent to his mother's side. Defense wants you to believe that within those three shots not one of them awakened Miss Faith to consciousness. According to evidence presented this is next to impossible. The gunshots were heard loud enough to awaken neighbors from their sleep and cause someone to call 9-1-1, but not loud enough to shake Miss Faith out of a minor state of *senselessness*?" she emphasized in a derogatory tone.

The jurors sat stone-faced while Joy portrayed Rock as this delusional liar who planned Daddy's attack days prior. She dissected the truth piece by piece and put it back together in her own manipulative way. Teller absorbed himself in every word, once in a while scribbling on the piece of paper in front of him. I was paralyzed. My insides felt like mush. It was more than a notion to indulge myself in positive thinking and focus back on the trial.

"It's all imagery ladies and gentlemen. Metaphors conjured up by Defense to build a case based around unrealistic evidence, evidence that not only hasn't been proven, but unseen, based solely on opinions and symbolisms." She walked hurriedly over to the evidence table and picked up the large plastic bags and returned to the jury box.

"Prosecution's evidence is clearly marked. The murder weapon baring Defendant's fingerprints, the bullets removed from the victim's body, the casings found by the victim's body at the time of the murder, credible evidence!" her voice traveled the courtroom and leveled off, "all proving beyond a shadow of a doubt that Mr. Rock committed the murder of his own father." She walked back over to the table, replaced the evidence bags and returned to the jury.

"Ladies and gentlemen before I take my seat I want you to consider the facts in this case. Defendant's own testimony states that in a fit of rage, not more than 24-hours after his father attacked him, he telephoned a friend and obtained a gun, stored the gun in the vicinity of his home, and at the allotted time retrieved the gun from its storage and confronted his father with it. Unarmed and scared his father stood helpless," Joy raised her hands in defense, "but it was too late, beaten and humiliated Defendant fired three shots." Joy secured the shooting position, clasped her hands together, extended her index fingers and stretched her arms toward the jurors, "Pow! One into the Bible held in the victim's right hand. Bang! One into his right shoulder, bang! one into his chest killing him instantly."

Vivid images of that night and loud sounds of guns going off flared Rock's memory. He could see Daddy lying in a pool of blood, Mama's face staring cold at him. The harder he tried to block the memories the more intense they got. He sat in agony. His body ice cold.

Joy dropped her hands to her side and cleared her throat. With the loud sound of her expensive pumps clicking across the hard floor she pressed on. "Now, is it possible that all of this pandemonium caused Defendant's young mind to become delusive, to see ghostly apparitions, things that weren't there? Perhaps, but those aren't the facts. The facts show that there was no one else in that room that night except the victim, the Defendant, and his sister. There is no iota of evidence to prove otherwise. Your verdict must be based solely upon the facts presented to you throughout this case and nothing more." She took in a quick breath.

"Was the victim painted as the model father in this case? No. Did he deserve the Medal of Honor or the greatest Dad award? Maybe not, but he was still a human being, and as a human being he deserves a certain amount of justice, which is why I am asking you, the jury of our peers, to serve that justice here today." She pointed across the room. "It was not up to the Defendant, Mr. Rock, to take the law into his own hands, to render judgment upon his father without a fair and just trial, therefore, he must be held accountable. The evidence clearly shows beyond all reasonable doubt that Mr. Rock pulled the trigger and fired the three shots that fatally killed his father that night." She paused, "premeditated murder. I ask that you return a swift verdict of guilty on all counts." She gave a quick nod. "Thank you ladies and gentlemen." Wearing a sense of confidence and with great stride she returned to the Prosecutor's table and reclaimed her throne.

Joy had given an excellent argument and somewhere deep within me I wrestled with the devastating notion of guilty in the first degree.

Judge Hallow addressed Teller. "Defense may present its argument."

Teller hesitated. He knew what this moment demanded of him so he closed his eyes and cleansed his thoughts of all that crippled him. Ms. Eloise, the hurt, the pain, his own debilitating past. Like a composer of music before the first note he freed his mind and prepared his spirit for what was next to come, and without expecting it, was gripped by a sense of peace that settled well within him.

Judge Hallow appeared to wait patiently for Teller to collect himself, but the tone of his voice hinted on irritation. "Counselor, your closing argument."

He opened his eyes, stood up, stuffed his hands into the front pockets of his pants and addressed the court. "Thank you Your Honor, Ms. Joy," he respectfully nodded, "Ladies and gentlemen of the jury."

Teller had been under a microscope throughout this entire trial, subjecting himself to nothing but ridicule and grief, and now, reaching the brink of finality, he stuck his chin out one last time. Throwing himself upon the mercy of the court he took one last shot at the chance for redemption.

The room suddenly felt deathly still. A thick silence choked the air, tension so dense a machete couldn't penetrate it. Teller approached the jurors and took in a deep sigh. With as much confidence as he could muster he paused, exhaled and pled his case, his voice calm and leveled.

"Ladies and gentlemen of the jury, I know that this case has become as much a part of your lives as it has mine, and if I am correct in my assumptions, everyone in here has become in some way personally involved or connected in their own way." He glanced around the courtroom at all the spectators who sat stoic. "I would like to share with you a personal part of myself that I don't normally share with anyone else, but under the circumstances I thought it important that I should." He paced the floor, his hands still tucked inside his pockets defying the urge to give in to his relentless compulsiveness. "During the course of this past week I had no idea what I was going to say to you this morning. No strategy, no plan of action, I came into this thing just as blind as you are, if not more. Things I couldn't explain or didn't know how to explain panged my stomach. I got all jittery inside and my nerves got the better of me, but then I remembered something my mother told me when I was a young lad, maybe about six or seven years old. She said, 'Teller, there are no difficulties in life, only challenges, and it is within those challenges that we find our inner strength, our ability to go on in spite of. No matter what befalls you in life it is your choice to sink or swim. If you choose to sink, it is at that time that you cease to exist, but if you choose to swim, it is then that you have chosen to live.'" He paused and turned to face the jury. "Well, ladies and gentlemen, I stand here before you today with not a difficult case, but a challenging one, a challenge to get you to see the unseen, to believe the unbelievable, and to walk by faith and not by sight, to give me an opportunity to swim and my client a choice to live by judging this case in a fair and unbiased manner."

My heart beat slow and irregular. Teller walked closer to the jurors and assembled himself where each one could engage him in their own individual way. Controlling every impulse he hoped he could gain the trust of at least one or maybe two of the jurors, but one would be satisfying enough to hopefully sway the jury into returning a verdict of not guilty for his client.

"Throughout this trial I have been ripped apart by the media and by many of you sitting in this courtroom today. Religious groups have labeled this trial as 'platypus,' which we can agree although a strange and abnormal creature, unique in its own right." He gave a slight grin. "It has also been painted as satanic, demonized and blasphemy to God's name. This is not a case of such things, this is simply a case that tests the very boundaries of Christian faith, a case that exposes Christianity's own hypocrisy and transgressions, bringing into question their own ultimate fate, a revelation that forces them to face their deepest fear in which they themselves will one day experience God's judgment only to suffer for their own individual sins. The idea of God's wrath manifesting itself from the spiritual into the natural is disgraceful to the Christian faith, after all God is a merciful God, He wouldn't kill, He wouldn't murder, He wouldn't destroy, God is a forgiving God, how dare anyone speak of such blasphemy, but just as the Bible speaks of God's mercy, it also speaks of His wrath," his voice alternated into a strong pitch. "'*Our God comes and shall not be silent, a fire devours before Him and around Him a tempest rages! He summons the heavens and the earth that He may judge his people! I am God, even thy God, and I will testify against thee, for the world is mine and the fullness thereof! Now consider this, you who forget God and discard my instructions and cast my words behind you, I will tear you in pieces and there will be none to deliver*!'"

Teller struck an unsettling chord. The demonstrative depiction of Psalm: 50, left thought provoking expressions across the faces of every one seated, each one fearfully contemplating their own destiny, everyone except for me that is. I was in no way moved by God's Word. My fate had already been determined. I wasn't awaiting God's wrath because His wrath dwelled with me every day of my life.

Teller lowered his voice and stared at the jury with closeness and intensity, their eyes tracking his every move. "God's wrath can be a scary thing, so rather than accepting its existence we choose to deny it. Why? Because denying it deceives us into believing we can avoid our own doom. '*Beloved, do not avenge yourselves, but leave the way open for God's wrath, for it is written, Vengeance is Mine, I will repay, says the Lord*!'" he cried out. "*It is written*," he emphasized, "*Vengeance is mine, I will repay, saith the Lord.* "That is what this case is about, and that is what enthralls us and scares us at the same time with this trial. It forces us to suffer our own fate, to brood over our own judgment and that, for many people, is a horrifying notion." He paused, clasped his hands behind his back and left everyone, for a brief moment, to weigh his own sins.

After a short respite and much conviction, Teller turned to address the jury. "Prosecution gave testimony after testimony as to what she believed led up to the murder of her client on March 17, 2008. Counsel has laid out the facts and presented evidence that could draw preconceptions of a cut and dry, open and shut guilty verdict in this case, problem is everything that she has presented to you throughout this trial has been a bias and unfair assessment of this entire case. As hard as it may be for you to grasp, this case cannot be tried in the secular realm. It must be taken out of the natural and into the spiritual in order to be put in perspective. You must step outside of yourselves and into the lives of these children, a life that was based solely upon the word of God. From the alleged abuse to the death of their father everything was centered around the living, breathing, and although unorthodox, word of God, and so must this trial. It is all that they know and it is all that they've lived."

I felt my entire body get hot. Not because Teller's statement wasn't true, but because it was. Each memory manifested itself one after the other until a feeling of deep despair filtered through me. Teller's voice rang hollow in my head as I trailed off to the past, only to return to an increased heaviness that attached itself to my chest like a tumor. Despite my pain, I relished in Teller's assertion.

"Forgive me if I sound a bit perplexed this morning ladies and gentlemen, but help me to understand. Christian folk can read the word of God, pray for His judgment against those that come against them, and then when their prayers for protection from their enemies are answered they suddenly become unbelievers. Faith turns into doubt and they begin demanding physical evidence, solid proof to show how these things have suddenly come into existence. Well, isn't that what faith is, the substance of things hoped for, the evidence of things not seen? Faith in itself provides the evidence and proof. We don't need physicality's when it comes to God. All we need is His Word. '*I am Lord and I change not*!' Isn't that what He said? Isn't that what the living, breathing word of God says? If you have faith that God will do what He said He will do then it will come to pass!" Teller stretched out his arms and raised his head toward the ceiling. "*Plead my cause O Lord, fight against them that fight against me! Destroy those who seek to destroy me! Arise and come to my aid O Lord! Let them be confounded and put to shame that seek after my soul! May their path be dark and slippery and let the angel of the Lord persecute them! May destruction overtake them by surprise! May they entangle themselves in their own nets and fall into the pit of their own destruction*!'" Teller lowered his arms and stood in silence for a moment. He spoke through winded breath. "I believe and I pray that this scripture is what Mr. Rock and Miss Faith had been praying for all of their young lives. Not to grab a gun and take the law into their own hands, but pray to a God who had promised them protection through His own words, that this indecency would finally stop, that God would do what He said He would do and deliver them from the claws of Hell that they had been bound in for so long." Teller went to the hearts of the jurors.

"Now, do I think God personally cares about our thoughts in this case? No. Why? Because God said, 'My thoughts are not your thoughts, my thoughts are higher than your thoughts.' Therefore, we must not seek to understand why God did what He did, but rather allow Him to do His Will. 'Vengeance is mine,' isn't that what He said? Isn't that what this trial has been all about? Who are we to keep God in a box, to limit His power to our standards?" Teller rushed over and grabbed the Bible off the table, raised it in the air and gestured it around the courtroom, speaking vigorously. "This is the handbook of life according to Christianity. Everything in it has either happened or will happen in some form or another whether we like it or not. Yes, the mercy; yes, the grace; yes, the deliverance; but also the wrath, the judgment, the vengeance, it is all God's whether we choose to believe it or not, whether we prepare ourselves or not, whether we try to justify it, evade it or rationalize it, it will all manifest itself into our lives at one point or another, and for these kids it was the night of March 17, 2008!"

The courtroom was rendered speechless. Mouths of spectators gaped in shock, while others remained close-fitted. Teller lowered the Bible amidst the still air and clutched it against his chest. He watched as the picture developed mentally into the minds of the jurors. With his heart beating a heavy drum he sighed deeply.

"If you would, I would like to tell you a story, a story about a young boy who had spent the first 18 years of his life in and out of foster homes. He never knew his dad, and his mother had died while giving birth to him. Every morning he would pray the same prayer, asking God why he was never given a chance at happiness, never to know a mother's touch or a father's love. 'A child,' he said, 'should never have to suffer such pain.' Awaiting God's answer, he continued through life. A troubled child, in and out of juvenile correctional facilities, lost in a system of monumental paperwork and economic burdens, known only as a case number for those foster families who took him in. Finally growing weary of all his misfortunes he became driven and determined to make something of himself. So he buckled down and graduated high school, then college, from there he went to law school and on to passing the Bar. One day he met the love of his life, a love in which he had never experienced before. After one year he was married and expecting his first child. He vowed to give his son what he never had. One day, while sitting in the nursery holding his young son, he remembered his prayer, 'God, why was I never given a chance at happiness, never to know my mother's touch or my father's love? My child,' he said, 'will never know such pain.' He sat in silence for a moment, finally, after years of waiting, God answered.

"My son, this was your mother's prayer, 'Father, forgive me for I have sinned, and through those sins I have infected my precious body. At the dusk of day I stand in the streets and in the open squares clothed like a harlot, searching out my prey, seizing and winning them over one by one with my smooth tongue and waywardness. For years I have spread my bed with fine linen, myrrh and aloe, and drank fine wine with other women's husbands, for this, I have taken fire to my bosom and paid the ultimate price of a loose woman. My seductiveness has made me with child, unknowing of the father, but knowing that he too shall suffer judgment, for you have said none who has touched me shall go unpunished. I pray today, not for my own selfishness, but for the life of my child, that you may not despise him, but find glory in the midst of disobedience; that he may be born blemish free from my infectious body. Please, God, do not reject him because of my appetite, but shine Your light upon him so that he may abide in your teachings and not in mine, for I have broken faith with You, and therefore must stand in my own judgment.' The boy sat weeping over his child, grateful that God had spared his life. 'So you see my son,' God spoke, 'I cleansed you of your past so that you may have a future.'"

Teller's faith had never been more challenged than at that moment. He found himself pacing back and forth while the courtroom sat fixated, every now and then engaging the jurors, praying that his story somehow broke through the veil of doubt and changed their beliefs.

I swallowed hard, the silence of the room spoke volumes as the story gripped at the hearts of everyone present with the exclusion of the jury, who's, from what I could see, blank stares and threatening demeanor proved otherwise. Teller waited patiently for the moment to pass then continued on.

"Sometimes we have people and things in our life that taint our very being. Parasites so infectious that if not removed it could kill us from the root. God has a way of taking the innocent and cleansing them of the organisms that seek corruption and harm upon their life. Destroying the unjust so that the just may live. Taking a woman whose body is infected by a disease that could be passed on to her unborn child and slipping him through the birth canal unscathed is a miraculous thing, but what's even more miraculous is preserving a child who is deteriorating from the corrosion of a parent and cleansing him of that putrefaction so that he may be washed clean and made whole again is nothing short of the glory of God. God's promise to protect us from those that mean us harm." Teller once again addressed the jurors.

"Do I believe, ladies and gentlemen, that my client's fate lies in your hands today? Of course, but I also believe that all things work according to God's plan and Defendant's ultimate fate lies in the hands of He who works through you. If you have never trusted God before I need you to trust Him today. He is not a God that He shall lie. 'Vengeance is mine, says the Lord." That is what I need you to put your faith in. That is what I need you to deliberate on. It is by faith, I pray, that you will return, after careful consideration, a verdict of not guilty and give my client the opportunity to live as God has summoned him to live. A life in which some happiness, some freedom, some level of security and trust should exist in a child's life. I thank you for your mercy in this case and ask that you allow the Holy Spirit to guide you in your decision." Teller connected with the jurors for a moment, his final words critical to Defense. He had given it his all and there was honestly nothing else he could give. He slipped in a curt nod before walking back to the Defendant's table. There was a brief silence. He took in a deep sigh and released slowly. His hands unsteady as he shuffled needlessly through his notes. I couldn't determine if his uneasiness stemmed from the struggle to control his OCD or the pressure to prove Rock's innocence. Either way his attempt to refute Prosecution's case appeared effortless.

The stoic expressions on the jurors' faces were enough to breed fear into the most poised person. Unable to read their emotions I began to shiver. The room suddenly became unbearably cold. I rubbed my hands briskly up and down my arms, first the right, then the left. Despite my efforts to keep warm I couldn't stop trembling. I gazed up at the ceiling petitioning a prayer, but once again it was fleeting, so I dismissed my appeal to summon God and opted to just sit in silence instead. Judge Hallow sequestered the jurors and deliberations began.

JUNE 23, 2008

TWO WEEKS LATER

At first awakening it feels like a dream. You're still in this half-sleep mode and then reality sinks in. It's all real. Your mother's dead, your father's been murdered and your brother's on trial for killing him. So you lie in bed, alone, barely breathing because breathing suffocates you, stifling you to the point of all consciousness around you. The pain clenches its claws of death around your very core, tightening its grip until the hold becomes so unbearable it sucks the very life out of what little existence you have left. Every morning you ascend into your unhappiness, like the pits of hell to the unjust you adhere to your fate of despondency. Your mind no longer tells you everything will be okay. It has become immune to any hope, rejecting it like a virus eating away at a vaccine of an incurable disease.

I huddled underneath the covers. A corpse encased in a shell, numb, unable to feel anything, incapable of making sense of the anguish that was going on inside of me. I desperately tried to will myself out of bed, but once again, the pain of facing another day overwhelmed me, my heart stricken, grief woven into my soul so tight the pressure made it almost impossible to move. Detached from everything and everyone around me I thought about Rock and how he was doing, if his heart ached as much as mine. It's been two weeks since jury deliberations and I have yet to visit him in jail. I struggled with his testimony, his confession of Mama's spirit being the cause of Daddy's death. I couldn't wrap my mind around it. It was too surreal. The imagery was stuck in the crevices of my brain. I was lost, a black hole, adrift in my own thoughts.

Unaware that my limp body had somehow become erect, I finally managed to scoot myself to the edge of the bed and dangle my legs off the sides. I couldn't feel my body, it was as though it had separated itself from my mind. At a complete loss of control I began to weep. The entire ordeal was too much to bear. On the brink of a nervous breakdown I buried my face in my hands and cried hysterically. My eyes were on fire. Everything hurt. My body was consumed with pain. I needed something to absolve me from this troubled state I was drowning in. Through the echoes of my distress I heard the phone ring, interceding my moment of grief. I hesitated. My nerves could not suffer anymore bad news. I cleared my throat and waited for the next ring to taper off. "Hello?" It was the County Jail. First the operator, then the connection, I paused for the familiar voice.

"Faith?"

I froze. My heart was pounding. I wanted to hang up. Not because I didn't want to talk to Rock, but because I was afraid. I had so many questions, fearful of all the wrong answers.

"Faith, you there?"

I swallowed hard, forcing the knot in my throat down to my stomach. "Yes, Rock, I'm here. How are you?"

"Scared."

I shut my eyes tight, trying to hold it all together. His voice was that of a frightened little child who had been left alone to fend for himself. My heart broke, wishing it was me behind those cold iron bars instead of him. "Everything is going to be okay, Rock. I promise."

"Faith, can you come see me. I mean, I really need to see you. I understand why you haven't been to visit, can't say that I much blame you," he struggled with his words. "But can you please come? There are things that I need to say and I don't wanna say them over the phone."

"It's okay Rock. I'm on my way. I'm sorry…I'm so sorry," my voice weakened. I slumped forward and cupped my hand over my mouth. The tears flowed uncontrollably. I felt horrible. I had abandoned my brother at the most acute time in his life. Faced with that fact at that moment was like facing a death sentence. I hated myself. The pain ripped at the fiber of my very soul. I wanted to die, I literally wanted to die. I was in this dark place, sucked in by this vacuum of doubt. I loved my brother.

I never fathomed that I would ever doubt his credibility, but I didn't know, I didn't know what to do or what to say to make it better. The only thing I could do was cry, sob helplessly while he sat alone waiting on 12 jurors to decide his fate.

"Faith, please," cries of a child echoed through the phone.

My head ached. The pain in the back of my neck was excruciating, a hammering of ice picks, grating, pounding at a nonstop beat. I nodded my head as if he could see through the holes of the receiver. "I'll be there, I promise, I'm on my way." The line clicked, disconnecting the child-like voice. The compulsion to get out of bed that hadn't been there before suddenly emerged. I rushed to get dressed. My foot entangled in the telephone cord knocking it to the floor. Ashamed of the unjustifiable reasons of not being by my brother's side resonated in the corners of my mind. No matter how much we suffered in life we always healed our wounds together. How selfish could I have been? Who was I to judge, to have the audacity to demand answers to questions he himself didn't understand? He was a child, a kid caught up in the web of an adult world, we both were. I hurried into the bathroom, brushed my teeth, washed my face, never once stopping to look at my reflection in the mirror, unable to confront the demon staring back at me. How could I? Before I could conquer my own fears I had to help my brother fight his, and that was a battle I wasn't about to let him face alone.

I arrived at the County Jail some time later. The stench of public transportation nestled itself into the clefts of my nostrils and lingered there for a while. I endured the protocol of going through metal detectors that were constantly triggered off by bobby pins, gold-plated jewelry, belt buckles and any other type of metal that accessorized the human body like a Christmas tree. The relentless, "step to the side, stretch your arms out," while security ran the hand held scanners up and down your body trying to locate anything unseen, internal or external, that would be a threat to you or anyone around you was irritating at most. Of course I understood the precautionary measures, but when you're impatient, stressed and suffering from a severe case of anxiety, you neglect to see the point of it all.

They sat Rock and I in this shell-of-a-room with a table and two chairs, placed so that we had no physical contact with one another. The room was cold and gray with a guard who stood cynically by, watching, observing our every move. Rock looked thin, pale, the whites of his eyes red from crying. I wanted to grab him, hold him in my bosom and never let go, but I couldn't. So I sat there, staring, waiting for him to say something, afraid to say anything for fear of saying the wrong thing.

"Faith…"

I forced the rock down my throat.

"Faith, I'm starting to second guess myself." Tears filled his eyes. "I know what happened that night seems unreal, so far out there that even you have your doubts, but I know what I saw, I know what I said in that courtroom was true." He shrugged and shook his head. "But…but, I'm starting to second guess myself. I'm starting to think that I was so upset about you and your state at that time that maybe I was seeing things that weren't there. That maybe in some way my mind was playing tricks on me. That maybe I wanted so desperately for Mama to be there that I saw what I wanted to see at the time that I needed to see it."

I stretched my arms across the table and laced his hands in mine. The guard carefully eyed us, but never interfered. A loss of words couldn't have come at a worse time. I found myself unable to respond. Part of me an emotional wreck, the other part fighting to keep from hyperventilating. I took in a deep breath and released it slowly. "Rock, are you saying that you are unsure of what you saw that night?"

He shook his head. "No, no I am not saying that I am unsure of what I saw. I know what I saw, but I am uncertain if what I saw was real. Was it a figment of my imagination? Some trumped-up story that my mind led me to believe was true? I'm not sure anymore." Releasing my hands he wiped his tears with the sleeves of his shirt. "I sit in that cell day after day, night after night, empty, decaying from the inside out. Scared of what might be. I pray to God until my head hurts and still nothing. I know He's listening, I know He hasn't abandoned me, but I am losing all sense of reality, Faith. I don't know what's real and what's not real anymore."

I sat stone-still, reluctant to speak my thoughts. I felt God had abandoned us a long time ago, but my feelings were less important than my brothers at that moment. He had already endured enough hardship and I wasn't about to inflict anymore then he could bear. I shook my head. "No, Rock, you're not losing your mind," my voice tapered off. The strain to keep from crying gave way. No longer torn between my brother and legalities I struggled to speak through the pain. "You know what you saw, and what you saw was a mother reaching beyond the grave to protect her children. Daddy was a bad man, he was a bad father, Mama knew it and the omniscient power of God knew it." My bottom lip trembled. "Now, I'm sure your testimony about the events that took place that night has raised some serious doubts and questions in the minds of many people, but out of all the bad Daddy done to us he somehow managed to give us one good thing, the virtue to never lie. If you say Mama was there that night then she was there." I closed my eyes in an effort to gain my composure. My face tightened as I primed myself to mask my true feelings about God, His all-knowing power, and why He was allowing my brother to suffer so deeply. "Now don't you go worrying yourself about what did or did not happen, you've done your part, now let God do His."

"I keep going over and over in my head Exodus 14:13, '*Fear ye not, stand still and see the salvation of the Lord,*' but I can't, Faith, I can't see passed the next minute let alone God's salvation. With everything that has happened in our life from the incest, the beatings, to being locked up in this hole...it's too much, it's all too much," Rock's voice elevated.

The guard stood alert. "God why has thou forsaken me?!" He stretched his hands toward the ceiling. Tears flowed down the sides of his face into the canals of his ears. I rushed to his side, my chair making a shrieking sound before it fell to its back on the floor. I grabbed Rock's arms and brought them down to waist level holding tight to his hands. "I can't see God anymore, Faith. I can't feel His presence. I'm scared. I feel so alone. Don't go, Faith, please don't go." He leaned his head against my abdomen and wrapped his arms tightly around my waist.

I reached down deep to find comfort for my brother. I had long given up on God, but Rock continued to trust His mercy, so I dug deep, shaking and fighting against all Godly emasculation and beseeched His word to give my brother the peace he so desperately needed. Stroking his boyish face, I wept Isaiah 40, "*Hast thou not known? Hast thou not heard that the everlasting God, the Lord, the Creator of the ends of the earth, fainteth not, neither is weary? There is no searching of His understanding. He giveth power to the faint, and to them that have no might He increaseth strength. They that wait upon the Lord shall renew their strength, they shall mount up with wings as eagles, they shall run and not be weary, and they shall walk and not faint.*"

Rock pulled himself up, pressed his wet cheeks gently against my forehead and whispered, "*Fear not, for I am with thee, be not dismayed for I am thy God, I will strengthen thee, I will help thee, I will uphold thee with the right hand of my righteousness,*" he quietly shut his eyes. "*Peace I leave with you, peace I give unto you, not as the world giveth do I give unto you, so let not your heart be troubled, neither let it be afraid...*" his voice tapered off into a whimper.

For a moment I had managed to comfort my brother. Neither one of us knew what tomorrow held so we stood there embracing each other amongst the cold gray walls, the cynical guard and the unknown, basking, if only for a moment, in sweet reverie.

JULY 2, 2008

PRESENT DAY

"**JURY DELIBERATES FOR 21 DAYS**." There it was front page news in big bold letters. I was fatigued and had no stomach for food so I settled for orange juice instead. Good thing too, considering there wasn't any food in the fridge to begin with. I decided to take a walk to the corner grocery store to pick up a few things. Seemed like a good idea at the time until right in the middle of the Market, housed between the Auto-Trader and Metro Times, were stacks of the Daily News publicizing intimate details of me and Rock's private life. It's one thing to be exposed in the courtroom but quite another to be violated in your own neighborhood. I made no attempt to bring attention to myself. Shaken as the rattled basket I was pushing, I paid for the groceries and hastily made my way to the exit. Quickly reaching down to retrieve my bags I emerged into the face of Ms. Leah, a long-time member of Daddy's church. Ill-eased, I faltered and drew back. Resentment clogged her face. Her thin veined fingers grasped the contaminated newspaper. She was a meddlesome old woman, always in folk's business, apparently because she had none of her own. Her demeanor warned altercation.

"You seem hurried," she said rudely evading my path.

"No ma'am." I stared off in the distance, regretting I didn't get as far as I hoped.

"How could you taint your father's image in such a shameful way?" she said in a coarse tone thrusting the paper boorishly into my face. "Pastor was a good man, a fine man, respectable as they come, that is til that demonic attorney of yours decided to befoul his name in that circus he calls a trial," her voice was full of contempt.

Demonic? I felt like I was face-to-face with Satan himself right here at this very moment. Terrified by the evil before me I stood mute, trying to put as much distance between the two of us as possible. Mounted between the closed sliding doors and the encroachment of Ms. Leah's questioning I digested my fate. By this time a small crowd had gathered in front of the store to witness my humiliation in all its glory.

"Well," she grumbled, "the church won't have such a thing. We have been down to that courthouse since that mockery-of-a-trial began and we will continue to do so until this mess has come to an end." She shook her head in disgust. "Lord, the blasphemy you children and that attorney of yours have put on God's name, it's a wonder the gates of hell haven't opened up and doused its coals of fire upon your very souls." She pressed the newspaper tightly against her chest. "Your poor Mama would roll over in her grave if she knew the indecent, vulgar light you children have put your father in."

I surveyed the wrinkles above Ms. Leah's thin puckered lips, the fine lines around her aged eyes. She was pale light-skinned, her thick green veins protruding through her emaciated frame. She wore an insipid floral dress that donned a white collar which did nothing for her pale complexion. The smell of cotton balls materialized, and her breath smelled of old cheese. I held my breath in an effort to avoid its unpleasant scent.

"I suppose you gone tell everybody standin here the nonsense your brother said in that courtroom was true." She leaned forward, her eyes flamed with bitterness. "I know as well as the entire congregation that Pastor never laid a hand on the two of you. The truth shall come to light and when it does you will have to suffer the agony of your own self-centeredness."

Threatened, I stepped back, the heel of my shoe caught a rock, twisting my ankle and knocking me, and the groceries I held, to the ground. I scrambled to pick up the cracked carton of eggs, smashed bread and dented container of milk. A burning sensation festered in the pit of my stomach rousing an imminent panic attack.

"Answer me, child!"

Speechless, my mouth suddenly went dry and my parched lips stuck to my teeth like velcro. Head down, I retrieved the remainder of groceries and threw them into the torn bags. I tried to stand up, but a defiant hand pressed against my forehead pinned me down, denying me the ability to rise to my feet. I hesitated only for a moment before a rush of adrenaline shot through my body. Tears erupted from my eyes and I became overwhelmed with anxiety. I fought to pull myself up off the ground, but the stronghold was too much. Against all will I fell to the pavement, the hard concrete tore through the bend of my jeans and broke the skin of my knee.

"You shall repent!" she screamed. "Repent for the unjust you have brought upon the church!"

Ms. Leah's unsettled laying-on-of-hands spurred images of Daddy's abuse, dispersing bitter memories through my mind like a plague. Screams caught my throat and came out as whimpered cries. In a fit of rage I swung my arms erratic, beckoning the release of her unyielding grip. Torn bags cased the pavement and bruised fruit rolled out onto the curb. Distraught, I searched my peripheral vision for help. The crowd stood impervious to the assault, watching from a distance with no intent to intervene.

"*All the sins and blasphemies of men will be forgiven of them, but whosoever blasphemy against the Holy Spirit never has forgiveness, but is guilty of an eternal sin*!" Her words bore a personal grudge.

"You let that child be, Ms. Leah!" Ms. Eloise weaved a path through the growing crowd. Her frail body supported itself on its wooden cane. She was a vision of benevolence against the cold presence of malice. "For God's sake, how can Satan drive out Satan? You leave that child be. The good Lord himself gone judge you by the same measure you judging this child."

I've never seen Ms. Eloise go as far as her front porch. Mama used to say particular circumstances compel people to do miraculous things, maybe this was one of those circumstances.

"All you standin round, gawking and carrying on, supportin this foolishness, she's just a child. Go on now. The good Lord won't tolerate no more of this condemnation. Leave this child be."

Ms. Leah's brow furrowed. I could feel her skeletal hand release me from her grip as pain radiated from the top of my head to the back of my neck. Her perched lips tightened. Disgust graced her face. She locked eyes with Ms. Eloise, searching for a sign of weakness. Age and fragility curled the stillness. The crowd slowly diffused and jeered remarks echoed in the distance. Despite the unease, I scattered to pick up the now tainted food and stood to my feet. From the repulsed look on Ms. Leah's face I knew my very presence harbored a bad taste in her mouth.

"May God forgive you and the heavens above have mercy on you for the iniquity of your tongue." Feeling no sense of remorse she turned and walked away.

Fear and anxiety consumed me to the brink of a heart-attack. It was all I could do to give the pounding of my chest time to catch up with the shortness of my breath.

"Now don't you go paying them no never mind, child, the devil comes in all shapes and forms, guess he just decided to come as Ms. Leah today."

Old age had taken many of Ms. Eloise's teeth, but a large grin managed to find its way through the few she had left. She locked arms with mine and we began our short journey home.

During our walk I couldn't help but to think how much Ms. Leah personified Daddy. The thought that one man could possess the capability to lead another down such a manipulative and destructive path was scary, almost hauntingly so. Daddy housed a congregation of two hundred plus people, to assume his twisted way of thinking influenced so many was disturbing. Was it possible Rock and I weren't the only two kids hiding behind walls of hurt and shame, locking away fears of traumatic and painful acts? I wondered how many of us sat as sheep among wolves, Sunday after Sunday, building walls as thick as blocks of ice, pretending to hear the Sermon but secretly suffering, terror gyrating in our minds like a train across hard steel tracks reminding us of detriments to come, each afraid to tell the other for fear of being exposed. I considered expressing my concerns to Ms. Eloise, but decided not to. I could barely take on Ms. Leah let alone an entire church. So I decided to discard my thoughts for now, at least until Rock and I was released from our own personal hell.

Stopping short of Ms. Eloise's home she loosed her embrace, a bothered look crossed her face as her eyes caught mine.

"Good Lord, child, why do you hold yourself in such bondage? You're like a mouse in a room full of cats. Don't go letting those religious folks trouble your spirit, most of them just using you and your brother as shields to hide their own dirty souls."

"You sound like Mama," I remarked, my head lowered in nostalgia.

Ms. Eloise put her small frail hand underneath my dropped chin and raised it erect. Some people were born suckin on lemons child and they gone die suckin on lemons. Always bitter, always sour, no matter what you do. It's not your job to make lemonade you here? It's not your job to live for their approval. It's only your job to live for God's." She released my chin. "You and your brother are just tape recorders for the truth is all, and many religious folks can't handle the truth."

I nodded just enough to mask the selfish dissatisfaction of her Godly remark. After all, He was banished from my life, not hers, who was I to interfere with that.

"Well, we'd best be gettin in, Miss Faith." She gazed up at the overcast sky. "Looks like God's gonna shed His tears upon us any moment now." She smiled and walked gingerly up the deteriorating stairs. "Rain washes away the darkness and gives way to light, my child. It's just God's small way of washing away the bad and making way for the good." Ms. Eloise paused for a brief moment, took in the atmosphere then nodded her head in approval. "Yes, ma'am, Miss Faith, water gives life to all who thirst," she smiled to herself, "you just have to be willing to drink of it is all," she said scrolling into the house with the battered screen door creaking behind her. I turned and ran home, barely escaping the down pour of the rain.

JULY 4, 2008

There are certain moments that define our lives, some happen in a split second, others cultivate over time, breeding like weeds in a field so deep mere pesticides can't contain them, moments that expose our vulnerability, depicting villains not of strangers, but family members who lurk in the midst of our weaknesses and insecurities, feeding off the frailty of inopportune times and unfortunate circumstances. These are moments that take us down a winding road with no way of knowing how it will all end. Moments that eat away at us, moments that leave us wondering, what if we had taken a different path? Would our life be different, or worse off than it already is?

I propped myself up against the kitchen counter and stared off in the distance, taken back to the days we had breakfast as a family, not a normal family, far from it, but Mama had a way of strengthening the family when everything around it seemed to be tearing it down.

She always had a way of doing the Lord's will, even if it meant doing Daddy's will as well.

The aroma of fresh brewed coffee, fried bacon and scrambled eggs permeated the air. Mama smiled through the pain as she moved slowly around the kitchen placing everyone's plate in its proper position before taking her usual seat next to Daddy at the head of the table…well, at least that's how she saw it. In my opinion, the table was so small either one of us could have been sitting at the head.

"Let's all bow our heads for a moment of prayer," she whispered. "Father, we thank you for another day of fellowship with family, for healing in our bodies and peace in our mind. We give You honor and glory for the means and support to receive this wonderful food. In Jesus' name we pray. Amen."

It didn't matter that the radiation treatments had distorted Mama's voice, or that the chemotherapy had replaced her long flowing hair with a pink silk scarf she wore so gracefully around her head, or that she was so weak she could barely sit in her chair. What mattered most was the harmonious unity she had the gift of bringing to a much needed broken family. The rare sounds of laughter and pleasant voices echoed around the table, clicking forks and plates with sips of coffee and orange juice synchronized like strings of violins and cellos performed before an auditorium of peaceful onlookers.

When everyone was done eating Daddy would indulge himself in the daily newspaper and Mama would perform her ritual citing of Maya Angelou's "Still I Rise." She swayed her hips back and forth on cue and gestured her frail arms round about in a dramatic fashion. Although the cancer had weakened her body she knew her performance relayed an amount of tranquility that brought us a sense of hope and freedom in our otherwise confined world. Rock and I propped ourselves up high on our elbows, our eyes as bright and enthralled as those of a little child on the wake of its first Christmas morning.

"You may write me down in history with your bitter, twisted lies,
you may trod me in the very dirt, but still, like dust, I'll rise.

Does my sassiness upset you? Why are you beset with gloom?
cause I walk like I've got oil wells pumping in my living room.

Just like moons and like suns, with the certainty of tides,
just like hopes springing high, still I'll rise.

Did you want to see me broken? Bowed head and lowered eyes?
shoulders falling down like teardrops, weakened by my soulful cries?

Does my haughtiness offend you? Don't you take it awful hard,
cause I laugh like I've got gold mines digging in my own backyard.

You may shoot me with your words, you may cut me with your eyes,
you may kill me with your hatefulness, but still, like air, I'll rise.

Mama moved with such elegance and poise. The sway of her body offered up the grace of a dancer caught up in the rhythm of her own world, a world free from pain and suffering, where peace was a state of mind, and sickness stood non-existent. She was just as enslaved and oppressed in her own little world as we were in ours, and that alone was enough for her, at the moment, to slip into sweet reverie.

My heart jolted from the sound of firecrackers being let off, the laughter ceased and the pictorial memories were once again lost in the yesteryears of fallacy and deceit. I found myself alone in the empty kitchen with my thoughts. I took in a deep sigh. It was all I could do to will my heart rate back to its normal beat. I gathered myself before walking over and peeking out of the small paned window into the smoke filled street of fireworks and stink bombs. A sense of sadness suddenly overtook me. Watching the kids frolicking in the streets without a care in the world was definitely a joyful moment, but knowing me and Rock had never known that type of happiness or freedom was equally as painful.

I noticed Ms. Eloise wasn't sitting on her porch as usual. Strange, she's never missed a 4th of July celebration, or any neighborhood celebration for that matter. I worried. Maybe I oughta go over and check on her. Just to be sure she's okay. I got as far as the front door when Teller pulled up to the curb erratically, hurried up the steps to the porch and immediately asked to come in. My heart thumped and my body became stone cold.

"Faith, its Rock," he had the tone of voice a person usually has when something terrible is wrong.

I swallowed hard, the knot caught my throat. I stood weak.

"Rock attempted suicide earlier today. He somehow got a hold of a sharp object and managed to stab himself multiple times before the guard found him in his cell. He's lost a substantial amount of blood. They've rushed him to Mercy Hospital."

I heard nothing after suicide. Every muscle in my body tightened, paralyzed from the sudden sting of Teller's words. By the time I was capable of moving, my feet buckled beneath me and I fell helpless to the floor. I wanted to scream but couldn't. Numbness gripped my throat and I was unable to cry out. The loud explosion of fireworks synchronized with the pounding of my heart, beating like a drum, hard, outside of my chest. I was beside myself with grief.

Teller did nothing more than stand cautiously by, conveying the seriousness of Rock's condition only through the frailty of his demeanor. He remained silent, standing there, leaving me to my own grief, disoriented, waiting for some sense of consciousness to return. After an emotional respite, he knelt down, tucked his arm underneath mine and slowly helped me to my feet.

Everything was in slow motion. A door opened, there was a dinging sound. The door slammed, the dinging stopped, the cranking of an ignition, and then silence.

I vaguely remember the big red sign with block letters reading "EMERGENCY" across the building, the smell of sterile linoleum floors and crisp white sanitized linen. The beeping sounds of heart monitors and machines, white coats standing over loved-ones turning hopes of healing into screams of despair and loss.

Teller and I walked down the long narrow corridor to Room 220. Two police officers in full uniform stood guard. Teller showed his identification. I waited mute until they gave a permissible nod to enter the room. Taken aback I drew short of the doorway. My heart took a raging plunge. The impact was so strong it was all I could do to keep myself from running to the nearest exit. Even in his hospital bed Rock lie imprisoned. His feet shackled to the base of the silver rail as a tube ascended from his throat, constricting and inflating his lungs, making his breathing sound heavy and irregular. The air smelled strongly of rubber tubes and alcohol. An I.V. drip hung from a pole leading to the direct vein of Rock's bruised and scarred hand. The pastel blue spread tucked neatly over the tight fitted-sheet covered his heavily sedated body, baring only his chest up.

The poorly lit room couldn't hide the silhouette of a small-framed figure sitting in the chair next to Rock's bed, gently clutching his hand in a frail, but rigid fist. My eyes narrowed.

"Hello, Faith," a feeble voice greeted me as a thin figure emerged from the dimness of the room.

Afraid to give way to my thoughts as to why Ms. Eloise would be in my brother's room I shut down all reasoning. A disconcerted look crossed my face.

"You're probably wondering why she's here?" Teller asked in a subtle tone.

I remained distressfully quiet.

The awkwardness provoked an uneasy silence. Ms. Eloise's aged-eyes rose to mine, red from crying. She appeared troubled, consumed with emotions that left her unable to speak. Her lips parted, but said nothing. Moments past and the silence grew increasingly tense.

"Start from the beginning," Teller said offering solace to an uncomfortable situation. He stroked her shoulder gently, rousing encouragement that had somehow gotten lost. Her eyes trailed the room until they fell solemnly back upon mine. She procrastinated a moment longer, and then, with much hesitation, came face to face with her torment.

"Faith, I would give anything to not have to tell you this. To not have to suffer you and your brother anymore pain than you have already endured," she swallowed hard. "Far too many times in life we don't always walk the way God intends for us to walk, sometimes we stray off path, get lost somewhere down the road. Some of us get to a point of no return and then there are those that find a way back, that seek redemption, a way to make amends for what they've done," her aged voice trembled with uneasiness. "I spent most of my life trying to get back on that path, trying to find a way to make things right, but equally so, I've spent a lifetime running, running from my past, from sins that haunt my dreams, that consume me like a rushing waterfall plunging over the edge to nowhere," her tone weakened. Tears coursed down her wrinkled face to the bottom of her chin before plummeting into the fastening of her hands.

I stood watch as she struggled to explain things I didn't understand. Her tone was full of sorrow and regret, painfully apologetic to say the least. My focus shifted from Ms. Eloise and Teller's effort to reveal obscurities that had already begun to bring me displeasure, to my brother lying in the hospital bed fighting for his life. The overwhelming notion to flee summoned me, but I feared losing my brother more than I feared what was to come, so I willed myself to stay.

"I've deprived and cheated you and your brother out of a life you've so truly deserved, and I beg your forgiveness." Ms. Eloise wiped the back of her hand across her running nose. "I'm tired my child, tired of eluding the truth, tired of hiding behind my wall of destruction, a wall built so high over so many years I've selfishly blocked you and Rock out of my life."

A knot tightened in my stomach.

"Faith..." A painful cry caught her throat. " Faith...your Mom...," she abruptly stopped, pressed her hand firmly over her mouth and let out a short agonizing snivel that sounded like a crisscross between a hiccup and a sob. My heart skipped a beat. "Your Mom was my daughter." She hesitated through the pain. "Me and Mister's daughter..." her voice faltered as she broke down in tears. Teller put his arms around her weak draped shoulders. She collapsed her head against his chest and wept.

Heaviness took hold of my body, denying me the urge to run. All breath left from inside of me. "Are you saying...," my voice broke. A tear of deceit crept down my cheek. "Are you saying that you are my grandmother...Rock's grandmother?" I asked breathless and full of contempt.

Ms. Eloise lifted her head. Her face had lost all color, her eyes troubled with hurt and pain, hesitant to go any further. There was a long silence.

"Answer me!" I screeched through the ferocious pain burning through my soul.

The squeal of my voice startled her to an alarmed jolt. "Yes." She nodded her head in disgrace. "Mister and I are your grandparents..." Her eyes dropped. She gave a heartrending pause.

"Finish it!" I screamed. Every organ in my being was aflame, burning from the inside out, peeling away at my flesh like a wildfire blazing out of control.

"Faith, please, things happened in that house that I had no control of. You must believe that, things that I am ashamed of." Her eyes begged forgiveness.

"Finish it!"

Trepidation gripped her like a noose. "Mister raped your mother!" The harsh reality resonated off the walls. "He raped his own daughter...my daughter! He's your father, Faith...oh God help me, he's your father," she gripped her chest and her voice trailed off and erupted into cries of shame. Mortified, she averted her eyes away from mine and buried them into the palms of her hands.

I stood scared stiff, my chest full and hot. The room closed in around me. The beeping of the machines got louder and louder. I pressed my hands hard over my ears to block out everything around me. I couldn't suffer any more pain. A shiver passed through me. Hot, then cold. I felt all life leave my body. I was trapped in the web of purgatory, caught between a nightmare I so desperately wanted to wake up from and a reality that I was incapable of facing. I gasped for air, tugging at the collar of my shirt that seemed to tighten itself around my neck, suffocating my airways, leaving me unable to breathe. Teller rushed to my aid, but I broke loose of his grip and ran over to Rock's bed, collapsing myself over his unresponsive body. I needed him to wake up. I needed his comfort. I wasn't strong enough to endure this alone.

In the hallway the officers took watch. The door opened, Teller gestured that everything was okay and they reluctantly returned to their post outside the room.

Ms. Eloise watched with difficulty as my world fell painfully down around me, hers equally as crumbled. She fought against the horror that coiled inside of her, knowing that no matter how deep the wound, she had to continue, so she carried on under her own distress.

"Faith, I've condemned myself for years over what Mister had done. The thought that I was unable to protect my own daughter sickened me." She blew her nose into the wet tissue that had become ragged and torn. "I wanted to tell you, but your Mom threatened to take you away if I did. I loved her too much for that. I couldn't bear to lose her again. I loved all of you too much for that. We needed to protect you, how could we protect you if she took you away?"

Something rose inside of me and I moved through the tightness of the room closer to Ms. Eloise. "Protection?" exasperated I forced the words through the grits of my teeth. "How dare you. Where was your protection when my father was revving his penis down my throat or penetrating the walls of my dry vagina for hours until it swell and bled, huh?" Hurt exuded out of me like the blood of a wounded animal taking its last breath. "Where was your protection when Daddy used Rock's face as a punching bag just because he forgot to put the cap back on the toothpaste or because he didn't clap loud enough during church service? Or what about the time he forced Rock and I to have sex with one another because his twisted mind mistook my show of affection as a sexual gesture rather than a term of endearment?" My face was wet with tears.

"Faith, please," Ms. Eloise reached out for my hand. I resisted.

"No! You're a liar!" Anger mounted up within me. "My mother did everything she could to protect us! She would never have left Rock and I believing that we were alone! She would never keep that kind of secret from us!"

"She did it to protect you, Faith, just as I did to protect her."

"You're nothing like her!" My voice was disdained.

"Faith she knew your daddy was touching you. She knew he was raping you."

"He never touched me! Not while she was alive! She was a shield, a safeguard from Daddy. She would protect me from the grave if she could!"

"She knew his intentions, Faith."

"Stop it!" I screamed. "She never knew!" I didn't know what to believe anymore.

"On the nights when your Dad would take out his frustrations on your Mom she would bring you and your brother down to me and Mister's house and we would talk while you kids were asleep. She told us how he would come into your room, watch you as you were sleeping. Make out-of-the-way gestures to you. It killed her. It literally killed her. She wanted to leave many times, and many times she did, but like me, she loved him more than she hated her circumstances so she always came back. Against everything she believed in, she stayed."

"Have you no soul?" I was fatigued. "My brother is dying in this hospital room and you dare disrespect him with your disgraceful lies about our mother."

"I beg of you, Faith, I'm not lying. I have proof."

Teller pulled a manila folder from his briefcase and handed it to me.

Unable to face the truth, I knocked the folder out of Teller's hand onto the floor.

"My child, please. I know how this must hurt, but to everything there is a season, and a time to every purpose under the heaven."

The passage of Ecclesiastes flowed off Ms. Eloise's tongue and burned liked acid to my stomach. I began to cry harder. Fragments of unwanted childhood memories came gyrating back, reminding me of Daddy's justified abuse under his own selfish biblical principles. He was unwilling to take any of the blame for his disgraced wrongdoings and Ms. Eloise was no different.

"Faith, please allow me to do what's right in God's eyes. Allow me to fulfill my vow to mend what I have torn down." She grabbed my wrist. '*When you make a promise to God don't delay in following through, for God takes no pleasure in fools. Keep all promises made to Him*.'"

I snatched from her grip. "Even the devil knows the Bible Ms. Eloise, so whatever it takes to pacify your heart you do it, but I made no promises to God. I have no obligations to you, only to my brother."

Teller stood in defense. "Allow her the opportunity for redemption, Faith, she deserves that much.

"I am trying to hold true to my word. I am trying to keep that promise." Ms. Eloise bared solemn eyes as she mustered up enough strength to make good on her oath, her face stricken with grief. "I've harbored secrets in this old heart of mine that would have sent many to their graves way before their time. I've asked God for many things over the years, and everything I've asked of Him has been done. He is not a man that He shall lie. He has made good on every last one of His promises to me, and now by His grace and mercy I have the strength to make good on mine."

I was impassive as always to the word of God, so whatever consolations Ms. Eloise tried to offer would only be cast into a dark wall. The hypocrisy of her repentance vexed my soul. I walked merciless across the room, rested my hands on the arms of her chair and leaned in close, clenching my jaws tight. "How dare you sit here with your contrite spirit and selfish motives and defend an unfaithful God. Your husband raped your daughter…his own daughter and impregnated her with the same penis he penetrated you with, yet you still have the audacity to sit here in devotion."

"That's enough, Faith," Teller's tone dropped.

"Did God make good on His promise knowing that the same tongue your husband rolled around so passionately in your mouth was the same tongue he rolled around the areola of his daughter's childish chest and underdeveloped body?"

"I said that is enough, Faith!"

I snubbed Teller's words. "Where was God when the same strong hands that held and caressed your body, groped your daughter's vagina night, after night, after night, until she vomited shame and embarrassment?!"

Darts of guilt shot through Ms. Eloise's strained body as she eased up out of her chair in a desperate attempt to evade my sharp tongue. Teller rushed to her assistance.

"Who do you think you are?" she sniveled under broken tears.

"The devil's spawn," I scoffed vengeful, "birth through the ruins of your husband's sick perversion."

"He wasn't a monster, Faith."

"He was a deviant," I retorted more disturbed by her defense of Mister's behavior than her selfish motives of betrayal.

Ms. Eloise paled. "There were things about Mister that you would never know."

"He was a revolting pedophile who exploited his own daughter for the selfish gain of ejaculation." My top lip trembled from resentment.

"Forgiveness is a hard thing, Faith. It is a hard thing, but it is decreed by God and is something that we all must do."

"Do you really believe Mister is perusing around heaven, abiding in the shadow of the Almighty just because you chose to forgive him?"

"I believe he's in heaven because of his repentance?"

"He's burning in the hot coals of Hell right along with Daddy and all the other filthy perverts who screwed their daughters in the name of God!"

"Faith, I know you're a victim in all this…"

Offended, I struck like a venomous snake, "Victim? Is that what you think I am…a victim…some casualty or injured little girl trying to recover from her Daddy's demented mentality?" A cold spirit overcame me. "Victims overcome! Victims find a way to live!"

"Faith I didn't mean…"

"Look at me!" I pounded my fist against my chest as tears welled in my eyes. "Victims have a soul! I'm a walking corpse! Dead from the inside out! Everything that defines a human being has been taken from me! Every virtue has been drained, and now you tell me that Mister, your husband, my mother's father, is my Daddy?!" I almost choked on my own repugnance. "Haven't we gone through enough?! Haven't we endured more than we can handle?!" I felt myself hyperventilating. "Were we birth out of such filth that no one is capable of loving us?!" I was in a fit of rage. I couldn't catch my breath. My chest was full and my heart felt like it was going to explode. "Disgust cannot begin to describe how I feel inside!"

Teller rushed over to console my pain. "No!" I lashed out thrusting away his support. "You come here, to my brother's bedside, with your wages of sin and wisdom from God and expect me to embrace you?! God has been as unfaithful to you as He has been to me, but yet you stand here, as broken as I am, with this fabricated faith and holier-than-thou mentality and expect me to believe it?!"

"Faith, please sit down." Teller pulled a chair from the corner of the room. I was irate.

"How dare you! How dare you come with more deception! You're nothing but a wolf in sheep's clothing! Was this supposed to help us?! Is this why my brother is lying in a hospital room fighting for his life because God told you to ease your troubled soul?! Is it well with thee?! Are you at peace?!" Nausea rose from my stomach. I felt choked. I swallowed hard to push back the sickness that filled my body. All breath left my lungs. Teller grabbed me in a tight embrace, I buried my head in his bosom and sobbed hysterically.

Ms. Eloise could only stare at me with shame and humiliation. A hard desiccated knot in her throat left her unable to speak. A rush of familiar emotions shared between three generations forced us to face one another's pain. Stricken, she started towards me, but stopped short of contact. She wanted to comfort me, to help me find solace in my afflictions, but she knew rejection would follow, so instead she walked heartbroken and helpless towards the door. I pried myself from Teller's grip and ran behind her. Everything within me demanded reasons. Distraught and confused I fell at her mercy.

"Why?!" I screamed through choked sobs. "Why didn't you come…why didn't you help us…why didn't you stop the pain?!" Questions tore from my mouth with no pause for response. "You knew he was hurting us and you didn't even care…no one cared…no one would stop him! Why didn't anyone care?!" My entire body was numb. I felt overwhelmed. Snot ran from my nose down to my lips. "Are we that soiled that filthy that nobody can love us?!" I squealed clutching my fist to my chest doubling over in pain. I couldn't form the words, I couldn't speak. I thought I was going to have a heart attack right there. It was as though my lungs had run out of air.

Ms. Eloise reached out for me, but before she could respond I collapsed into her arms like a wounded child.

Rock's body began to convulse. The erratic sound of the heart monitor startled me. I turned to see my brother shaking violently. He appeared to be having a seizure. Fear charged me and I lunged towards him screaming. Teller caught me from behind and wrapped his arms around my waist, incarcerating me in the vault of his grip. I struggled to get loose, desperately beating my fists against his tightly bound hands. Doctors and nurses in white coats and scrubs rushed into the room, gesturing us out. Everything went silent. I was terrified. My soul literally left my body.

"Get her out of here!" The doctor's lips were moving but I couldn't hear the words. Everything about me was distant and in slow motion.

Teller pulled me out into the hallway where Ms. Eloise was already seated. I fought against his clinched arms until the pain in my side left me too sore to move. I fell limp in his arms as he eased my back against the wall and sunk me into a crouched position on the cold hard floor. Bringing my knees to my chest, I rested my head into the shelter of my own embrace. I closed my eyes to block out the pandemonium surrounding me. The entire ordeal left me exhausted. My eyes burned from crying. My thoughts kept going back to Rock lying helpless in that hospital bed…to Ms. Eloise's confession…to Mama dying from cancer…to Daddy's abuse…to Rock…to Mama…to Daddy. My mind was spent. I felt like I had actually suffered a nervous breakdown. I had been pulled in so many different directions in such a short amount of time I was literally coming apart at the seams. Feeling sick to my stomach I excused myself and went to the restroom.

The smell of hospital bathrooms was enough to make anybody sick. It housed a stench of body odors and fluids that reminded you of every person that had come and gone throughout the day, not to mention the disgusting streaks of bowel left in the toilet as a souvenir from someone else's defecation. I squatted to avoid touching the infectious toilet seat, wiped away the excess urine from my vagina and flushed the toilet with the soles of my shoe. The loud boisterous suction alerted the entire hospital that I was done with my business. I avoided the jaded image in the mirror, fully aware of the self-deprecated reflection staring back at me. I washed my hands with the antibacterial soap, which I swore smelled more medicated than the hospital itself, and reluctantly walked back out into the hallway to rejoin Teller and Ms. Eloise.

The scene outside Rock's room had calmed and an older doctor wearing blue scrubs, a white coat and plastic coverings over his shoes was talking to Teller and Ms. Eloise. I couldn't hear the conversation from where I was standing, but he appeared relaxed and composed. The officers were still on guard but managed to huddle up in a nearby corner of the hall away from all the commotion. I wanted to get in on the conversation but was too afraid. I could feel panic bubbling up inside of me. I couldn't deal with any more bad news…no way, so I kept my distance. After a few moments of conversation the doctor smiled politely, gave Teller a pat on the shoulder and walked away.

"How's my brother?" I asked, my throat tight with worry.

Teller focused in on my bushed face. “They’re doing everything they can, Faith. He’s stable but the next 24-hours are very crucial.”

“Can I see him?”

“Sure,” Teller said in a guarded tone.

I took in a deep burning breath and walked slowly into Rock’s room. The sound of the ventilator shook my nerves. The scene was an all too familiar one. We’d spent many a night by Mama’s hospital bed, Daddy praying her back to health and asking God to heal her by His stripes. Needless to say our prayers never got answered, and as usual I was the only one who’d admit to God’s unchanging hand.

I walked around to the other side of the bed away from all the cords and machines and carefully cuddled up next to Rock’s motionless body. I laid my arm gently across his chest and nestled my head into the small nook between his neck and shoulder. A rush of warmth penetrated my body and I suddenly found myself longing for my younger brother’s touch. We’d been apart for nearly a year now and his love was the only true love that I had ever known from a man. It was an innocent secret discovered after a night of consoling one another following Daddy’s ill-treatment. I buried myself deeper into Rock’s chest, closed my eyes and lost myself in thought.

My mind was consumed with the memory of that night. Rock’s pure hand reached out and touched my contaminated body. I could feel the warmth of his touch against my icy skin. My heart beat like a drum as I struggled to suppress the desire to hold him close to my breast. He brushed his soft young lips against mine. I eased my soiled body quietly into his and engaged in the most sensuous kiss. A warm sensation filled every organ within me and I wrapped my legs and arms around him like a baby clinging to its mother’s bosom. The caress of his hands was so gentle. The security of his embrace erased the revolting events of the day and submerged me into a moment of freedom and pleasure. Every sordid ruin Daddy had implanted in me was released with each breathtaking stroke of Rock’s body. It was a surreal moment that healed wounds and broke down walls of fatigue and pain. The need to feel accepted and loved exonerated all immoralities, and for one yielding moment made everything right.

A low almost inaudible choking sound snapped me back to the present. After a heart stopping moment I rose from the bed. Rock was coming out of sedation. His eyes blinked rapidly and he gagged from the tube descended in his throat. I ran out of the room to get help and rushed back to his bedside with Teller and Ms. Eloise in tow. I leaned in close so he could focus on my face. Tears welled up in my eyes and I smiled from a great sense of relief.

White coats and blue scrubs once again plagued the room, forcing us back out into the hallway. My thoughts hinged to Mama's death. There was no drama, no big scene, just peace and quiet, but the magnitude of losing her was inconceivable. I remembered being afraid of so many things, it was as if the veil of protection had been torn and God had given Daddy total accessibility to us.

Ms. Eloise's voice broke the still. "Shall we summon a prayer, Miss Faith?"

I dismissed her words, never considering her request.

She gave me a pensive look. "How long will you hold onto your father's transgressions? No one should harbor that amount of hatred in such a pure heart."

I stood in the company of my own bitterness, uttering nothing that would give Ms. Eloise the impression that I had somehow received an epiphany of God's unwavering favor.

"Is it not enough that God has shown Himself miraculous through the rising of your brother? Is He not worthy of at least that?"

I put miles of thought between me and Ms. Eloise. Her voice dissipated in the quietness of my mind. The weight of her vain request sunk deep into the finality of my hollow soul. She knew I would never assent to her prayer call so she summoned one herself.

White coats emptied out of the room like roaches exposed to light.

The older doctor lingered behind checking vital signs and flickering beams of light into Rock's dilated pupils. He removed the clipboard from the foot of Rock's bed and flipped through the leaf of pages attached, occasionally licking his thumb in the process. He fished for a pen at the pocket of his jacket and signed his name to the bottom of each form. His sloth demeanor only added to my frustration as I waited with expectancy for his report on my brother's condition. The heavy feeling of not knowing troubled my restless spirit and left me feeling anxious. Teller stood close by while Ms. Eloise whispered a prayer of healing so devout the only thing left was the laying on of hands and sprinkling of holy oil.

After a few more debilitating moments the doctor joined us in the hallway. He cleared his throat. His neck mimicked that of a turkey as the excess skin jiggled around while he spoke. "He appears to be fine. Vitals are good and he's breathing on his own. We removed the ventilator with careful observation still warranted. Overall he's stable."

"Is he responsive?" Teller asked, his tone concerned and edgy.

Apprehension soured my stomach and nerves gnawed away at my insides. I decided to stand mute, my breath quick and short.

"Mr. Rock is a lucky young man. The injuries he sustained were severe, but he's doing pretty well, considering. He's alert and asking for his sister." A gratifying smile adorned his face. "I'll check back later." He walked away charged with purpose and fulfillment.

A sense of urgency caught me and I hurried into Rock's room. His eyes were open and they were the most beautiful hazel green eyes I had ever seen. I cradled his cheeks in the palms of my hand and gently kissed his chaste lips, leaving behind beads of moisture from the wet of my tears. Our eyes locked and for the first time in a long time I wasn't afraid, all caution disappeared and I was able to relax in a moment of security. But as usual, all good that coiled within me was short-lived, quickly frayed by the unsettling look on Rock's face.

"What is it? What's wrong?"

"Did she tell you? Did she tell you about Mister…about Mama?" his voice low and whispered.

My eyes answered him with a deep agonizing stare.

"I begged her, Faith…I begged her not to tell you such depraved things." Tears rolled down the sides of Rock's face onto the foam-like pillow supporting his head. "I couldn't cope with it. I couldn't cope with it being you."

"Shhhhh." The sudden notion that Rock would try and take his own life for the benefit of protecting mine was too unbearable to think about. All the abuse Daddy had ever inflicted upon me could never be comparable to that amount of pain. I would have never been able to survive. I would have taken my own life before living without his.

Weakened by his self-inflicted wounds, Rock fell silent, drifting in and out, his energy depleted. Emotionally consumed and worn myself, I pulled up a chair next to his bedside and waited out the remainder of the night.

JULY 7, 2008

I hated hospital food, especially breakfast. The regurgitated looking oatmeal, powdered eggs and greasy bacon curled my stomach and left me feeling nauseous. Although the compassionate and thoughtful attitudes of the staff more than made up for the displeasing meals, it did nothing to salvage my sour stomach.

Rock's been hospitalized for three days now and I've never left his side. Teller had court business to tend to and Ms. Eloise's age limited her mobility to travel back and forth to the hospital. She called every day for prognosis and never failed to remind us of her more than willing assistance if needed. Rock and I had yet to address the situation with our so-called grandmother mostly because we were too busy dealing with the trial and nursing him back to health.

News of the extended deliberations and Rock's hospitalization burned through the television like wild fire. Every media outlet known to man was either camped outside the hospital or broadcasting live from the studio. Reports of Rock's attempted suicide were over exaggerated by rumors of dramatic events cooped up by the media to rake in viewers.

"Homicide turned Suicide," one of the theatrical headlines read. I flicked through the channels. "Acquittal by Suicide," another one read. Unable to deal with the offensive reporting of media greed and defamation of Rock's character I hit the power button, disabling the uncivilized connection between us and the outside world.

It was just after eleven and Rock had been gone all morning for tests. The extra cot the hospital so nicely provided for me was hard and uncomfortable. I punched the flat paper-like pillow and fluffed it underneath my head. I turned on my side, leaned over the edge of the bed and pulled open the top drawer of the nightstand next to my cot. A green pocket-sized Bible lay adjacent to an unopened box of Kleenex and travel size lotion. I snubbed the fallacious contents that were obviously put there to manipulate feeble minds into believing that somehow they would be healed by His stripes. I slid the drawer closed, rolled over on my back and stared at the ceiling. The water stains on the wall formed outlines of different shapes and figures. One resembled an insect while the other sketched the face of a man. I shifted my eyes to the open door where the officer stood guard. The tread of footsteps across the linoleum floor echoed through the hall from family members and visitors dropping in on loved-ones. White coats and multi-colored scrubs strolled back and forth on either side of the corridor. Electrocardiograms rolled by on carts while I.V. poles wheeled pass with patients in tow.

I stretched out on the bed in a desperate attempt to catch up on my sleep. Chronic insomnia weighed me down and left my body feeling lethargic and worn. In an effort to block out all the distractions I shifted my body to its side and closed my eyes, curled myself up into the fetal position and finally drifted off into a much needed rest.

I'd been napping only moments when a gentle hand gripped my shoulder and gave me a faint shake. My eyes caught the figure standing over me and I leaped from the bed disoriented, my breath nearly snatched from my windpipe, my body shaken and anxious, unsettled by the sudden disruption of my sleep. An urge to scream overcame me but weakened as I steadied myself. The room suddenly took still and I felt a sense of intoxication rush through my bloodstream. "Bishop?" his name caught my throat and I nearly choked on my own saliva. He stood taut, his hands tucked tightly into the front pockets of his snug jeans. A smile filled his boyish face which seemed to have matured over time. His dimples sank deeper than usual into the impression of his cheeks and made him more attractive than ever.

"Hi, Faith," his voice raspy yet gentle.

Bishop had a way of looking at me that made me feel comfortable and uncomfortable at the same time. I didn't know what to do with myself so we just stood there, staring back at one another like children, each waiting for the other's initiative to play. I shifted my weight from my right leg to my left and gazed down at the floor. Giving him a hug seemed like the most logical thing to do so I lunged forward and gave him an embrace that seemed to imply more than a happy gesture, judging from his reciprocation, the feeling was mutual. Our channels were quickly interrupted by the squeaking of Rock's wheelchair being pushed back into the room.

An uncomfortable pause lingered, more uncomfortable than the one before. Rock's face held a stare of disbelief as the nurse wheeled him over and settled him back into bed. Bishop and I stood inaudibly by while she reattached the I.V. tube back into the small catheter protruding from the vein of Rock's arm. She silenced the beeping sounds of machines as she went about her tasks pushing buttons and reconnecting cords. She pulled up the bed railings.

"Are we comfortable?" she asked kindheartedly.

Rock gave an uneasy nod.

She shared a smile before quietly exiting the room. Rock's face was hard as bricks.

"What's up my man?" Bishop cut into the awkward silence.

Rock looked floored, he couldn't speak.

Bishop's smile broadened, but then grew serious. "What's up, man?" he asked again, this time giving Rock a slight nudge on the shoulder.

Rock sat silent, blame taped his face.

"Come on man, this silent treatment wouldn't have anything to do with that trial now would it?"

"Have you been following it?" Rock's eyes studied Bishop's face.

"Are you kidding me, man? Everybody who's anybody's been watchin that trial. You'd have to been sleeping under a rock not to know the details of that case. It's on every channel there is. Reporters are camped outside this hospital like roaches."

"I told them you gave me the gun." A tug of betrayal gripped Rock's body. He blurted out the guilt before he had a chance to process what he was saying.

"I know."

"I made you an accessory. What are you doing here?" He whispered peeking over at the officer standing outside the door.

Bishop crouched down beside the wheelchair. "Look man, you did what you had to do. Don't worry about me, besides, your lawyer took care of it. He got me in to see you, anyways, when have I ever let anything come between our friendship…huh? He gave a supporting smile and nudged Rock on the shoulder again. "Maybe later when you're done faking this whole hospital scene I can kick your butt in some more street ball or something, what do you say?"

Bishop's allegiance brought a wide grin across Rock's face, soon after the chatter and laughter of teenage boys filled the room. A sense of freedom overcame me and at that moment I couldn't help but like Bishop even more. I yearned to feel the innocence he portrayed, the impulsivity of being young, the carefree mentality to live life the way it's supposed to be lived, without bitterness and regret. But that wasn't my life and as hard as I tried to think otherwise the harsh reality of the trial stormed me. The hatred of Daddy, the loss of Mama, the threat of losing Rock, the fear was still there, all of it circling around me like a devastating tornado ready to touch down and wipe out everything in its path. I couldn't forget that twelve strangers had been deciding over Rock's fate for weeks now and each one held our lives in their hands. Unsettling as that thought was, I wanted a verdict now more than ever. As scared as I was I was ready to accept the inevitable conclusion that God had cut me and my brother out of His holy plan a long time ago.

JULY 7, 2008

LATER THAT DAY

Apparently Teller had some news he wanted to discuss with me, so I met him at a discreet location not too far from the hospital, which worked out fine because it gave Rock and Bishop more time to spend with one another. Police placed barricades around the vicinity of the area and the hospital had set up a back entrance where I could come and go without being spotted by all the media channels. I pulled the round brim hat down as far as I could over my forehead and hid behind the dark shades Teller bought me from some vendor downtown, not exactly vintage but they served the purpose just as well. The temperature was in the high eighties and it was scorching hot underneath the layers of clothing I was wearing. Didn't bother me much though, I was used to dressing in layers on the off chance Daddy was on one of his vile kicks. It wasn't so much that the heat was so grueling, but the congestion of people that made me uneasy. I wasn't use to being around large crowds and was beginning to feel a little suffocated. I pushed my way through the multitude of people, half breathing, trying to catch some air. The honking of horns and voices on cell phones got louder with every step. The high rise buildings hovering over appeared to be closing in around me. I spotted an area that looked to be less congested so I waited for the traffic light to turn green and hastened across the street, the heat of the sun trailing behind me.

In a desperate attempt to cool myself I dipped into a small building across the way. I pushed through the glass door and found myself standing in the middle of what appeared to be a quaint little bookstore. The tiny subtle bell over the entranceway warned of my presence. The dimly lit store smelled of old worn-out books that infused the air of a stale, but welcoming scent. Wooden tables that looked to have aged over the years set adjacent one another. Pictures of historical writers lined the walls around the entire store, tacked with a single nail and wired hanger. The small-paned windows were stained-glass of red and blues with wooden trim, and each sill adorned a single colorful figurine, which radiated an angelic-like glow off the natural light peering through the windowpane. I paused for a moment to catch my breath. Anxiety had made its way to my nervous system and I felt like I had overdosed on caffeine.

"May I help you?"

I turned to see a pint size woman who obviously got bored with retirement and decided to take on a few hours at the bookstore to have some sense of fulfillment in her life.

"Oh, no thank you, ma'am. I was taking a breather is all…" I stopped mid-sentence. My throat tightened. I could see the pages securely encased in the glass frame hanging above the front desk. It took a moment to focus, but the all too familiar words leaped out at me and I suddenly found myself back at our kitchen table watching Mama performing her customary dance.

"May I?" I asked as I drew closer to the wall for a better look.

"Signed by the famous Maya Angelou herself," information that was obvious, but apparently a conversation tool that was readily available to be said. "We have several books filled with her most renowned poetry. I could show you where they are if you'd like."

I snubbed her kind gesture as I fingered the black and white photos of slaves surrounding the glass case, a young woman being torn from the arms of her pleading mother, fathers and sons bound together by iron collars around their necks, women impregnated by their aggressors, toiling the field in the summer heat. There they were, kindred spirits, encircled around the poem like the moon orbiting the earth, rising amidst the hatred and obstruction of humanity, rising against the very dirt and dust in which they toiled, bowed heads and lowered eyes lifted and strengthened by the soulful cries of freedom and equality. "Still I Rise!" I had it memorized word for word. Mama had recited it so often it was engraved in my soul.

I closed my eyes, engrossed in the moment, desperately trying to hold on to Mama's voice that was slowly fading away in the distance. "Still I Rise!" Screams of a fearful child rang out in my ears, outstretched hands reaching for a mother that wasn't there, silent tears from a broken heart who could no longer protect, a bleak reminder of what was and uncertainty of what's to come.

"Ma'am?"

I opened my eyes to find the pint size tour guide staring directly in my face.

"Ma'am, would you like to purchase the poem? We have it in audio as well as paperback?"

I stood there, letting the moment pass, and then, very slowly I turned and walked out. Leaving the pint size woman to fulfill her purpose, and me, to meet Teller and somehow try to find mine.

I was dripping wet by the time I got to my destination, sweating in places I never thought possible. Teller handed me a glass of water and a box of tissue. I dabbed what I could from my face and arm pits then sat down to enjoy the coolness of the room. I barely took note of the papers being shuffled around on the table. My mind was a million miles away. Teller gave me a dry stare, then a more intense look before going back to flipping through the pages. He took in a deep breath and let out a frustrated sigh.

"I think we're looking at a hung jury here."

My body temperature was just beginning to level off, but escalated again. "What is that?"

He shifted in his chair. "It's when the jury can't reach a unanimous verdict."

"What does that mean?" I asked through the hotness.

"It means that Judge Hallow will declare a mistrial and the prosecutor can either negotiate a plea bargain with Rock or pursue a new trial."

"There's no way my brother's gonna cop a plea, and another trial, no way."

"Under any other circumstances I would say a deadlocked jury is the best thing to happen to a Defendant, but in this case, to try it again would be legal suicide. It was difficult enough the first time around. To try and get fair and partial jurors after all the national media attention this case has gotten would be close to impossible."

There was a moment of uncomfortable silence, followed by dead air, and then something inside me broke. The nonchalant attitude of Teller's response, the ambiguity of Rock's fate, or maybe heat exhaustion, but something within me ruptured and threw me into a full-blown rage. I grabbed the goblet off the table and hurled it across the room, hosing down the wall with pieces of glass and water. Books, magazines and papers toppled to the floor as I flipped the small coffee table over to its side. Teller rushed over, but I backed away as if suddenly confronted by a vicious dog prepared to attack.

He stretched his palms out in front of him. "Okay, Faith. Okay. Everything's going to be alright!" he moved cautiously toward me.

My face was pale and burning hot. I tore passed Teller with no thought of where I was going. He grabbed me by the waist-side and held on tight. Kicking and screaming I pushed all my weight into his torso, lifted my legs with such force and drove my feet through the window directly in front of me, shattering glass everywhere.

"Faith calm down!"

I scratched and clawed at his hands in a desperate attempt to break free.

Teller tightened his grip. "*Hear my prayer, oh Lord, and let my cry come unto thee! Hide not thy face from me in the day when I am in trouble, incline thy ear unto me, in the day when I call answer me speedily*!" He prayed for God's mercy, "*For my days are consumed like smoke, and my heart is smitten and withered like grass*!"

Teller's words scorched through the heat burning in my bones. I struggled to get loose. The flashback of an all too familiar scene whisked me into a frantic state. I lost all awareness and found myself hysterically trying to escape Daddy's incestuous claws. I screamed over the traumatic memories of justifiable scriptures and sinful hands.

"*Mine enemies reproach me all the day, and they that are mad against me are sworn against me! But, thou, oh Lord, shall arise and have mercy upon her, for the time to favor her, the set time is now*!"

I raged on. The chokehold of a father, the sodomy of his own son, the ungodly sins of a Man of God, consumed my mind. I pierced my fingernails into the skin of Teller's hands until he broke grip. I ran towards the window and propelled my hands through the broken glass. Teller grabbed me from behind and pulled me away from the shattered window. Ripping off his tie, he wrapped it tightly around my bleeding arms. Exhausted and crying, I leaned against his stiff body and slowly slid down to the floor and rested my tired spirit at the soles of his feet.

Teller stood in silence for a long moment. His chest heaving from exertion, he scanned the marred room of a young girl's fear and the uncertainty of a brother's future. A representation of mutilated lives scarred by the biblical principles of a righteous God caught up in the wrong hands of an unrighteous father.

Disturbed by my troubled spirit, but rightfully justified, Teller settled down on the floor and held me from behind in a benevolent embrace. He issued no words of admonishment but instead sat sorrowfully amidst the ruins of the room that had suffered deeply from the lesions of my soul. I couldn't help but to wonder if the sadness he felt was for me or him, or maybe both, either way he reached into the darkness of the moment and christened it with an unwarranted scripture that brought nothing but memories of pain and grief.

"*The Lord is my shepherd, I shall not want.*
He maketh me to lie down in green pastures, he leads me beside the still waters.

He restores my soul, he leads me in the path of righteousness for his name's sake.

Yea, though I walk through the valley of the shadow of death, I will fear no evil,for thou art with me, thy rod and thy staff they comfort me.

Thou preparest a table before me in the presence of mine enemies, thou anoints my head with oil, my cup runneth over.

Surely goodness and mercy shall follow me all the days of my life, and I will dwell in the house of the Lord forever."

I wanted to denounce his words, argue my zero tolerance for pseudo-biblical innuendos, scream that God's protection had somehow bypassed my life and provided me with nothing but hurt and pain. But I didn't, I said nothing, I was simply too tired to fight. So, devoid of all Godly emotions I closed my weary eyes and drifted off into the warmth of sweet reverie.

JULY 8, 2008

NEXT DAY

My injuries were not severe enough to seek medical attention. I would have fought against it anyway had Teller forced me to go. Rock being hospitalized was enough. I decided it was best for Teller to drop me off at home rather than back up to the hospital, considering the circumstances and all, so I called Bishop to ask if he could stay with Rock and give me a night's rest, he was kind enough to oblige. My presence would have just agitated the situation even more anyway. I assured Teller I was fine, blocked out all worrisome thoughts, put on three layers of clothing, curled myself up in a cocoon-like position and fell off into a much needed sleep.

I awakened to the loud ringing of the phone. The old clock on the nightstand with the big red numbers read 8:30 a.m., but I wasn't sure seeing that my eyes had not come into complete focus yet. I wiped the sleep from my eyes and leisurely picked up the receiver.

"Hello."

"Hi, Faith, it's Teller. I'm up at the hospital with Rock. He's being discharged this morning. They're preparing to take him back over to the jail as we speak, just thought you should know."

"What?" Still half sleep. "They're releasing him? But, he's a minor. Shouldn't they have called me first?"

"That's why they called me. As his attorney I had to be here for the process of discharge and transfer."

"Ok...um…I'm on my way." I searched the floor anxiously for my shoes, the phone rustling in my ear. "It's going to take me a little time…I mean I have to take two buses to get there…but I'm on my way."

Teller cut me mid-sentence.

"It's ok, Faith. By the time you make it to the hospital the transfer would have already been completed."

Dead silence on my end.

"Look, it's Sunday, you wouldn't be able to see him anyway. Why don't you take the day and relax. I'll pick you up first thing tomorrow morning and bring you over during visiting hours."

I suppressed the urge to protest. "Can I at least talk to him?"

"I'm afraid that goes against policy, Faith. But I will be sure to tell him that you called and you'll be up first thing in the morning."

Wordless, I clutched the receiver tight in my palm, pressing it firmly against the coil of my ear. The deep wound of letting my brother down, yet again, registered within me and I found myself feeling numb. Had it not been for my own voice echoing inside of me I don't think I would have recognized that I had been talking at all. "Can you tell him I love him?"

"Already did," Teller said genuinely smiling.

I waited for Teller's end of the dial tone. I couldn't reconcile the thought of disconnecting myself from my brother again. Caught up on a rollercoaster of nausea and disappointment I buried my face in my hand and wept in condemnation.

The day had started off as gloomy as the weather outside. The wind was gusty and a roll of thunder had already rumbled through the overcast skies. Mama use to tell us that thunder was just God moving his furniture around in heaven, but somehow, at this moment, that didn't bring me much comfort.

I curled back up on the sofa hoping to get another hour or so of sleep. I buried my head in the bend of my arm in an effort to shut out the pounding of the storm. The thundering had subsided, but the rain beat heavily against the murky silence of the barren house. After a minute or so the downpour calmed to an almost threatening and eerie drizzle. I uncovered my face to see lightning flash through the windows of the kitchen and illuminate its dimness. A sense of fear overcame me and I suddenly felt the strange presence of another person. I stood up from the couch and moved slowly towards the entranceway of the kitchen. A vague figure appeared to be sitting at the table. I heard the rustling of paper, like pages being turned. The gust of wind against the frail structure of the house stopped me short of the doorway. The sound of broken tree branches or objects of some sort tumbled across the roof. Startled, I turned back towards the living room when a strange distinct voice stopped me cold.

"Faith, girl you hear me calling you! Come in here right now before I come in after you!"

I stood rigid. The hairs on the back of my neck erect. The petrified sound of the ghostly voice filled me with panic and provoked my fear. I turned and caught sight of an unearthly figure. His face was buried into what appeared to be the Bible. I started in towards the kitchen to get a closer look, but then a sudden flash of lightning pierced through the window, struck the book and set it ablaze, revealing the stranger's identity. It seemed to be an older man dressed in a long black cloak with a hood attached. Two horns protruded out the top of his head. Chains were bound on his hands and feet, but extended far enough out to allow him to maneuver around. His face was concealed by the bow of his head. The spirit-like figure rose from the table and moved in closer. He appeared to be levitating about an inch off the ground. As he got closer he lifted his head. His face was severely scarred and burnt. His pupils were completely extracted and you could only see the whites of his eyes.

I stood paralyzed as I stretched out my hand to remove the hood of his cloak. The lightning from the storm once again lit up the night sky, casting a smoldering beam upon his ghastly face. Horrified I let out a loud stifling scream. I turned to run when Daddy's ghostly image grabbed me by the roots of my hair and flung me across the room. I tried to scrape past him on all fours, but he backhanded me across the face and I collapsed head first back onto the ground. Kneeing me in the small of my back he pinned me down and ripped off my panties.

I screamed a deathly cry as Daddy rent his robe from top to bottom.

He was a skeleton of dry bones. I clawed my fingernails into the floor until they bled. I lifted my head to see Mama standing before me holding an ax. She swung a forceful blow, decapitating Daddy and then disappearing into the night as quickly as she appeared. The revolting scene left me unable to scream. Nausea rose from the pit of my stomach and I choked on my own vomit.

"Faith, girl you open this door right this second! Faith do you hear me!?"

The loud banging jerked me from my sleep. The house was hot and humid and my clothes were soaked clear through with sweat. I rushed to the door, panting like an injured animal. Ms. Eloise was standing there, eyes as wide as a deer in headlights.

"Are you okay girl? I have been knocking for eternity."

"Yes," I said catching my breath. "I was just sleeping is all."

"My God, I thought something had happened to you. Mr. Teller called and asked me to check in on you, said you had an accident of some sort yesterday."

I gestured for her to come in. "I'm fine, Ms. Eloise, just a few minor scratches, nothing too serious," I said with irritation.

She limped in with the assistance of her wooden cane. I latched the door behind her.

"Child, you're as pale as a ghost. Looks like you've been wrestling with the devil himself."

"I'm fine," I snapped disoriented. "Um…Teller…Teller will be here soon. I'm going to see Rock today."

"That's tomorrow, dear." Ms. Eloise looked on concerned.

"Oh…right…I'm sorry. I got thrown off from the morning nap," I said in a confused tone gesturing towards the bathroom. "I'll just…I…I just need a minute." I quickly walked away.

Back in the bathroom I took a moment to gather myself. I doused my gaunt face with a palm full of cold water and stared at the reflection in the mirror, a picturesque of vacuity cloaked over a heavy body of stone, a burden that was becoming too hard to bear. Deep scars hemorrhaged my body with sins that could never be cleansed. Tainted blood coursed my veins and flowed through the blood vessels of my hollow shell. I lashed onto thoughts of never being whole, never being able to have some sense of normalcy. I pressed my hand over my mouth and choked out tears of self-pity. The pain was too great, the damage too profound. I slid down the base board of the wall into a realm of defeat.

"Faith, are you ok?" Ms. Eloise called from down the hall.

"Yes, I'm fine." I dried the tears from my face and dawdled back into the living room.

Ms. Eloise had taken the initiative to sit down. Her eyes settled in on me. I sensed she wanted to discuss what I've been avoiding for days, but I had no desire to push her into the conversation and she had no desire to give me a pass.

"This is the first time we've had a chance to speak since the hospital, Faith."

My face darkened. I don't know if it was just in that moment, but I had no interest in addressing this issue.

"Would you like to talk about it?"

I avoided a response. Christians have this belief that if they can justify their wrongdoings then all is forgiven. This conviction that as long as they repent all the hurt and pain they've caused others are just supposed to go away, as if somehow they've been set free by the confession of their tongues and the deceitfulness of their hearts.

Ms. Eloise scanned the spoiled rooms of the desolate house. Depravity rooted itself so deep into the crevices of the walls that it tapered off into the foundation of its rotten core.

"Unsettling, isn't it?"

"What?"

"The profaned feeling you get just sitting in this old house. The way it pulls you down into this relentless hole, black and unforgiving, gnawing at you until you have no other choice but to give in to its unyielding grip."

Ms. Eloise's expression went faint. "It carries a heavy weight, yes. So hefty that at times you wonder where God was in all of this. How could a God with so much mercy look down upon all of this pain and do nothing."

Coldness crept over me and the silence returned.

"No man carries his burdens alone, Faith. God is an all-knowing God. He sees our suffering. He knows what we go through. He's a vengeful God and He takes care of his own. God never said that we wouldn't have problems, but He did say that He would see us through those problems."

Resentment filled the silence. "Is that what He was doing during all this suffering, seeing us through our problems?"

"Faith, all suffering is not of God."

"God is suffering!" I screamed through the intolerance. "It's all through the Bible. Look at Abel, he brought God the best of what he had and God still allowed Cain, his own brother to kill him. He told Moses to free the Israelites and what happened, they suffered more in the desert with God than they did as slaves to Pharaoh. And what about Job, He was a righteous man, obedient to God, and yet God gave Satan free reign to inflict nothing but suffering upon him just to prove his devotion. So don't sit here and tell me that all suffering is not of God because every night in this house the word of God brought nothing but suffering, and you or your all-knowing God did nothing about it!"

Her offensive words shrank into a miniscule of nothing, dismissed in the hatred of my soul. Aversion kicked in and my insides churned into this ugly place. My stomach felt like I'd swallowed a mouthful of bitterness. Bile's of anger made its way into my throat and I gagged on its spitefulness.

Ms. Eloise sat quietly in her own reproach, trapped in a tower of guilt and shame. Praying for the right response, but knowing there was no right one to give. She had to trust God, even with this. "Faith, I know the indignities that went on in this house, the irreverent acts your father decreed in the name of God. The profaned scent circulates this house like a decomposed rat trapped in the base of the walls. Each and every room reeks of the foul smell of his semen, and no matter how much you scrub, how much you wash, you could never rid the dwelling of that horrible stench. "

Her vine of contempt stretched out across the room intertwining two branches whose tree was birth from the same hardened roots of a loathsome foundation. Underneath the surface we were no different than the other whose lives had been broken by the sins of a father. Despite our tangled web she was still this treacherous person who deceitfully shunned her grandchildren all these years, and I had no other thoughts but that.

"You can appease your heart all you'd like, Ms. Eloise. It still doesn't negate the fact that you did nothing."

"I swear, Faith. I sat on that porch many of days and nights and I swear I could hear the screams haunting me from this house! I don't know if they were the screams of my daughter calling me from the grave…I don't know…but I swear…I swear they haunt me to this day!"

The wretchedness of my spirit wouldn't allow me to embrace the sensitivity of her words, so I snapped. "Do you have any idea what it was like in this house, to have everything drained and torn out of you until you're reduced to a fragment of nothing, to have every day bring another day of torment and pain?!"

"Yes, I do!"

"No you don't! You allowed it to happen! You knew what he was doing and you kept him around, you let him back in!"

"Don't judge me, Faith! I did what I could to keep you and your brother near! I did all I could to keep you safe!"

"You were never there!"

"And for that I am ashamed!"

Something immediately snatched me back to the realization that it was Ms. Eloise in front of me. She had somehow in the midst of my outburst taken on the image of Mama. My words threw me into a moment of consciousness. Panic overcame me and I was forced to face certainties that I never wanted to face, but somehow, deep down, I knew. The dull ache of betrayal cramped my stomach and my veins pulsed with fear. It felt as though my entire body had literally shut down. Ms. Eloise held a stare that warranted resolution, but I just couldn't do it. I just didn't have the strength. Feelings I suppressed for so many years ripped at my soul and tore me apart. The thought of knowing Mama was aware of the personal hell me and Rock endured crippled me. I was a mess of trouble and grief. Resentment pierced me from every angle and I just wanted to be left alone.

Ms. Eloise looked at me with such familiarity. Maybe I was a symbol of Mama, a wound of self-punishment, a cryptic memory of who she once was, I don't know, but whatever it was it left her afflicted. She rose to her feet, burdened, and limped quietly to the door. The storm was beginning to pick up outside. A loud boisterous thunder cracked the sky. We kept quiet for several moments and then Ms. Eloise turned with conviction, her face laden and strained.

"There is no reparation possible for the sins that were bestowed upon you and your brother, but I swear I will spend the rest of my tomorrows mending my wrong, right."

I was all out of fight so I sat silently with my eyes fixed on everything but Ms. Eloise, my conscious bearing no thought of her remorseful words. I stared into the cold dead air. My hardcore demeanor was just enough to threaten her into a moment of contriteness before she turned and walked out into the malevolent storm.

JULY 9, 2008

MONDAY MORNING

The visitor's room felt much colder today. The chill of the air spawned like a web, the floor bit of hoarfrost beneath my feet, the world around me sluggish and reserved. Perhaps it was just stress, but pain radiated up my neck to my temple area causing a debilitation that left me unable to move my head. I massaged the back of my neck with my right hand, but still no relief. I took notice of the guard in the corner who appeared to be studying me hard and openly, his face an expression of stone, concrete as the walls around us, a visage so deep it appeared to give homage to his own personal incarceration.

I don't know how long I waited for Rock, but it felt like hours. Suddenly I heard the turn of a key and I swung my body around to see my brother and Teller come through the large vaulted door, my neck still blistering with pain. Warmth ricocheted through my veins and I rushed over to embrace him like a lioness protecting her cub. I examined the bandages around his wrists, and then his face, his eyes a domicile of fatigue and restlessness. I rubbed my hand across his cheek.

"Rock, are you okay?"

"I'm good. I spent the night in the infirmary. They took good care of me, sis." His response cast a bitter light upon my weaker than thou sisterly role.

I gave a faint smile. In some odd way I couldn't help but to think that that was an indirect jab to my ego. Rock had suffered a rough night and had gone through the majority of it alone, so rather than jump on the defense I graciously humbled myself and tried to focus on the situation at hand.

Teller tapped away on his cell phone. The clicking seemed to circulate around the stillness. Messages were coming in quicker than Teller was putting them out. I've never seen anyone's fingers move so fast. He gestured in the direction of the small table, Rock and I grabbed a seat and waited patiently for the clicking to stop. Teller gave eye contact, speaking direct and to the point.

"The judge will be meeting with the jurors today. If a verdict has not been reached we're looking at a hung jury. If so, we will be faced with a new trial and that can definitely be cause for concern. As I stated to your sister before, Rock, this case was hard enough to try first time around. A second run at this will be detrimental for both of us."

"Detrimental for us or detrimental for you?" a questionable look seized Rock's face.

Teller leaned forward. "We are chasing a ghost, son, can you understand that? This entire case has been based around a spirit, an apparition that may or may not exist…"

"That does exist," Rock quickly interrupted.

"According to who, a 17-year-old boy who's been abused all his life? A friend who gave you a gun for self-defense? Neighbors who, despite windows being open, never heard screams? Or how about a sister who was lying right there, but still can't back up your story?"

"What about a God who's all-knowing, a Protector who came to our aid when no one else would?" Rock heaved a heavy sigh against the dense silence. "I know this is a hard thing to reconcile with, Mr. Teller, and I understand your skepticism. Who wouldn't be in this case? But I also know there's nothing too hard for my God, and at the right time when He sees fit He will show His glory. That's what He does, that's who He is."

"I have done all that I can do. Do you understand that, Rock? I have covered all avenues, researched every book from biblical to paranormal. I have visited every psychic, spiritualist, mystical and supernatural advisor I could think of. I have spoken to every teacher, friend and church member who knows of you or anything about you. There is nothing left for me to do. No one else I can talk to. A second trial cannot be won."

"Says who, man's report? I don't live by man's report I live by

God's, and if God's report says I am a victor and not a victim then that's what I am. That's what's gotten me through this trial and that's what's gonna bring me out, not you, not the jury, not the judge, but God and God alone."

Teller's eyes bucked as he pondered Rock's comments for a moment. It wasn't that he wanted to take credit away from God, but he was the one in that courtroom every day fighting for my brother's life and in some selfish way he needed Rock to acknowledge that.

"Son, I applaud your faith, I do, and at this point that may be the only thing that's going to get you exonerated, but if we do not get an acquittal this time around the Almighty Master would have to try this case himself if you were to have any chance in hell at winning a second trial. That is not a prediction. That is not an educated guess. That is a statement of fact."

"It's an opinion of law."

"It *is* the law."

"Based on what, a system of principles and legalities concocted by man to set people like me up for failure?"

"That's daddy talking," I intervened.

"No, based on a system that has allowed Prosecution to build its case against you around circumstantial evidence, and circumstantial evidence can build just as strong a case as direct evidence, which can lead to a guilty conviction most of the time." Teller understood Rock's precociousness, but he also needed Rock to understand that he was still a kid who was facing maximum term of life in prison, and as mature as he thought he was he was in no way prepared for that.

Rock stared at Teller for a moment, his mind trying to come to terms with the weight of it all. Fear had begun to creep in and in some way he felt it had inadvertently made its way into Teller too.

"So what do you want me to do, Mr. Teller? Give up? Let the devil win? What if there's a hung jury, what then?"

"He's gonna give up on us just like everybody else that's what," I quickly interrupted. Don't you get it, Rock? That's what he's saying. If the jury can't come to a unanimous decision he's gonna quit the case, the court will appoint us some stank attorney who's gonna do some half-ass job and you'll be thrown into jail anyway. When will you understand? We'll never be a part of something good, just wasn't meant to be." I was agitated so I stood up to gather myself, but it really didn't help the matter at all. I was feeling as though Teller was looking for an out and that out was a hung jury. Betrayal once again gripped me and Teller became just another notch in the belt of our deceitful lives.

"We're still in God's holy plan, Faith." Rock's response was as naive as his belief that God was going to bring him a not guilty verdict, me, I wasn't as simple-minded. Although this hung jury thing was gonna send Teller packing he had truly done a wonderful job in closing arguments, so if anyone was gonna get him acquitted it was going to be Teller, not God.

The mood in the room quickly shifted. I thought I was going to break down at that very moment. My spirit had been so weakened by all of the disappointment in my life I had become immune to any sense of hope. No matter what happened to me and Rock there was one thing we could certainly be sure of and that was being let down by anyone who had ever had the displeasure of having any type of emotional connection to us.

I turned my back to the both of them. I needed a breather. This God thing was a heavy load to carry. Besides, my neck still ached and my body felt exhausted from the weight of it all.

"Faith, why can't you see that God's grace, His mercy will see us through this?" Devotion stained Rock's face.

I swung around. Not him too. I had enough to deal with without another one of Ms. Eloise's God-will-see-you-through speeches. I took in a peeved breath. "Rock your faithfulness to God is beyond measure. I don't know if it's because you believe that nobody could experience such vast amount of pain without at least a diminutive of good coming out of it, or you just need that small ray of hope. Whatever it is you hold on to that, you've earned it, but if you're looking for God to suddenly become this savior and rescue you from all this torment you're sadly forsaking yourself. You know as well as I do that God ain't never saved me or you from nothing, so why would He start now." I knew my words would somehow leave Rock's heart scarred, but I needed him to face the truth.

"Faith, I don't think this is the right time to discuss your displeasure with God," Teller mediated.

"Well when do you suggest would be the right time? When they impose sentence upon him? In the middle of the courtroom after he's found guilty? Or maybe after you've dropped him as a client seeing that you've already admitted you can't win this case anyhow."

"I didn't say that, Faith," Teller's tone verged on offensive.

"But you did imply it?" I tensed up. "You think you're doing us a favor by fighting for our freedom every day in that courtroom? We've been fighting for our freedom since birth. The injustice that my brother and I have suffered stems far beyond that courtroom. The disfavor God has shown us would never be seen by Man because Man is too busy going about their own lives to see the inequity in ours!"

Rock rose into a disheartened rant. "Faith, why must you always vex my spirit?!" The heaviness of his tone pounded into the bitterness of my words and left me breathless. His face blackened with disappointment, and for the first time I regretted my indignation. "Everything we've endured, all the pain, the beatings, the scars, I've been there for you, supported you, comforted you, even when I didn't have the strength I managed to sustain you, but now in my moment of need you've tried me, convicted me and thrown away the key!" Rock's cheeks stung with tears.

I fell silent and still, the thought that I would trouble Rock's spirit troubled mine as well. I stood in the selfishness of my own reasoning, spinning out of control, unconsciously taking my brother with me. My cynicism had violated my loyalty in such a way that in that moment…that brief moment, I was ashamed. How could I be there for Rock when I couldn't see past myself? The idea that he would misunderstand my intentions for anything other than love shook me to my core and left me with a deep sense of regret. I wanted to say something to ease his mind, to lessen the strain of the moment. I walked over and gently rested my forehead against his, cupping his face in my hands.

"I'm so sorry Rock…," I paused, "my only sin is protecting you and I've somehow managed to screw that up."

His hands lifted to mine. "Faith I know amidst all this pain you still bear scars, so do I, but it's God's job to protect, not ours."

I raised my head and drew back. His response threatened my words and once again the situation became tangled. "When has God ever done His job, Rock? When have we *ever* received His protection? His unmerited favor has never been sufficient enough to show us any type of mercy. " I retorted

"He saved us from Dad, Faith, isn't that enough?"

"You're in jail for killing him, Rock! How is that being saved?!"

"Why must you continue to cast judgment, Faith? I'm standing here in front of you, He spared my life. Can't you find some solace in that?" His maimed voice grew.

"If God was so intent on sparing your life why would He save it just so you can rot in this hell hole?!"

"This is man's doing, not God's!"

"God has a say in everything!" I screamed in opposition. "Isn't that what Christian's say?! One moment it's God's will then it's free will, next the devil's busy then God takes us through! Which is it, Rock?!"

"It's God's grace being sufficient enough for us to trust Him!"

"God's grace is as contradictive as His word!" Defiance expanded in my chest and clinched my heart like a vice. "He tells us to pray and when we do He never answers! He tells us to wait and when we wait He never comes! He tells us to ask and when we ask He never gives, and then Christians hypocritically rationalize all this psycho-babble with, God has a bigger plan or He knows what's best for us!" Rebellion hyperventilated within me.

"He does know what's best for us, Faith. I didn't kill Daddy! God's mercy will prove that!"

"God has never shown us any mercy, Rock!" My screams echoed through the emptiness of the room. A quiver shuttered through the marrow of my bones. Concern brought Teller to his feet and the guard stood watchfully by.

"I am a product of depraved immorality, conceived by the insemination of my own grandfather, for that God has shown me nothing but contempt!" The vile act sickened me as I choked down the shameful thought of Mister and Daddy's semen flowing through my body. "I was created out of the abomination of sin. The offense of my perverted conception has turned God away from me! I am nothing but a disappointment to Him! How can He show mercy to a person He never created?!" I bent over in pain, my stomach cramped from crying, barely able to speak over my own agonizing sobs.

"We're all God's creation, Faith, made in His own image. None of us are perfect and all of us must answer to our own misdeeds. You can't hold yourself accountable for Mister and Daddy's iniquities. It's not your fault, you're not to blame." Rock reached out to embrace me, but I recoiled.

"My God, why has thou forsaken me!" The thought of being conceived by such vulgarity rose from deep within me and erupted into a volcano of disgrace and humiliation. "Isn't that what Jesus cried out on the cross?! Isn't that what he asked?!" There was so much dishonor festering inside of me I was inebriated with shame.

Rock pleaded his case. "God never abandoned Jesus, Faith. He briefly looked away. The purity of God would not allow Him to look upon all that sin that Jesus bore for us, He had to turn away, but He turned back, and when He did we had everlasting life, a life that you have yet to embrace."

Sobs extracted from my burning throat as broken words formed between cries. "He separated Himself from His *only* son because of sin! I am an anatomy of sin, who am I to deserve any mercy?!"

He reached out for me again, but I rejected his embrace. "Please, Faith, I pray for your misguided heart. God has not deserted us. We don't serve that kind of God."

I was unglued, an emotional wreck. The flood of tears blurred my vision, I moved my attention away from Rock and around the chilled concrete walls, the guard's eyes caught mine and I could have sworn there was a brief look of repulse, a distaste that stared back at me like I was some contagious virus. His less than enthused glare caused me to focus my attention back to Rock, but I could still feel his sickening gaze piercing through me like a laser. I shut my eyes in despair as tears fell from my closed lids. Thoughts of Daddy's mean and hurtful words soared within me and I started to believe that every cruel thing he had ever said to me was truth. Remnants of deep hurt and pain ran through my mind. I locked my eyes tight, forcing flashes of lights to replace distressed memories behind closed lids.

"Faith this has got to stop. You're not the only one suffering. Mama suffered. I'm suffering. Ms. Eloise is at home right now battling with her indiscretions. Far be it for us to say she's hurting any less than we are. She feels like she owes us the very air she breathes, but yet nothing she does will ever erase the pain of Mister raping her only daughter. Don't you think she's suffering just as much as you? Don't you think her afflictions are just as much to bear as ours?" Rock's voice was thick with emotion and defense.

"She did nothing!" I screeched through burnt red eyes.

"She stuck around, Faith. She never left us, she never left Mama. She protected us with everything she had, you have to believe that." His voice calmed. "Yes, we've endured a lot, Faith, but we survived, we're still here."

"This is not surviving, Rock, this is existing!"

"Well I'm doing the best I can with what I got. Just like Mama, just like Ms. Eloise." His agitation settled in on me, his calmed tone now harsh.

"She sat on that porch day in and day out and watched us rot in that sickening hell-hole and did nothing, nothing but rock back and forth in that old rocking chair of hers as Daddy had his way with us. She was no better than Mama! How can you forgive that?"

"My God, Faith, what in the name of all that's holy do you *want*? Why must your bitterness come with such a high price?" Rock's voice was laced with frustration. "As hard as it may be for you to believe, Ms. Eloise and Mama protected us the only way they knew how and that was to stay as close to us as they could to keep Daddy away as much as possible. For you to insinuate that they in some way abandoned us intentionally is far worse than any wrong Daddy has ever done us."

"They were never there, Rock. No matter how much you try to convince yourself otherwise, they weren't. Not then and not now." My voice tightened as I wiped the tears from my depleted face.

Rock gave a keen stare. "God would never leave us vulnerable, Faith. Even in the middle of Daddy's vileness, God was up to something. He kept Mom and Ms. Eloise there, guardian angels sent by Him to shield and protect us from Daddy's evil approach. Why is it so hard for you to believe that?" His eyes remained locked on mine. I stared back in distaste. "*God is faithful in His protection; 'For He shall give His angels charge over thee, to keep thee in all thy ways,'* Psalms 91. That's where I find my comfort. It's where I find my peace. You're gonna have to figure out some way to find yours."

Teller left me and Rock to our own recourse. He appeared miles away from the visitor's lounge, quiet, preoccupied in his own thoughts, as if something was troubling his mind.

My heart pounded like a jackhammer. I was a mess of nerves.

Rock's idea that I was my own worst enemy, the engineer of my own self-destruction left me painstakingly strained. I had done all I could to forgive…all I could to move forward, but I couldn't…I couldn't just pick up the pieces and move on as if nothing happened. Not without knowing that the two people I despised most would always be disgustingly a part of me. Not without being appalled by who I truly was. How was I supposed to find peace when I was at constant war with myself? Daddy and Mister were both dead and each of them and their own repulsive way dwelled inside of me. How was I supposed to find solace in that?"

Rock pushed his hands deep into the pockets of his oversized jumpsuit. Drawing in a deep breath, he filled the silence. "Faith, I get it. I understand. Nothing in our lives have come without complexities, everything about us is complicated, emotionally draining, but you can't let Daddy's iniquities continue to course your veins and harden your heart? Daddy can't control us anymore, sis, he's dead, and every sin and every wrong he ever done us died with him." His voice was filled with self-assurance.

No longer wanting to drive a wedge between me and my brother I stood mute. The morning had gotten off to a rough start and had proven to be a jaded and torn day. It was evident that God and I hadn't been on good terms for a while now so I saw no point in dragging out the whole spiritual thing any longer than it needed to be. Instead, I pulled in close to Rock and buried my head gently into his chest. His soft hand ran up and down the nape of my neck, consoling my intolerant spirit. A sweet calmness seized my body. I nestled into the warmth of his embrace and for a moment's time, quieted the storm that raged so deeply within me.

I wasn't sure what was going on in Teller's mind, but he remained oddly still as though something had disturbed his spirit. Somewhere between the screaming and yelling deep remnants of past conversations with Ms. Eloise seemed to reconcile his thoughts. Revelations of Rock's testimony and visions of Mama's ghost paralyzed him in his seat.

Obscure voices and faces of witnesses discharged themselves and ate away at him like a cancer, each bringing more revelations than the one before. Haunting images of shadows and apparitions pummeled the air. Sounds of gun shots pierced his ears and tapered off into the echo of a child's scream, first low and faint, then loud and agonizing. The disturbing figures moved about as if being beckoned by the vociferous cries. Another gunshot, this time illuminating the dismal room, images of pained faces appeared, first Daddy's, then Rock's. Teller noticed the cold hard steel at his feet. He knelt to retrieve the gun. A disturbing figure caught his eyes and he found himself confronted with Mama's ghost, a look of protection marked her face. The stark image knocked him abruptly to the floor and he crawled backwards against the wall. She remained deathly still, her position stooped. She cased him with vengeful eyes. A flash of light cut through the room and the ghostly figure quickly altered to Ms. Eloise. Her wrinkled face carved of retribution and despair, an eerie smirk of vindication chiseled her lips. She picked up the gun and gripped it firmly in her feeble hand, her apparition now erect, levitated off the floor. She turned towards Teller, pointed the gun in his direction, and fired. Alarmed, he pulled himself to his feet, the wall supporting his stance. A terrifying fear took hold of his body and he stretched his hands outward, quickly averting his head. His heart pounded viciously in his throat. Everything shifted to slow motion, the dawdled bullet aimed straight for his chest. He steeled himself before impact, heeding the moment Rock swore witness to.

"*It is a fearful thing to fall into the hands of the living God*!" Ms. Eloise howled.

The contact of the bullet pierced Teller's chest. He could feel the hot steel burning through his body. The ghostly figure rushed in. Her cold spirit passed through him like a bolt. The hairs on his neck stood erect. He clenched his chest and fell to his knees. Daddy's Bible appeared before him, one single bullet pierced its cover. He felt a hard tug, his hand grudgingly reached for the Bible, but something broke its grip.

Bound papers tore from the binding and swarmed the air of the room. A strange presence pulled Teller to his feet.

"Absalom!" A deep piercing voice rose above the turmoil. Teller quickly turned behind him, but saw nothing.

"Absalom, do you seek my life?!" The voice reverberated off the walls into the darkness. Petrified, Teller turned again, but saw no one. A loud shot rang out. A thunder of light flared the room. A sharp pain blazed his torso. The wetness beneath his feet caused him to look down. He was bleeding. His hand gripped the Bible now pressed tightly against his chest. His white robe, dripping with the stench of fresh blood, bled down to his bare feet. Trepidation took hold and he stumbled backwards into the life-sized mirror housed between the corroded staircase and dry rot floor. He turned quickly to catch a glimpse of himself, his reflection, that of Daddy's blood-stained frame, but before he could give wake to his panic the beeping of his phone roused him back to the visitor's lounge. Discombobulated, his heart raced to catch up with his breath. Beads of sweat broke out across his forehead and his eyes strained to make sense of where he was, vaguely taking note of Rock's and my confounded scrutiny. He somehow gathered himself and glanced anxiously down at his phone held taut in the sweats of his palmed hand.

"THE JURY HAS REACHED A VERDICT." The words came across like a defibrillator, pumping life back into Teller's body, driving a rush of adrenaline through his veins. He raised his head, still halfway between his thoughts and reality. "The verdict is in."

Teller's mention split the air, causing Rock's jaw to tighten. The unsettled look on his face was evident of fear, but suppressed itself through the senseless faith of God's devotion.

My entire body grew heavy. Every muscle ached with the possibility that my brother would be taken away from me. A rush of heat crawled down my neck and spread clear through to the middle of my chest. I reassured myself it was stress and not a heart attack from the mingled feelings of uncertainty over Rock's final judgment. I stood in place, unmoved. My feet buried in quicksand, gradually sinking in despair.

"The jury will convene in the courtroom in one hour. Get my client to the courthouse and I'll meet you there." Teller addressed the guard and bolted across the floor towards the exit, the bottom of his shoes rebelling against the hard cold floor.

Rock was handcuffed and led out of the room to the holding cell. His head turned and his gaze caught mine. Although I couldn't judge what was in his heart, his eyes held the stare of a frightened child, a fear that can only be felt when one is confronted with his own ultimate fate. I rummaged for the words, but fell silent. I could no longer will myself to move. I tore my eyes away and remained frozen in stance as warm tears fell from beneath my closed lids.

"*Be still and know that I am God*, Faith! *Be still and know that I am God*!" Rock blurted out the words as he glanced over his shoulder one last time before sentencing, his voice echoing in the distance.

I crossed my arms tightly across my chest, lowered my head, and submerged myself in immeasurable woe, offering no rebuttal to his declaration.

45 MINUTES BEFORE VERDICT ANNOUNCEMENT

Teller turned the car's air conditioner on full blast. The afternoon sun was at its highest peak making the temperature in the car hotter than the heat outside. Anxious and with less than an hour til verdict, he rushed over to Ms. Eloise's house. He had exhausted every avenue possible to prove Rock's innocence and now he would try one last attempt to exonerate him completely. Brief flashbacks of what transpired that night played out in his mind. He felt the sweat of his palms grip the steering wheel as he tried to reconcile the events in question that night. Despite the chaos that was going on in his head he would remain rational. If he could get Ms. Eloise to confess before the ruling, Rock could be set free and released of all charges. His revelations did nothing to alleviate his concerns. After all Ms. Eloise was an elderly woman who would spend the rest of her short years in prison, and Rock, Rock would once again have to bear the ruins of deceit. After all the pain he and Faith had suffered this would prove to be a dreadful outcome either way. He took a sharp right turn and sucked in a deep breath. The warmth of the sun burned even more so and the pits of his arms began to sweat. With the air conditioner blowing on full speed and no relief from the glare, he pulled down the visor to block the blistering rays of the sun. The visions in his head came back quick and strong, exposing dark secrets of a tragic situation that could once again leave a family torn. He pulled up in front of Ms. Eloise's house and shut down the engine. Leaving the keys in the ignition he rushed up the broken stairs.

"Ms. Eloise! Ms. Eloise! May I speak to you a moment?!" he yelled banging on the unhinged door.

"Ms. Eloise, please, it's Mr. Teller! May I have a moment of your time, Ma'am?"

He noticed the door was slightly ajar. He reluctantly pushed it open and walked in. Immediately inside the doorway he could smell an unpleasant and disheartened scent. He walked cautiously into the dimly lit house taking care not to disturb anything that may be used as evidence. The room was scorching hot. The small fan rattling in the window did little to cool the temperature inside.

"Ms. Eloise?" he whispered, "Are you alright?"

A beam of sunlight peeped through the cracked blinds and revealed a small figure sitting quietly in a rocking chair. Her backside faced Teller, but he could see the top of her head ascending a few inches over the chair. Her gaunt hands clenched the ends of the armrests and a blanket appeared to be draped over her legs. Condensation had settled on a glass of ice cold lemonade that was now warm and watered down, atop two milk crates next to the chair.

"Ms. Eloise?" Teller had moved in close enough to see the elderly woman's head tilted slightly upward, her body rigid. A knot pressed his throat, his words choked on a low painful sob. He gradually lowered himself to one knee and buried his face in the sorrow of his hand. Ms. Eloise was colorless, her lips were blue and her eyes were wide open. She looked so thin. Her frail body leaned lifeless against the back of the chair. He gently clenched her wrist to check for a pulse, nothing. No heartbeat, no breath. He couldn't determine how long she had sat there, but her body was ice cold. He pressed his hand tightly across his closed eyes and wept silently in the quietness of the room. A wave of emotions washed over him and he found himself for the first time questioning God. Each question coiled with anger and reproach. How could God allow such a thing? He had been a good and faithful servant and yet he hit a brick wall at every turn. He was carrying the weight of Rock's fate on his shoulders and his questions were only met with the stillness of the room.

Lifting his head, he caught one last gaze of Ms. Eloise's cold state. He rubbed his hands gently across her cheeks before closing her eyes with the tips of his fingers. Teller reached inside his coat jacket and pulled out his cell phone. Amid the haze of tears he willed himself to dial the numbers that would regrettably leave him once again fighting for his client's innocence; yet, free Ms. Eloise from the burdens of a world that seemed to offer her nothing but suffering.

A voice on the other end answered. "9-1-1, what's your emergency?"

Each word pulled like a noose around Teller's throat, tightening his airways, suffocating him as he spoke. "Yes, ma'am," his voice low and somber, "could you please send an ambulance to 555 E. Randolph?" He pulled himself up off the floor and stood erect. "There's someone here who's unresponsive." He pushed the end button on the phone and stared benevolently at Ms. Eloise.

Through the dark haze of death a light seems to shine that brings about tranquility and freedom that could not be received by any other means but one's own demise. It cleanses the soul of the deceased and washes away all that was wrong and somehow makes it right. The rhythmic sound of a beating heart, the warmth of the human body, all quieted by the inevitable route that we all must take to reach our destiny of immeasurable joy that only death, through all its hurt and pain, can bring us.

Leaning at the waist, he graciously kissed Ms. Eloise on the forehead. "*We know that all things work together for the good of them that love God, and to them who are called according to His purpose*." He offered up a silent prayer and kissed the top of her head one last time before walking out and leaving her to finally rest in peace.

THE COURTHOUSE

VERDICT WATCH

Teller arrived to the courthouse dismayed. It was a frenzy of reporters and spectators screaming and yelling, some demanding justice for the victim, others vindication for Rock. The media bombarded his vehicle. Camera's flashing, microphones shoved in his face, reporters yelling over one another desperately trying to get a statement. Sheriffs pushed their way through the mob in an effort to get Teller safely into the building. He shunned off questions with a quick gesture of the hand and moved swiftly into the courthouse. He charged into the room with great strides and took his seat next to Rock. His heart pounded hard in his chest. Despite his emotional strain, he reached out and cradled Rock's shoulder, giving him a slight nod and curt smile. Rock seemed relieved by Teller's arrival, but his tardiness sparked concern.

Crowds swarmed the courtroom, many lined up against the wall to take part in the trial of the century…at least that's what the media headlined it. I glanced around the room. Everyone appeared to be in their elected areas. Spectators conversed with one another while reporters periodically referred to their note pads. Joy focused her attention on Judge Hallow who appeared to be very annoyed.

"Would Counsels approach the bench?"

A hush fell over the courtroom. Stark eyes focused on Teller and Joy as they adhered to the request. Teller a bit winded.

"Nice of you to join us, Mr. Teller," Judge Hallow peered from underneath his glasses.

"My apologies, Your Honor," Teller stood in respect.

"Were you aware that all Counsels on this case were supposed to be in my courtroom thirty minutes prior to verdict, or were there other matters more important you needed to tend to?"

Joy stood mute, her arms folded across her chest waiting for Teller's response.

"I'm sorry for my tardiness, Your Honor. I had an emergency that needed my immediate attention," Teller pressed hard against the sorrow choking in his throat.

Judge Hallow, although displeased, responded in a tone that seemed to empathize with the distress in Teller's voice, "Very well, Counselor, you may be seated."

He and Joy returned to their seats and settled in for the verdict.

My mind was frayed. I was a ball of nerves which made it almost impossible to sit still. I focused my attention once again around the room. Everyone looked so stern, so cold. I fought the impulse to run. Where? I wasn't sure. I just knew I needed to get out of that courtroom. I felt like I was suffocating, like there wasn't enough air to fill my lungs. I took in short deep breaths, forcing myself to breathe. My lungs felt restricted. Unable to get the necessary oxygen needed to exhale. I felt lightheaded, dizzy. A choking sensation overcame me and I struggled to clear my airways. Hotness rose through my chest and I belched warm bile that I grossly managed to force back down. My body ached all over. My face felt flushed and heat radiated from my body like steam rising off hot asphalt.

I shifted my attention to Rock who seemed to be consumed with his own thoughts. I caught his peripheral vision and he turned just enough to give me a faint smile which made me more anxious than ever. I took in a hard breath and released. I was literally unraveling at the seams. I fanned my hands in a desperate attempt to relieve myself from the steam of heat exuding from my body. I felt like I was sitting in the middle of a sauna. Maybe if I redirected my thoughts I'd find some relief, so I turned my focus to Joy, who appeared to have the confidence of a lion. Her self-assured demeanor only added to my anxiety and my body temperature rose to astronomical heights. The only answer was to remove myself from all the stressful elements surrounding me, and I intended to do just that. I stood for the exit.

"Bailiff, will you please escort the jury in."

I froze in my stance. Judge Hallow's words broke through the heat and a cold sweat lined my body.

Everyone stood in sync. Quietness fell, and vigilant eyes shifted in the direction of the jurors. They invaded the courtroom like an army marching to war. Their focus never wavered, each one expressed domination in their own right. Obedient and compliant to the rules of the court they seated themselves in an orderly manner.

Judge Hallow waited for each one to take their perspective places before addressing the courtroom. "Ladies and gentlemen you may be seated."

For a moment I felt out-of-body. My knees wouldn't bend. I knew once I sat down Rock's fate would be sealed. So I stood, desperately trying to stop time. If I refused to sit I would somehow delay the inevitable. The verdict couldn't be read and Rock would sit up front, a free man…for as long as I stood…but only if I didn't sit down, so I fought the impulse to sit. A flush of tears filled my eyes. My vision distorted. Everyone gazed at me with confused stares, but they didn't know. How could they? They were not about to lose the only person they had in their life. They couldn't possibly know how that felt…so I stood, paused in the moment of my brother's freedom. I would never sit, I just couldn't.

Judge Hallow gestured for the bailiff to address the issue, but Teller raised his hand in protest. The judge gave a nod of permission and Teller approached the fragile situation. He never said a word. His empathetic look and understanding smile spoke all the things my heart felt. He took hold of my hand and his warm spirit filtered my soul. My lips quivered as I tried to hold back the tears that poured uncontrollably down my face. We stood for a moment, gazing back at one another, never whispering a word. Our hearts connected and I felt that Teller, in his own strange and revealing way, understood my pain, that maybe he himself had suffered the same grief. Those thoughts had somehow calmed my fears and the compassion of his being slowly descended me back into my seat.

Teller gave a reprieved smile and returned back to his rightful position next to Rock and the proceedings began.

"Ladies and gentlemen of the jury, I would like to take this time to thank each and every one of you for your diligent service to this court. I understand that this was a long and grueling process and not an easy one at best. It took you twenty-eight exhausting days to reach your ruling, which confirmed to me, and all involved in this case, that your decision was not taken lightly, that it was thorough, complete and carefully thought out. This court also recognizes that you have been sequestered through the duration of these proceedings and are anxious to return to your family and homes. I will do my best to get you back as quickly as possible." Judge Hallow kept his poise and remained attentive to the jurors.

"At this time the court would like to take a moment to address two issues. First, was this a unanimous verdict amongst each and every one of you? Please respond to this court by stating, 'yes or no.'"

The jury orchestrated a harmonious, "Yes".

"Second, was this final verdict reached under any duress or coercion by any inside or outside influences? Please respond to this court by stating, 'yes or no.'"

The jury once again synchronized, "No."

"Thank you. Bailiff would you please hand me the verdict?"

My heart ceased to beat. The entire room appeared to stop breathing.

Judge Hallow opened the piece of paper. His face showed no expression. He turned to Rock and Teller. "Would the Defendant please rise?"

Teller clamped a hand around the back of Rock's neck and gave a tight squeeze as they stood to their feet. Rock's position was solemn. It had been a trying journey and he was weary and exhausted. Teller's role had been completed and it was God's will from this point. A will Rock was all too ready to accept.

Judge Hallow shifted his attention back to the jury. A tall slender man stood up. Clean shaven and well dressed. He clasped his hands firmly in front of him and centered his attention on Judge Hallow, who, himself, did not waver.

"What say you in the matter of State vs. Mr. Rock?"

I braced myself for what was to come.

"We the jury find the Defendant…"

There was silence and then the words rushed in like a tsunami.

"**NOT GUILTY.**"

Pandemonium engulfed the courtroom. A tidal wave of emotions pursued. People hurried outside to announce the news, reporters flicked on cameras to be the first to broadcast the verdict. Mothers, who had in their own way adopted Rock as their own, cheered in relief. Screams of disappointment and joy resonated from outside. Hordes of people crowded the courthouse steps to protest their views. Religious folks voiced their disapproval while the opposition retaliated.

Mayhem was just as flared inside the courtroom as out. Strobes of light discharged the room like electric volts. Photographers stumbled over one another trying to capture the emotional moment. Rock's breath labored, his face held an incredulous stare, his pulse a mess of rapid beats. He tried desperately to slow his insides down, but everything within him was moving so fast. He could feel himself screaming, but no sound was coming out, only slow and shallow breathing. The fear of spending the rest of his life in prison collided with the overwhelming realization of freedom, and he collapsed relieved into Teller's arms, locking him into a weighted embrace. Teller squeezed tighter. The thought of a different outcome flowed straight to the crux of Rock's heart and released itself into an emancipation of tears.

Teller, locked in his own reservations, quietly repented for his own measure of misgivings. He had faltered one time or another and at some point questioned God's approach, but he was of contrite spirit and his remorseful soul quickly brought him back to a place of compliance and submission where God remained in control. We all fall short of the glory of God, and that was a passage Teller, himself, knew all-too-well.

Joy interrupted the humble moment with a firm hand shake that seemed to warrant a truce. Teller slowly released Rock's grip and turned to greet an endorsing smile.

"Congratulations, Counselor, you put up a helluva fight." Joy's commendation seemed to break down barriers that erected between she and Teller over the course of the trial. The code of ethics had been restored and once again Teller was seen as a respected Counsel in the eyes of Prosecution. "If I was ever going to lose a case I'm sure as hell glad it was this one…off the record that is." Her unexpected accolades jarred Teller into a humble state. He offered the only thing he could at that moment, a charitable handshake and reciprocating smile.

"Thank you, Counselor."

He stood in Joy's good graces for a moment's time before she freed his hand and made way of her business. She left with a celebratory demeanor that appeared to support the victorious outcome of Rock's innocence, despite her travailed efforts to prove otherwise.

From behind the tall chestnut bench, Judge Hallow cut a watchful eye. The expression on his face was of highest regard. An unprecedented smile spread out into a wide blissful grin that lasted long enough to indulge Teller in a congratulatory still. He had never felt such gratification than at that moment. It was short-lived, but one he would relish a lifetime. With nothing more to say Judge Hallow stood, banged his gavel, and exited the courtroom. He had given Teller exactly what he needed without saying a word, reverence in its fullest form.

I stood in the shackles of my own disgrace. I thought about my dearth of compassion, my malicious intents, the uncertainty of my brother's innocence, every emotion within me welled-up and I ran. I fought my way through the crowd and rushed to my brother's side.

Standing was almost impossible, so I fell to my knees. Hugging him tightly around his waist I buried my head into his abdomen. Warm tears streamed down my face and I couldn't bring myself to let him go. I felt the grip of his tender fingers caressing the back of my head, a feeling that will never again be broken or threatened. I searched for my words but they were lost in a voiceless pit of emotions, caught in the maw of unspeakable relief. Rock and I had lived with anguish all of our lives, so much that I had lost all hope for a better life. Our fate had been sealed and I no longer had the energy to wage war against a battle that had already been lost. Where affliction is a constant presence, a casualty of your existence, you lose your will to fight. You wait in expectancy for the next misfortune. If you wait long enough it eventually comes, but this time it didn't. Hardship was replaced with consolation and I didn't know how to receive it, so I desperately held on to it. Cradling it with the claws of fear, fear of losing it, fear of it dying like everything else in our lives. I felt its breath, its vivacity. It was as much alive as I was and I refused to let it go. The relentless tears flowed, not tears of sadness, but finally tears of joy, a stream of countless years of hurt cleansed by two words, "Not Guilty." Not guilty of Daddy's vile acts, not guilty of Mister's incest, not guilty of Ms. Eloise's abandonment, not guilty of Mama's injudicious love. We were finally found innocent, a word that carved its way into my soul and flowed down into a waterfall of emancipated tears.

Through haze covered eyes I noticed two figures standing in the back of the courtroom near the entranceway. I squinted to clear my blurred vision. The figures were of Mama and Ms. Eloise, standing together, smiling. Mama's hands clasped tightly against her lips, while Ms. Eloise's wrinkled face adorned an expression of peacefulness, unlike the weariness it displayed in life. Radiating like angels they wore the reverent smiles of justice, standing in admiration that the righteousness of God had prevailed. I stretched forth my hand to touch her, but Mama, in all her splendor, did not reach back, instead she gave one last heartwarming smile before she and Ms. Eloise slowly turned and ascended into a sparkling gleaming light that could only be described as a kaleidoscope of beauty and tranquility.

"Don't go Mama," I whispered under the quietness of my breath, "please don't go."

Rock eased himself down to one knee and offered a kiss of solace on the top of my head, a warmth that shielded my body and seeped through to the core of my soul. Greeting him with a tight embrace I leaned in to the comfort of his chest. The rhythmic sound of his heartbeat reminded me of his faithful love and I was once again lost in the security of his arms.

Taken by his own inner peace, he cradled me tighter and whispered in my ear. "*For by grace you have been saved by faith, and this is not your own doing, it is the gift of God.*"

ONE YEAR LATER

The belief of the world is that we have two roads to choose in life. We can decide on the good road, or the bad road. But I believe there's a third road, a road for those of us with no choice, a road that we are thrown into against our will by the ones we trust, the ones that are chosen to protect us, the ones that take our ignorance and innocence and shove us into the pits of life's hell with no remorse. Through no fault of our own, we are thrust into circumstances that challenge our strength and belief that somehow we will succumb to the person that God has purposed us to be, the belief that somewhere in the midst of our despair we are worthy of love and compassion. Some of us meet that destiny, but sadly some of us don't. Rock and I were fortunate enough to find that place, a place of relevance and blamelessness, a place that took us off a winding road of darkness into a glorious light that for the first time set us free.

A year has passed and I've reconciled with God. I've learned through the revelation of His Word that there's no greater cruelty than stealing the purity of a child, especially when it's stolen by those who were meant to shield them from the harms of the world. Nobody knew that better than Ms. Eloise. Teller told us of her unfortunate demise, but we knew in our hearts that God had finally answered her prayers and granted her the peace she so desperately desired. I would like to think that in the writing of her last letter to us she had found serenity. That in the still of her loneliness she had asked God for forgiveness for the measures she had gone through to protect us.

> "God is a peculiar God," she wrote, "One of peace and One of wrath. He is the beginning and the end, the Protector of all. His vengeance comes at a price, and for your father it was an unfortunate cost paid through the depths of your mother's despair. Unforgiveness is an evil that tears at you and rips at your very soul. It breaks you down

to a fragment of nothing and all you can bear is retribution upon those who have wronged you. I suffered that iniquity and for that I have paid the price. I only ask that you beg my forgiveness. Do not grow weary of your father's death, for it was not Rock, but the profane disrespect of Galations 6:7, that executed his fate. '*Be not deceived; God is not mocked*; *for whatsoever a man soweth,, that shall he also reap.*' The disobedience and desires of his flesh led to divine punishment, and it was only through that divinity that he was unable to escape fatality. Your mother was not sent as an executioner, but as an angel to take charge over thee, a messenger to carry out God's command. A mere vessel used in God's vengeance of the spoil that was perpetrated upon you and your brother. This, the night of your father's murder, I bore witness to. Summoned by God, I beheld his death by the hands of your mother to avenge all wrong suffered by you and your brother, a vengeance unavoidable and beckoned by God.

Children are the most innocence of God's creation, of whom your father so immorally defiled. "*Beware that you do not despise or feel scornful toward or think little of one of these little ones, for I tell you that in heaven their angels always are in the presence of and look upon the face of My Father Who is in heaven.*" May you now find faith in knowing that the protection of God is always with you."

We buried Ms. Eloise next to Mama. It was our way of fulfilling her last request that she would once again be reunited with her daughter. Mama use to say that a rose represents the beauty of the world that's hidden behind the thorns of life, for us, Ms. Eloise was that rose.

Although we will forever be stained by our past we will not be defined by it. We had all fought the good fight, finished the course and graciously received the crown of righteousness. In my moments of quiet I would like to think that my grandmother, through the repentance of her letter, did not suffer, but slipped away into a place sweeter than sweet reverie, a place where she could finally sit amongst Mama and the other angels and bask in the glorious realm of God.